The house, when Daisy and Primrose returned to it, was in an uproar. The first thing they noticed, as they hurried upstairs to change their rain-soaked garments, was that there were posies all about the place, large bouquets sending heavenly fragrances in all directions. Daisy stopped to smell a few, and to call for some larger vases. Flowers were her passion and she could not bear to see them crammed stiffly in ornamental bouquets.

It was Primrose, then, ascending the stairs, who almost collided with a striking-looking Lily in a walking dress of smart military style.

"Primrose, I shall never forgive you for adventuring without me, but you shall not believe the excitements we have had today! Lord Holden, Lord Witherspoon, Captain Stanley and Sir Lancelot Danvers all left cards; Mr. Stanridge has been composing sonnets—quite horrible, really, but still they celebrate my eyes, so I cannot help liking them just a smidgen—and we have had two proposals of marriage!" On this dramatic note, she clasped her hands in glee and awaited, breathless, her sister's response.

It was indulgent. Primrose kissed Lily's forehead and brushed away some of the dark, silky strands that had escaped their rather grown-up top knot. "Gracious, Lily, you quite overshadow all our tame adventures! And who, may I ask, is *we*?"

"We?" Lily looked puzzled.

Primrose endeavored to be patient, for she loved Lily dearly, despite her robust innocence coupled with a hearty narcissistic streak that bordered, at times, on conceit. "You said *we* had received two proposals of marriage. Do you mean you and I, or you and Daisy or all of us collectively?"

Lily beamed. "Oh, any of us will do!"

BOOK YOUR PLACE ON OUR WEBSITE AND MAKE THE READING CONNECTION!

We've created a customized website just for our very special readers, where you can get the inside scoop on everything that's going on with Zebra, Pinnacle and Kensington books.

When you come online, you'll have the exciting opportunity to:

- View covers of upcoming books
- Read sample chapters
- Learn about our future publishing schedule (listed by publication month *and author*)
- Find out when your favorite authors will be visiting a city near you
- Search for and order backlist books from our online catalog
- Check out author bios and background information
- Send e-mail to your favorite authors
- Meet the Kensington staff online
- Join us in weekly chats with authors, readers and other guests
- Get writing guidelines
- AND MUCH MORE!

**Visit our website at
http://www.zebrabooks.com**

RAVEN'S RANSOM

Hayley Ann Solomon

Zebra Books
Kensington Publishing Corp.
http://www.zebrabooks.com

To my dearest Clivey,
more wonderful than the most romantic of my heroes.
To Rhaz, Raphael, and Raoul, my little gentlemen,
I love you all.

One

Bills, bills, and more bills. Denver, Lord Barrymore, pulled out the pockets of his elegant, satin-lined waistcoat and fingered a sheet of paper that seemed permanently wedged in the stitching. He tugged a little harder and drew it out. A much-creased memento of Lord Derbyshire's gaming party. Wherein he had lost a thoroughbred mare, a hundred guineas, and a prized ruby pin. He unfolded the paper with gloom. *This* debt was not so easily settled, for it was for a prodigious sum quite beyond his immediate means.

He cast aside the suspicion that old Lord Raven had *known* he was in deep waters when he'd issued the challenge to him in the first place. There was something about those wizened black eyes that dented his fabled composure. *Now* he was summoned to Raven Place and there wasn't a way in the world he could make good the debt of honor. It would be a debtor's jail for him, for certain, and disgrace besides.

"Would my lord be wearing the jade velvet this evening?"

"Bother the velvet, Hoskin!"

"Very good, sir. Am I to understand you are in Queer Street again?" The valet's jaw did not move a muscle as he picked up a wide-brimmed, rather jaunty beaver hat and began brushing it down with vigor.

"The devil take it, is it that obvious?"

"Only by the number of tradesmen who are dunning you at the back door. Mrs. Quivers is sending them the rightabout, my lord."

In spite of his troubles, Lord Barrymore's lips twitched.

"Then very likely I shall not be bothered by them again for a month, at least!"

Even Hoskin, singularly averse to humor of any sort, grinned for a split second.

"Very likely not! Mrs. Quivers is giving them a regular, jaw-me-dead ear wigging, I can tell you that! Dunning a viscount indeed!"

"A very *broke* viscount." Denver's tone was rueful. "You probably have not been paid for a sennight."

"Tush! As if I care the snap of the fingers for that! You shall come round, my lord, you always do!"

"It shall take a miracle, this time, to set me to rights. I am afraid I have rather overreached myself."

"Stuff and nonsense." Hoskin laid the hat to one side and opened his lordship's trinket box. Sadly, much of the contents, by now, were paste. He tutted a little, then clicked it shut with disfavor.

"At the very worst, my lord, you shall find yourself an heiress. And now, I implore you, may I suggest the dark superfine with the satin trim?"

Hoskin, a valet of quite considerable talent, turned his mind to more momentous matters. It would be horrendous, after all, if the debonair Viscount Barrymore should ever be glimpsed in an outmoded frock coat. As for his cravat . . . Well, if it was not tied *à la mathematique* it would be criminal. Quite criminal.

The viscount allowed him to tangle expert fingers around his throat and high, perfectly starched shirt points. This was from a matter of polite, good-natured habit rather than from any burning desire to appear as modish as his man intended. All very well for *him* to talk of heiresses, of course—they did not, sadly, grow on trees.

Nor, to his precise knowledge, were they in the habit of favoring fortune hunters with nothing to recommend themselves but a tolerably handsome countenance, a rather middling sort of title, and a couple of dirty coal mines.

Of course, he had not yet made the delectable acquaintance of a certain Miss Lily Chartley, nor of her equally engaging sisters. *That* pleasure was still to come. As Hoskin kept prophesizing, my lord would come round. After all, he always did.

"Grandfather is sporting the most *devilish* smile this morning."

"Worse than usual?" Two pairs of eyes regarded this announcement with interest.

"Oh, *decidedly* worse! Either of you know why?"

Miss Primrose Chartley sank into a wing chair and bit hard into one of the fresh apples that had been set by Mrs. Bartlett upon the occasional table. It was deliciously crunchy and tasted especially good, since she'd missed breakfast and was famished.

Her sister, delicate, as usual, in a pale pastel dimity speckled, here and there, with the sparkle of a seeded pearl, frowned. It was only a *slight* frown, so her countenance was not overly marred by ill temper. Indeed, a person would be hard-pressed to annoy Daisy, who was a dear, trusting soul by nature. The slight furrow on her brow indicated concern. She tut-tutted as she pushed back one of her bright, sun-filled ringlets.

"You *also* thought that? I brought him in the *Gazette* about an hour ago and the gleam in his eye was unmistakable. If I was a flibberty gibbert like Lily, I would have been *quite* unsettled."

Lily grinned from across the room. "Did you ask him *why* he was in such suspiciously good spirits?"

"Well, of *course* I did!" Daisy sounded indignant.

"Well, what did he *say?*" Lily bounced most reprehensibly on the lavish cushions, causing Primrose to frown and remark that she would crease her elegant—and very grown up—muslin morning gown. This had the desired effect at once, so that when Daisy answered, Lily was the picture, once more, of serene graciousness.

"Oh, there can be no talking with him! He merely cackled uproariously in the most *infuriating* manner and told me I was a baggage."

"Well, you *are!*" The oldest and youngest of the Miss Chartleys giggled. They spoke as one, which caused Daisy to roll back her *heavenly* blue eyes and threaten to depart the room upon the instant.

"No!" Primrose pointed to a profusion of morning blossoms that she and Lily had been gathering. They were sadly mangled in a huge, silver epergne rising from the center of the room.

"You shall have to help us with the arrangement. I can't stand delphiniums. I can never get them to sit properly."

"That is because you don't wedge them in with enough greenery. Here, I'll show you." Daisy set down her copy of *Lady of the Lake* and obligingly walked over to the offending epergne. It had several rather drooping stems sticking out from it and was decidedly in need of her green-fingered touch. As she deftly set the arrangement to rights, she thought she heard a few rasping coughs muffled by the distance of a gallery and several great chambers.

"It is getting worse, isn't it?"

For once, all three of the Chartley sisters looked grave. The youngest, Lily, wiped away a sudden tear. It had welled up *quite* unbidden in her clear, impish green eyes. Now she fiddled anxiously with the ribbons of her modish new gown and sniffed.

"He is getting worse. Dr. Hall leeched him yesterday and he didn't even have the energy to throw so much as a *book* at him." Her tone was doleful as she reflected on this extraordinary state of affairs.

Primrose chuckled in spite of the situation's gravity.

"Dr. Hall must have been tremendously relieved! I believe he must have the patience of saints to continue ministering to him."

"Yes, though he is now canny enough to stand at the far side of the room when his decoctions are administered. It is left to poor Richmond to coax the evil smelling stuff down the old man. He has handed in his notice three times this week!" Daisy sighed, though there was a faint curve to her lips.

"Three times? I could have sworn it was four! I am not surprised, though everyone knows he is *devoted* to Grandfather."

The coughing seemed to progress to a spasm. Primrose set down her apple. Though she appeared as calm and unruffled as always, a slight glimmer of alarm nevertheless nagged at her features.

"I think I will go and check on him again."

Her sisters nodded. "Yes, you go. You have a soothing way about you."

Miss Chartley nodded. Unlike Daisy, she was statuesque rather than delicate, with fine cheekbones and a healthy glow about her that spoke of brisk vitality and excellent health. She tossed her bonnet onto a chair and shook out her short, cropped locks. The copper brown gleamed in the sunlight.

"Go ask Mistress Ainsley to make up some chicken broth, will you? And perhaps Mrs. Bartlett will take up some of the lemon cordial. His throat is likely *aching* from the exertion."

"Of coughing or shouting?"

Primrose's eyes twinkled. "Doubtless both!"

Daisy looked doubtful. "Are you certain it is broth he needs? If he swallows that, then we shall *know* he is ill!"

"Let us hope he pours it out the window, then. Hush! Can you hear him?"

There was now no doubt that the rasping was worse. Primrose strode briskly down the hall, schooling herself not to run. Lord Raven's interests would not be served by a wild and indecorous sprint through his home.

She hesitated when she arrived at the heavy oak door. The old man would not appreciate meddling, particularly if he suspected that he was being cosseted. Still, the coughing was now a peculiarly distressing wheeze and there seemed to be no sign of any of his personal attendants.

She knocked briskly then took a deep breath before bearding the lion's den.

"Grandfather! Can I fetch you a glass of water?"

The old man glared at her from his bedcovers. Even at death's door, he would have choked to admit how glad he was to see her. He *adored* his three lively relatives but would have swallowed gall before so much as *whispering* as much to them.

Of course, after so many years of living under his roof, the Chartley sisters were more than used to his bushy-browed frowns and his ominous tut-tuts. They knew perfectly well that under the mountain of ill humor hid a man of sterling virtues and infinite kindness. Who, after all, had taken them in when they'd been orphaned, had educated them, fed them, housed them, clothed them, bullied them and generally defended them against all ills for longer than memory served? Why he, of course. And all with an outward guise of quite dreadful temper and terrible wrath.

Primrose no longer shrunk in fear. Rather, she chuckled inwardly and smoothed down the pillows so that they were light and airy.

"I suppose you take liberties because you think I am in my dotage!" Lord Raven eased his head back on the goose feathers and steadfastly refused to admit he was any more comfortable. Since Primrose did not in the least expect such an admission, his stubbornness passed unremarked. This seemed to niggle at his lordship, for he felt it necessary to point out that he was used to three pillows, but since Richmond had deserted him, he supposed he would have to suffer with two.

"Richmond has not deserted you, sir. You sent him on to London."

"Did I? And how do you know *that*, my little flower?"

Primrose noted how his eyes gleamed with sudden animation. So there *was* something afoot! She had known it!

Her reply was tart, which pleased his lordship, for he liked to feel his granddaughters were heartily endowed with spunk. Not at *all* like some of the dreary, missish wallflowers he had encountered in the past.

"If you wished it to be a secret, sir, you should not have called out the grooms from their slumbers and sent poor Richmond out in the pouring rain."

"He was in a carriage, if you please, young lady! With those newfangled gas lamps he should be perfectly comfortable!"

"No doubt your most overwhelming desire!"

His lordship's lips twitched at her irony. Then he guffawed a little, coughed to the point that she grew alarmed, and set his head back against the great crested cushions.

"No doubt! But come, you have not disturbed my peace to talk of Richmond."

"No, but I confess I would like to know why he was dispatched with such haste."

"I *wager* you would! He is to fetch Mr. Anchorage at once."

"Mr. Anchorage? But he is your lawyer! Grandfather, you should not be conducting business when you are ill!"

"I shall please myself, little Miss Primrose! But no, this is not business, this is pleasure!"

"I thought lawyers were dreary creatures with never a lively thought in their heads."

"They *are*. That is why he is bound to be shocked when he hears why he has been summoned. I have not had so much good fun in years."

"Grandfather, you are a rogue! And what are you up to now, I wonder?"

Primrose's eyes twinkled, for she could see Lord Raven was in high good humor and further from death than she had feared. His eyes were bright and there was a pinkness about his cheeks that she found pleasing. Perhaps a little meddlesome mischief at the long-suffering Mr. Anchorage's expense was the very thing to revive his spirits.

"I am rewriting my will."

"How gloomy. Can you not think of sunnier matters?"

"Certainly not! I have you three baggages to think of. And why your mama chose to name you all after flowers I cannot fathom! Lily, Primrose, and Daisy. Ha! It is enough to give me hay fever thinking on it!"

"Be sure not to sneeze in *my* direction, then. I have no desire to spoil my new gown."

"New gown? What fustian is this? That is *Lily's* old gown, darned a hundred times, no doubt, and trimmed with a bit of newfangled ribbon."

"How observant you are, Grandfather! I only meant that since it has been refurbished, it *feels* new. No sense throwing away a perfectly good garment!"

"I'll warrant that is precisely what *Lily* intended to do with it!"

"Yes, well, she is so very beautiful, it is understandable she wants to set off her looks with something more fashionable than last summer's gown."

"Ha! She could do with a smidgen of your common sense."

"Very likely, but . . ."

"And you, young lady, could do with a bit of her vanity! Go buy *yourself* a few gowns for a change! Do I not supply you with enough pin money?"

"Oh, a quite shocking amount!"

"Well, then? Is it necessary to look like such an old maid? I warn you, the house is very soon going to be flocking with suitors. I shall expect at least a dozen to be buzzing about you."

Primrose looked at the old man sharply.

"Grandfather, I shall assume you are not yet deranged. Your sharp wit attests to the contrary and relieves my most immediate fears. Which leaves me to surmise that you are up to something *quite* preposterous. A dozen suitors indeed! The suspicion quite *sinks* my spirits!"

For an answer, Lord Raven cackled quite uproariously, his yellowing teeth offering no comfort to the most sensible of his granddaughters.

She wiped some dust off his bedstead. "I shall not press you, sir, for I do believe you *mean* to infuriate me!"

The earl wiped his eyes with his handkerchief and though his hands trembled, his gaze was quite steady.

"My dear Primrose, you must allow me my small diversions. Beneath your calm exterior you are such a *spirited* thing. You can not, I hope, wish to deny me the pleasure of raising your ire? You are so much like your papa when your eyes flash."

"Grandfather, you are a wicked old man!" Primrose frowned ominously but her light, laughing tone removed the sting from her words.

Lord Raven settled back on his pillows and closed an eye. He entwined his bony fingers together and contrived to look inordinately pleased with himself despite a worrying degree of breathlessness. He sat up, coughed a little hoarsely, then returned to the pillows.

"These cushions are as hard as rocks. And my hot brick is cold."

Primrose did not stir from her seat. Bricks were heated at the coal fire and pillow feathers were always plucked from the finest of estate geese. Lord Raven was merely being quarrelsome

"Oh, get along with you! Wake me when Mr. Anchorage finally appears."

"Very well, Grandfather. And you will drink your broth when it arrives?"

"That puky stuff? I shall pour it over the housemaid if she has the temerity to bring it up."

Primrose suppressed a small smile and stood up, relieved. Grandfather, she was sure, would live another day yet.

The Marchioness of Rochester clipped her fan shut loudly. Her reprehensible son did not so much as *look* up from his detestable book. Some dry old verbiage about steam engines, as if horse-drawn carriages were not quite sensible enough! She was of two minds to write to Olivia Darcy at once. Her eyes twinkled for a moment. Olivia's loathsome brats with their fluttering eyelashes and insipid little simpers would be a suitable punishment for him. The young Marquis of Rochester, like his father before him, did not suffer fools gladly,

"*Do* pay attention, Gareth! If you do not make some attempt to pick yourself a bride this Season I shall have to do it for you. I thought the Darcy sisters might . . ."

"*What?*"

"Aha!" The marchioness pounced on his book and unrepentantly lost his page. "I *knew* that would capture your attention!"

"More likely to give me indigestion. Stop teasing, Mama. When I meet someone who is sensible, intelligent, bright, and beautiful, you shall be the first to felicitate me."

"And how do you expect to meet such a paragon if you refuse every suitable invitation? Lady Castlereigh is much put out that you did not attend her soiree. Emily Cowper is barely speaking to me, and as for Lady Turlington . . . She has three daughters to dispatch and she was *relying* upon your handsome nature to give them a good sendoff."

"And why was that? I believe I have never so much as clapped *eyes* on the chits."

Lady Rochester had the grace to blush. "Well, I fancy I might have led them to believe . . ."

"Oh, Mama! Can you not stop promising my attentions to the whole world? Last Season with the ladies Delia, Eugenie, Clarissa, and Harriet was quite enough!"

"Well, their mothers were my particular friends!"

"Mother, you are too popular by far! If I were to dance with the daughters of all your particular friends I would be frequenting Lobb's every day!"

"The bootmakers? Don't gammon me—it would take more than a couple of quadrilles to wear a hole in your elegant hessians!"

"I shouldn't like to put it to the test, though. The results might prove expensive."

"Tch! As if you care a soux for expense! You would not have paid off your latest ladybird with a handsome carriage and four snow white horses if money was the smallest consideration."

"Mama!" Lord Gareth Rochester's tone was shocked, but his eyes twinkled with exasperated affection. "Is there *nothing* that gets past you? And how thoroughly disreputable to mention such matters!"

"Mmm the pot calling the kettle black. Gareth, *when*

do you mean to settle? I quite *yearn* for grandchildren and there is the title to consider. I would turn in my grave if it ever passed to Cedric."

Something in his mother's tone stopped Rochester from making the flippant retort that immediately sprang to mind.

"Mama! I shall make a deal with you!"

Lady Rochester did not quite like the quizzical sparkle in her son's eye. She knew, for a certainty, that it meant trouble was brewing. Lord Rochester, whilst charming perfection personified and the very best of sons, nevertheless had an occasional wild streak that had caused both his parents a fair bit of flutter in the past. She was thus cautious as she mildly raised her noble brows and asked for elucidation.

"I shall marry the precise maiden you select for me. No doubt she shall have *all* the credentials you require. My only specification is that she be neither cross-eyed, cross-grained, nor a shrew."

"Gareth! You cannot mean such a nonsensical thing!"

"I most certainly do! *You* want an heir and *I* want some peace!"

"But to be so cold-blooded . . ."

"The marriage mart *is* cold-blooded. You are the first to admit it."

"Yes, but . . ."

"If you have qualms, forget the whole thing and let me live in peace."

Lady Rochester looked at the stubborn set of her son's jaw. She sighed. So much like his father, he was! There would be no making him see reason.

"Very well. I shall present you with my choice at the end of the Season."

Gareth grinned. "Excellent. *That* should keep you out of mischief! And now, I shall bid you farewell."

"Where are you going?' Lady Rochester's tone was sharp. "You are not forgetting Almack's tonight?"

Gareth shuddered. "Mama, I shall do everything in my power to do precisely that! Those rooms are overrated, they serve the vilest of drinks, the food is more often stale than not, their master of ceremonies is the greatest jackanapes I have ever come across, and the ladies are insipid."

"Gareth! You shock me!"

"Very well, Mama, you shall have to be shocked. *You* go. No doubt you will have an edifying time finding me a bride. I, however, shall not."

"Your uncle is in Bath, Gareth. He cannot escort me and I *despise* going with Jaspers. He fills me with misgiving."

Her son's deep sapphire eyes softened a little. "I can't blame you, Mama. He is a surly creature. Shall I give him his notice?"

"No, for I know that he is excellent with your cattle."

"Indeed he is. He has an unerring eye for detail." Gareth sighed loudly. "I suppose, then, you shall have it your way. I shall take you."

Lady Rochester smiled gently. She rang for a fresh brew of tea. Years of practice had taught her, she knew, how to tame her man.

True to his reliable self, Mr. Anchorage wasted no time in expediting Lord Raven's wishes. If he thought them strange and rather crackpot, he had the wisdom to hold his peace, commenting only *very* mildly that the proceeding was "unusual." For which trouble he received an acid retort from the old man, wheezing himself into fits from the comfort of his great twelfth-century four-poster bed.

"You are certain this is your wish, my lord? It would be more practicable, perhaps, to split the estate into three equal shares. Alternately . . ."

"A pox on your musings, man! Hand the paper up that I may sign!"

"You shall need witnesses, my lord."

"Well find them, then!"

"Richmond?"

The valet stepped out from the shadows. "Ha, I *thought* the walls had ears! No doubt you find my last will and testament very edifying!"

"Certainly I do, sir." Richmond's answer was as smooth as silk. He did not blink at the aspersions cast upon his character. He was used to them and inclined to feel that a thousand of Lord Raven's curses were worth a hundred of any *other* employer's praises. Besides, he *had* been eavesdropping. He would be an extremely unnatural sort of fellow had he *not* been.

"Excellent. Then you shall stand as witness and call that other lazy good-for-nothing in to do the same."

"Betty, sir?"

"Who else?"

The valet bowed. "Very good, sir. I believe she is sweeping out the upper chambers. I shall find her at once. And may I say, sir . . ."

"*Yes?*" Beady eyes snapped in his direction.

"For the purposes you have in mind, I would suggest the jewelled tricorne rather than one of your beavers. It has a sense of occasion, I feel."

"By Jupiter, Richmond, I believe you are right. Did you hear that, Anchorage? Write it in, write it in."

The long-suffering lawyer looked daggers at both master and servant. They were both, in his opinion, as mad as hatters. The tricorne indeed! Still, if my lord wished to play ducks and drakes with his fortune, it was not his concern. All he needed to do was write. And so he did.

Two

"Lord Holden, Lord Witherspoon, Captain Stanley, and Sir Lancelot Danvers have all left cards. The blue receiving room is filled to the brim with flowers and I have left Mr. Harold Stanridge below stairs. He is this very moment rehearsing a piece of poetry to your glorious eyes, Miss Lily."

"Is he? How delightful! They are not as round as Daisy's, nor as fashionable a color, but I *do* believe they are worthy of a sonnet or two! I shall go down at once!"

The housekeeper pressed her hands together nervously. "I do wish Miss Daisy and Miss Primrose were home! These are strange goings-on. I am quite at my wit's end.

"Stuff and nonsense!" Lily bounced off the chaise longue and patted down her second-best walking dress of azure lawn. "It is perfectly obvious that we have 'taken.' Perhaps we shall be as famous as the Gunning sisters!"

Mrs. Bartlett looked bemused. Faint rumors were circulating in the kitchens but she hadn't the heart to depress Lily's irrepressible spirits. Still, she would be hopelessly remiss if she permitted her to have a tête-à-tête with one of the most gazetted fortune hunters of the Season.

"I should send him away, Miss Lily. It is not fitting that he should meet with you unchaperoned. Wait for Miss Primrose to return. *She* shall know what to do!"

"But she will be an age! If she went to Hookhams she

will be there forever! You *know* how long she takes to select a book! I *never* have that problem, for there is always a juicy Gothic at hand, or at the very least a second volume of something."

This logic may have been incomprehensible to the housekeeper, but it made perfectly good sense to Lily, who never, *never* got beyond a first volume of anything.

Mrs. Bartlett stood firm. "She will not be long, for she only ordered up the curricle and the skies are darkening. She would not risk Daisy catching cold in a passing shower. Mr. Stanridge can wait. If your eyes are *indeed* like gem pools—whatever *they* may be—they will undoubtedly be worth kicking his heels for."

Lily at once saw the sense in this, remarking that it was very romantic indeed that poor Mr. Stanridge had to suffer so. Mrs. Bartlett declined the tart rejoinder that more likely Mr. Stanridge was suffering from indigestion. The manner in which he had wolfed down her cream tarts had been reprehensible bordering on rude. Still, it was what one could expect from a fortune hunter with not a farthing to fly with. No doubt he had missed his dinner.

"What *else* was he saying?"

"About your eyes?"

"Oh, about anything! Did he mention my cheekbones? I put a dash of color on them yesterday . . ."

"Miss Lily!" The housekeeper was shocked. Nevertheless, she was kindhearted enough to mention that Mr. Stanridge had spouted at length about "crimson lips with the hallowed sheen of overripe berries," a dubious metaphor that appeared to send Lily into transports. Mrs. Bartlett sighed as she looked at the ormolu clock on the mantel. It was fine time Miss Primrose was home.

Lord Armand Valmont glanced skyward and frowned. Undoubtedly it would rain, and whilst he did not in the

least mind getting soaked to the skin, the sky was darkening and the paths he intended to cross were misting
up so that he could see almost nothing of the rolling
green hills and sandy paths that guided his way.

He would have to stop at the White Dragon and seek
shelter, for it was useless getting lost upon the Westenbury
moors. His arrival home would simply have to wait. He
tugged soothingly at the reigns and coaxed his midnight
stallion round. The sky was flashing ominously and he
feared a sudden lightning storm. Dancer was already beginning to whinny softly, her nostrils flaring for danger.

White mists seemed to descend from nowhere, almost—but not quite—obscuring an oncoming carriage in
the distance. Lord Valmont very quick-mindedly stepped
onto the turf. *He* had had the advantage of seeing the
curricle, but he was not certain, by its speed, that the
reverse was true. Moments later, his misgivings were jus-
tified as the little tilbury sped out of control and lost a
front wheel.

"Bother!"

The sound was as clear as a bell and, rather surprisingly
for this area, feminine.

My lord was just contemplating making his presence
known when a second, equally delightful—and *just* as
feminine—tone was heard to reply.

"Do you think we have lost him?"

"Oh, undoubtedly! What a churlish fellow! I wonder
which one of us he meant to abduct?"

"Oh, undoubtedly both! Poor man—he must have his
flowers confused. He kept calling you Violet."

"And you Daffodil!"

Something seemed to be amusing the pair, for though
their little tilbury was rendered useless, the first was
chuckling rather throatily and the second was giggling in
a manner that Lord Valmont *should* have found irritating,
but instead found singularly intriguing.

"Ahem!" He stepped out onto the road and startled the pair, who were engaged in a rather indecorous descent. Even with the mists swirling about them, Lord Valmont was able to appreciate a very pretty turned ankle coupled with a quite delectable . . . but no, this was not the time to reflect upon such matters.

"On guard, sir!" The tone was ferocious and he found himself contemplating the taller of the two, who was brandishing a parasol with an alarming metal point in his direction. He could not quite be certain, but he could swear her eyes flashed fiercely.

Suppressing a smile, he dropped his hands at once and announced that he was entirely at their mercy, for he never as a point of principle, crossed either sword or parasol with the gentler sex.

Whereupon he elicited a rather rewarding smile from his aggressor and an aggrieved "Oh!" from the more delectable of the duo.

"You would prefer it were otherwise?" He looked at her in surprise.

"Well, we were having such a tremendous adventure, sir! It seems a trifle tame that you are now to rescue us. It would be a lot more fitting if you were an accomplice or a highwayman or some such thing."

"You may thank the Lord he is not! We may have outwitted our abductor, but *he* was mounted on such a pathetic, mangy little nag it would be a strange thing had we not! *This* gentleman, on the contrary, is mounted on an Arab. If he wanted to pursue us, he would have no difficulty at all."

As if on cue, the gentleman, by now quite enthralled, cleared his throat and commented that strictly speaking the beast was only *sired* by an Arab, but of course, if pursuit were a question, he should have no difficulty.

Whereupon the elder of the two glanced at him steadily, then smiled in sudden amusement.

The sister, however—for he surmised she was such—looked quite mulish. Then she effected such an *adorable* pout that the gentleman was inclined either to laugh outrageously or to lift her off her feet and kiss her thoroughly. That, of course, would have been even *more* outrageous, but my lord, with restraint, desisted in both.

Instead, he told her with a *great* show of earnestness that he was the fabled Barnacle Jack, but because she was so pretty, youthful, and intoxicatingly innocent, he was going to spare her her life.

Whereupon the young lady cast a suspicious eye upon him. Oh, they were heavenly, those eyes! As deep as cornflowers and round, so round! Round, rimmed with lashes as honeyed as the silk-soft ringlets that crept delightfully over her cheeks and caused her to brush them away with impatient white-gloved fingers.

"Barnacle Jack? You are not gammoning me?"

"I? Good heavens, no! I am the terror of these parts, though I beg you will not betray me."

The lady blushed. She actually blushed! Valmont raised triumphant eyes to the more sensible of the sisters. She furrowed her brows reprovingly, but he was not deceived. He had caught her answering dimple in the mist light.

"May I steal a kiss before I ride off into the mists forever?"

"No!" The copper-colored miss's head shook decisively. Unfortunately, her words were not echoed by her sister, who appeared mesmerized by the tall, infinitely handsome stranger. She stared at him with saucerlike eyes and pressed her hands up to her chest, for the dull thudding of her heart ached quite dreadfully.

Then, casting a saucy glance at the sister, who looked like a thunder cloud, Lord Valmont put his arms about the little one's waist and kissed her far, far more gently than his inclination demanded. When her hands crept shyly up to his neck, he emitted a strangled oath, for his inclinations very much interfered with his consummate good sense.

Fortunately, he was not left in this sublime state of chivalrous indecision long, for a dull thud and a mild to moderate pain caused him to drop his arms at once.

"Primrose! How *could* you!" His sweet defender looked mortified. *He,* of course, looked merely sheepish. The wench was brandishing the parasol again. He supposed he should be grateful she'd not poked him with the sharp end.

"Daisy, you are behaving no better than Lily! I had credited you with some sense! You cannot go about the countryside kissing every stranger you see!"

"Pardon me, ma'am, if I might interject at this point?" The Honorable Lord Valmont ceased rubbing his distinguished temple and looked at the sky.

"On a point of issue, I am not a stranger, I am Barnacle Jack. On a further point, I am certain Miss—Daisy, is it?"

"*Chartley*—Miss Chartley." Primrose's tone was repressive. The cutpurse seemed not to notice, and continued blithely with his argument. "Miss, ah, Chartley does not go about kissing every *cutpurse* she encounters upon the common road, however much she may treat strangers in general. I am right, am I not?"

He smiled engagingly at the one and challengingly at the other.

"You are absurd, sir!" Primrose's response held the faintest trace of a smile. Lord Valmont was encouraged and turned his dark, penetrating eyes upon the delectable Daisy. She blushed, but held his gaze with such sweet simplicity that he was inclined to repeat his earlier offense. Still, he realized with a slight inward sigh, however much he may proclaim to the contrary, he was a gentleman. Gentlemen did not take advantage of sweet innocents, however tantalizing the temptation. With a steadying breath, he pointed to the sky and continued his conversational tone.

"Also, though I am, of course, loath to point it out, the rain shall be pouring in seconds. I hesitate to mention this, for a thorough drenching is no doubt highly commendable by adventurous standards. However, I am an *amazingly* obnoxious fellow, quite hell-bent on throwing a rub in the way and I *cannot*—cannot—see my way clear to allowing you to catch your deaths. Therefore I propose we walk at once to the nearest inn. It is called the White Dragon, but to all of its intimates, it is known as"—he leaned close to Daisy—"the 'Devil's door.'"

Her eyes widened as he hoped they would. Primrose's lips twitched a little, then she settled them into stern lines once more.

"Very well, sir! You shall rescue us. We shall abandon the tilbury and walk alongside the horses, for we have no riding clothes and no sidesaddles. Do you know if the mail coach passes in this direction? I should like to pen a letter to my sister to set her mind at ease."

His lordship smiled, glad that despite an aching forehead, there was no hard feelings to mar this unusual encounter.

"I believe so, though if you use that method you shall wait all day. The mail coach only arrives from Tollingsbrook at some time past four. Leave the matter to me. I shall see that a message arrives at your home without delay."

Daisy sighed in bliss. No doubt the cutpurse knew of several secret shortcuts and had a *crew* of villains ready to fly like the wind. Primrose was cannier. She judged that several shining coins would soon be passing hands. If anyone was "flying" to London, it was most like to be the taproom boy.

The letters, penned in haste, arrived sometime around eleven. By this time, Lily was in a passion of impatience and had gone so far as to disobey Mrs. Bartlett in the matter of entertaining the various suitors who seemed to hang about Raven Place in droves. Sadly, she had missed the edifying spectacle of Mr. Harold Stanridge's poetic recital, but she was more than compensated by Captain Knightley's abundant charm and the Baron of Dawcett's fulsome compliments. If he made the mistake, now and again, of referring to her as "Miss Primrose" or "Miss Daisy," she did not appear to mind, but rather, flirtatiously slapped him on the wrist with her fan and corrected him. Mrs. Bartlett, finding herself in the position of chaperone, chortled a little when she realized the sensible man was now taking no chances. By the end of his requisite fifteen minutes, he was very properly referring to Lily as "Miss Chartley" a safe and blanket term that was bound to give no offense.

Lily was just curtsying to Mr. Campion when the letters arrived. Abstracted, she agreed to give him the first waltz at Almack's that evening, though she had not yet procured the necessary permission. Mr. Campion seemed as pleased as punch, doffed his stylish beaver in Mrs. Bartlett's direction, and was gone before the housekeeper could make any objections.

"Oh, Mrs. Bartlett, *look!* Of all the rotten luck!"

"What *is* it?" Mrs. Bartlett looked alarmed. She had been serving in Lord Raven's household for thirty years or more and loved the Chartleys dearly, though they were her social superiors and quite above her mild-mannered touch.

"The letters are from Primrose and Daisy. Oh, it is dreadful, dreadful, dreadful!"

Mrs. Bartlett looked grave. "Are they ill? Have they met with an accident?"

"No, yes, oh . . . but how I *wish* I were with them! You read it."

Lily thrust a letter into Mrs. Bartlett's hand. The housekeeper took her *pince nez* from her pocket and slowly read the words.

> *Dearest, dearest Lily,*
>
> *You will never guess what an adventure we are having! We were abducted by the nastiest man, but Primrose drove the tilbury to an inch until we were ditched—or something of that nature, the wheel or something—and now we are being rescued by the most ghoulish—heavily under crossed—cutpurse with oh, the kindliest of eyes! He kissed me . . . I had better leave off, Primmy is impatient for the pen.*
>
> *Love, etc.,*
> *Daisy*

"Good heavens! Has the child run mad? It sounds like something out of one of those dreadful novels you ladies persist in reading! Is there anything more intelligible from Miss Primrose?"

"Yes, but it is not half so informative. Oh, Mrs. Bartlett! To think I chose not to go to Hookhams today! It is really too bad!"

"You should be thanking your lucky stars. Let me see the letter from Miss Primmy before I speak to your grandfather about calling in the runners."

"Bow Street? Oh, but that is famous!"

"Hmmph!" The housekeeper did not bother to reply. Rather, she extended her hand for the missive and waved the under butler away rather crossly.

"Go, Hammond! I cannot think of menus when I am all at sixes and sevens!" She smoothed out the single folded wafer and nodded crisply. Primrose, at least, wrote legibly.

> *Lily, dear!*
>
> *We have met with a small accident but are perfectly comfortable. We are situated, for the present, at the White*

Dragon Inn, on the outskirts of Westenbury. Could you send for a wheelwright and possibly ask the groomsman to send on a chaise? We hope to be home late this afternoon, in spite of some decidedly inclement weather!

Yours, etc.,
Primrose

"Well!" Mrs. Bartlett sounded reassured. "How very like Daisy to make a pother out of nothing! Highwaymen indeed! Very likely she is suffering from indigestion and merely daydreaming her time way. I shall set about decocting some soothing syrup of burgundy and rye."

Lily looked gloomy. "Yes, no doubt it *is* all a hum! I shall scold Daisy dreadfully when she returns. It is *wicked* to tease me so!"

"Indeed, dear. Now remove, will you, that glum look from your countenance. It does not do your high good looks any credit at all."

Lily needed no second telling, especially since the butler was announcing a fresh set of eager-looking suitors. He was preceded by a housemaid carrying an enormous array of cowslips and roses, thus adding substance to Mrs. Bartlett's muttered prediction that Lord Raven's home would soon look like nothing short of a hothouse.

Three

Lord Raven tossed on his pillows querulously. "Richmond, if you do not tell me what is going on below stairs, I shall turn you off without a character!"

This threat held no terrors for the strong-minded valet, who'd spent most of his working life in Lord Raven's ill-tempered—but thoroughly satisfactory—employ. It was a threat he heard a dozen times or more in a working day, but not one, he was perfectly certain, that ever would be dispatched. Lord Raven, despite his perverse temper, was too much the man of honor.

Now he stepped over to the bedstead, wiped the crusty old face with a warm, wet sponge, and muttered, soothingly, that the earl would doubtless be well pleased with the shenanigans that was turning his well-ordered home into a state of chaos.

"Well?" The earl's bellow came out as a wheeze, but Richmond understood his intention perfectly. He stepped over to the highly polished ebony bed stand and with a flourish removed the *Morning Post*, which sat upon it crisply.

"I fancy *this* must have something to do with the commotion below stairs."

"Ah." The earl's eyes were bright as he regarded the paper with interest. "So you have seen the insert?"

"Indeed I have, sir! As have, no doubt, the whole of

London society together with a great deal of seedier undesirables."

"They shall be weeded out." The earl waved his hand dismissively. "Well, why are you dawdling in that reprehensible fashion? Let me see!"

Richmond opened the paper with practiced ease and flicked over the pages until he came to the item that had at *once* attracted his critical eye. *So* useful that he, like Mrs. Bartlett, was the type of superior servant who could both read and write.

"Ah." The earl nodded in rare satisfaction. "Perfectly worded. I am surprised. That Anchorage person is a scoundrel."

"He is your lawyer, sir," Richmond objected mildly.

"Pshaw!" The earl made a rather dismissive gesture. Nevertheless, Richmond could tell he was pleased.

"So what is happening? I wager a dozen young men are squirming out of the woodwork."

"Oh, easily that, my lord! Your announcement is the talk of the Ton. If I may say so, sir, you are a wicked old man."

This pleased the earl tremendously, for he offered Richmond a sweetmeat before demanding to speak to Primrose.

"I fear you cannot, my lord! She was abducted by a knave."

"What?" The earl turned purple and sat up with sudden vigor.

"Indeed. You are not to concern yourself, sir, for by all accounts she and Miss Daisy have been rescued."

"Ah." The earl's unscrupulous eyes twinkled. "By a gentleman, I presume?"

"Oh, no, my lord! By a cutpurse."

The face darkened once more. Richmond's tone was bland as he dusted some flecks of fluff off his lord's heavy brocade.

"You are gammoning me!"

"Indeed, no! Mrs. Bartlett had it off Miss Daisy herself. Evidently the man has some credentials to his credit . . ."

"These being?"

"He kisses rather expertly . . ."

"Richmond!" This time the earl's wheeze was replaced by a roar. The valet blinked.

"My lord?"

"Send for Mrs. Bartlett! There is no dealing with you!"

"Very well, my lord." Richmond bowed and departed the room in haste. He knew, with the certainty of long service, that he was in danger of having a potted plant hurled at his head. He permitted himself a faint grin. The earl's quirk of madness might be the very thing to raise his spirits and set him on his feet again.

The "cutpurse" had little difficulty finding a private parlor for the two ladies, who despite their very best efforts to skip alongside the horses, still found themselves drenched to the skin, their merry bonnets in ruins, and their fashionable half boots all but soaked. Still, they maintained the best of spirits, especially when confronted with a hearty meal of sautéed chicken livers, roast dumplings with apple sauce, and a generous helping of minted lamb.

The waiters were tumbling over themselves to help, the innkeeper on such pins to please that his ingratiating manner became rather intrusive until the cutpurse wisely shut the door in his face. Primrose raised her brows at this decided action, for certainly there was not the necessary three-inch gap to preserve their combined reputations. Still, she decided, dining with a gentleman masquerading as a cutpurse was proving a novel experience. One quirkish enough, she felt, to risk a little flexibility in observing the conventions. There was no doubt in the elder Miss Chartley's mind, you see, that Barnacle Jack was a gentleman. True, his manners were outrageous and his flirtatious style quite beyond the pale, but there was a certain directness of manner that pleased. If he was not a gentleman born, she was no judge of anything.

Daisy, of course, had no such dampening suspicion. On the contrary, she was quite enraptured with her roguish villain, something that disturbed the perceptive Miss Primrose a little. Adventures were one thing, but attaching too much significance to a chance encounter quite another. Relieved, she noted that the Raven chaise had arrived, an abominably ostentatious thing, gilded in gold with vivid blue wheels and an interior of matching hue. Even the plush squabs were of royal blue velvet, commissioned only recently in keeping with current fashion.

The earl, when not upon his deathbed, enjoyed squandering his quite *inordinately* indecent fortune. Lily bravely helped him. Primrose sighed. There was no hoping, now, that they would be able to glide out unremarked. The White Dragon would probably be speculating about their noble visitors for *weeks*.

She nodded to Daisy, who looked anything but noble in her clinging gown. It becomingly revealed her many feminine perfections, a fact that Barnacle Jack did not mind in the least.

"Wretched man! You need not look so smug!" Primrose frowned reprovingly at his impudence.

For answer, she received a wide-eyed grin and a quite unabashed compliment on her *own* high good looks, which served to make her crosser still.

"Flummery, sir! Now say farewell to Daisy, for I suspect we shall not meet again."

"No?" The words were soft and rather whimsical. Primrose glanced at him sharply, her tone unusually firm.

"No!"

Daisy sighed. "How I *wish* you were not a cutpurse!"

"How contrary of you! I could have sworn you desired the reverse this morning. No, that was a highwayman. But of course, I double as a highwayman at night."

"Don't be absurd, sir! I could not have wished such a thing! Well, perhaps I did, but that was before we were acquainted! Can you not reform, sir? I would not like to see you hang from a noose."

Barnacle Jack's eyes sparkled with merriment. "Indeed, no! I have always found that particular prospect singularly unappealing! As to reforming . . ." He shrugged. "I am a rogue at heart."

"Probably the truest thing you have uttered all day," Primrose remarked under her breath. The cutpurse regarded her with a certain amused sympathy.

"Hush, you shall disillusion the infant and I shall be *quite* overset!"

He turned from her and smiled quite deliciously at Daisy. "I shall help you into your carriage and beg your direction. Then, on a moonless night—or no, perhaps the moon shall be full—I shall be heard riding across the moors proclaiming your name."

"Daisy?" Daisy giggled, though her round eyes widened at the beguiling tone.

"I wish my mother had named me Ariel or Athena, or something heroic! Even Camellia or *Rose* would have been more suitable."

"Well, it just so happens that I adore Daisies." Armand pushed back the guilty thought that he hadn't set eyes on a daisy for years, and if he had, he would not have known it from a petunia or a common garden variety iris. Still, his words seemed to be having the desired effect, for the younger Miss Chartley was beaming at him with starlit eyes.

"Our direction is . . ."

"Daisy!" Primrose looked shocked. "Have you no decorum? You are worse than Lily!"

"She is quite right, you know." The cutpurse put his finger to Daisy's protesting lips. "It would never do to divulge such secrets! You have no idea that you can trust me. Indeed, I hardly know whether I can trust *myself!*" This last was directed apologetically at Primrose. She stared at him hard, then smiled, a sudden softening pity entering into her expressive eyes.

"Doubtless our paths shall cross again, *Barnacle* Jack!" She stressed his name slightly satirically, causing his lips to twitch appreciatively.

"Ah." He grinned as he realized he was being given tacit permission to seek them out if he could.

"May we recompense you for the meal and the mail charges?"

Dark eyes flashed scornfully. "Do you seek to insult me?"

"Felons are not notoriously plump in the pocket."

"Oh!" He was reminded of his ridiculous role. "I prigged two *prodigiously* fat purses only this morning. I shall be rich, therefore, at least until sunrise tomorrow. Go, whilst the rain has stopped. Tell your man I have handed the bays over to the inn's ostler. He will await your convenience."

Daisy smiled. "You are thoughtful! Not at *all* what I would expect from . . . from . . ." She blushed, for she hesitated to call him a common thief.

Lord Valmont's eyes darkened disgracefully. Then, without warning, he whisked the bemused young lady off her feet and kissed her with practiced ease. When he released her, Daisy's head was spinning and she looked quite liable to swoon.

"You are *more* than a rogue, sir! *Look* what you have done!" Primrose clicked her tongue crossly.

He grinned. "It would have been *such* a shame to disappoint her." He pushed one of Daisy's amber gold ringlets aside and addressed her in thrilling tones. "You see, Miss Chartley, I *am* a villain!" Whereupon he kissed her fingers—they had somehow or other got themselves ungloved—winked at Primrose, and strode from the room without a further word.

The house, when the sisters returned to it, was in an uproar. The first thing they noticed, as they hurried upstairs to change their rain-soaked garments, was that there were posies all about the place, large bouquets sending heavenly fragrances in all directions. Daisy stopped to smell a few, and to call for some larger vases. Flowers were her passion and she could not *bear* to see them crammed stiffly in ornamental bouquets.

It was Primrose, then, ascending the stairs, who almost collided with a striking-looking Lily in a walking dress of smart military style.

"Primrose, I shall never forgive you for adventuring without me, but you shall not *believe* the excitements we have had today! Lord Holden, Lord Witherspoon, Captain Stanley, and Sir Lancelot Danvers all left cards; Mr. Stanridge has been composing sonnets—quite horrible, really, but still they celebrate my eyes so I cannot help liking them just a smidgen—and we have had *two* proposals of marriage!" On this dramatic note, she clasped her hands in glee and awaited, breathless, her sister's response.

It was indulgent. She kissed Lily's forehead and brushed away some of the dark, silk strands that had escaped their rather grown-up topknot.

"Gracious, Lily, you quite overshadow all *our* tame adventures! And who, may I ask, is *we?*"

"We?" Lily looked puzzled.

The elder Miss Chartley endeavored to be patient,

not too hard a task, for she loved Lily dearly, despite a robust innocence coupled with a hearty narcissistic streak that bordered, at times, on conceit. But then, she *was* so lovely! She had sumptuous dark hair that, when loosened from the topknot, fell about her shoulders and almost down to her waist in a positively abundant display of shining luster. Her eyes were sultry, a deep green that whispered of promises and was bordered by long, ebony lashes with distinguished brows as accents. Her complexion was creamy, with just the faintest hint of rose touching the high lines of her cheekbones. She stared, now, in blank incomprehension.

Primrose decided to spell her meaning out. "You said *we* had received two proposals of marriage. Do you mean you and I or you and Daisy or all of us collectively?" This last was meant only as a little satirical humor, but turned out to be the closest to Lily's bright-spirited meaning.

"Oh, any of us will do!" Lord Darnley and Gresham were quite specific about that point.

"Well, that hardly sounds specific to me!" Primrose continued her ascent up the stairs. "Does Grandfather know?"

"Of course, he received them! He has been chortling quite disgustingly ever since! Gave them a regular flea in the ear—Betty heard him and reported it to Mrs. Bartlett, and she—in confidence of course—"

"Of course." Primrose smiled. Her sister missed the irony and continued happily "—told me!"

"Well! And what did she tell?"

Miss Chartley had arrived at her chamber.

"Oh, he was in high fettle, led them on preposterously, listened to Lord Darnley's dowry proposal and Lord Gresham's declaration of undying love—then guffawed rudely in their faces and told them that if his granddaughters were such gap straws as to want to marry such pathetic specimens of masculine pulchritude, he would not cast a rub in the way."

Primrose chuckled.

"Mrs. Bartlett must have most faithfully recounted events, for I can hear him using those terms exactly!"

"Oh, *no!* Mrs. Bartlett said he was using some hideous oaths but she could no sully my ears by repeating them."

"Mmm . . . I'll warrant." Primrose was thoughtful as she pushed open her door and beckoned for Daisy, who was only now appearing upon the landing. "Come inside, we shall have a council of war." At which Lily's eyes sparkled solemnly and Daisy seemed well pleased, for she'd just contrived to overhear this last remark.

"Something is afoot. In the last day, we have been abducted, proposed to, and inundated with morning callers. Grandfather hinted—rather slyly I felt—that I could expect my share of suitors. Any ideas?"

"Grandfather is up to something!" Daisy seemed delighted at the brilliance of her perception. Primrose sighed. "That much is obvious! But what? It must be something remarkably cunning to have him in such high grig with peers of the realm falling all over our feet!"

"It is!" Unexpectedly, Lily jumped off from the neatly arranged counterpane she'd been bouncing on and pointed to Primrose's crisp, unread copy of *Society News.* "I'll wager it is in there, too. It was definitely inserted in the *Gazette* and the *Post.*"

"*What* was?" Her sisters chorused in unison. Primrose restrained herself from boxing Lily's pretty little ears.

"Oh, Grandfather's bequest. He is heaping his whole entire fortune like coals upon one of our heads. We are either to inherit nothing at all, or the vast total of riches he has accumulated over the years. Something about change and railways or something. Primmy, it is a *prodi-*

gious sum! I had simply no idea! He is cackling merrily and calling it 'Raven's Ransom,' for indeed, it *is* large enough to be a king's ransom, I'm certain."

"Yes . . ." Primrose looked thoughtful. "Does he mention which one of us is to inherit?"

Lily laughed. "Oh, that is the dreadful thing! He doesn't know himself!"

"What?" Again, both Daisy and Primrose spoke as one.

"He doesn't, truly! He is a wicked old rogue! He has announced that the inheritance will only be formalized as a dowry when all three of us are married."

"And then?"

"And *then*—" Lily looked mischievous, rather enjoying drawing the rapt attention she was receiving. "And then Richmond shall enter his book room carrying a jewel-encrusted tricorne hat."

"Yes?"

"In it shall be cards bearing our names. He shall draw one and settle his fortune on whoever that name shall be."

You could hear a pin drop.

"Well!" The sensible Miss Chartley was for once struck mute.

Daisy giggled. "We shall have every fortune hunter in London courting us!"

"They would have to be gamblers, too, for it is all or nothing with the odds against."

Primrose looked gloomy, though she *did* admire Lord Raven's cunning. He was using *one* fortune to respectably wed three penniless orphans. Still, the thought of a fortune-hunting husband with a predilection for gaming did not exactly rouse her spirits. Grandfather should have consulted her. Undoubtedly, there would have been a wiser way. There was enough to distribute the largesse perfectly evenly between them. She sighed. Inveterate gamblers *never* seemed to realize that others might not share their enthusiasm for the hazards of chance. There was nothing for it. She would talk to the Earl of Raven. She only hoped she could scotch the nonsense before any harm was done.

When she peremptorily knocked on his door a little later, however, she realized her mistake.

"Wiser?" The old man chortled wickedly and reached for a sip of prime brandy to soothe the ensuing fit of coughing. "A *pox* on wiser! I have not had so much entertainment in years!" His yellowing teeth glinted with gold in the curtained half light of dusk.

"And by the by, young lady . . ."

She looked at him with exasperation mingled with a slow pride. He might be curmudgeonly, but his wits were rapier sharp and his scheme, whilst loathsome and reprehensible, *did* have the merit of making a twisted kind of sense. A gazetted fortune hunter would not, given the odds, take the risk of marrying poverty. A peer of the realm, in need of—but not *desperate* for—funds might well consider the risk worth seizing. There were many, she knew, of the ilk of Darnley and Gresham.

"Yes?" She fixed her gaze on Lord Raven, who was propped up on his pillows consuming a lavish repast of kippers, coddled eggs, and sugared oats.

"By the by, the next time you find yourself rescued by a dashing cutpurse on Westenbury lands, have the goodness, I beg, to furnish him with your direction! I have a fancy to cross swords with a fellow who is more than a mere milk-and-water mannequin! Those last two—Lords Darnley and Gresham—were pathetic!"

Primrose was not surprised her exploits had come to Lord Raven's ears. There was nothing, it seemed, that escaped him.

"It is Daisy you should address, sir! I believe she was *quite* enamored of the man, though I am a little suspicious of his professed profession. I should hate to disappoint you and present you with some pink of the Ton who has nothing, whatsoever, to do with the high toby."

"Pink of the Ton, eh?" The earl stroked his chin thoughtfully. "He was an impostor?"

"Daisy did not seem to think so."

"Daisy does not think, period! What do *you* think?"

"I would be surprised, sir, if a well-spoken man with unimpeachable address, impeccable accents, and snow white hands ever did anything more fearsome than ride his steed across the downs at a canter."

The earl chuckled. "Was he tall, dark, and handsome?"

"Of course. All fairy-tale villains are."

"Codswallop! You are confusing heroes and rogues. Tell me, were his eyes green?"

"No, they were hazel brown."

"Ah, noticed, did you?"

"The man was imposing."

"Doubtless, doubtless. Westenbury, you say?"

"Yes."

The earl looked thoughtful. "Ride an Arab?"

"Yes."

"About five-and-twenty?"

"Grandfather, you talk as if you know him!"

"Hush, child! I am merely lucky in my guesses."

"You have the devil's own luck."

Raven guffawed. "Very possibly." There was a moment's pause as he viewed Primrose speculatively. "Then he was the model of propriety?"

"Did *I* say that?" Primrose did not flinch, but looked at her grandfather straight in his beady, knowledgeable, and altogether far too rakish eyes.

"Propriety was not his second name, my lord. His behavior was reprehensible and his manners altogether far too rakish to be permissible."

"A rogue, was he?"

"Absolutely." There was a moment's silence.

"A *personable* rogue?"

"Oh, *very* personable. Daisy practically swooned every time she caught a glimpse of his *entirely* ample proportions."

The earl chuckled. "Sounds like a man and not a milksop." On that point, Primrose was unfortunately forced to agree.

Four

Lord Rochester's very able valet stared at his lord and master as if he had something akin to the pox. Indeed, his revulsion was so intense that he was hard-pressed not to visibly shudder. Even so, his hands trembled as he set down the elegant garment, studded in lapis lazuli, that he had been about to suggest for the evening.

"My lord." He swallowed hard and averted his gaze from the slovenly garb the marquis had chosen to effect. The greatcoat had fewer than three capes and though undoubtedly warm, was hardly the height of noble fashion. Likewise, my lord's riding boots were past their first stare and his unmentionables were exactly that—unmentionable.

"My lord! They turned the Duke of *Wellington* away from Almack's because he was not wearing full-dress costume!"

"I am aware of that, Reece!" The marquis grinned a particularly engaging sort of smile and turned to the mirror. "They shall undoubtedly turn *me* away, shall they not?"

"More like to call in the watch!"

"Ha, I love it when you are moved to sarcasm! Yes, I believe the outfit shall suffice."

"My lord!" Reece's tone was somewhat strangled. "I shall never hold my head up again if you persist in garbing yourself like a common groom! *You* shall be turned away from the door and *I* shall be the laughingstock of all my peers. I am convinced you cannot be so cruel!"

The marquis stared at his reflection in the glass. It looked rather raffish. He set his beaver to an angle, adjusted it ever so slightly, then declared himself satisfied.

"Mama shall have fits!"

"Undoubtedly, my lord." The valet's tone was dry.

"Excellent! I shall take the place of her coachman, tonight."

"What?" Reece's jaw dropped quite comically.

"She dislikes Jaspers, you see."

Reece did *not* see, but he held his peace with a disapproving sniff. The marquis continued. "It is really quite simple. She desires me to take her to Almack's, so I shall."

"I am certain she meant *escort,* my lord!"

"Ah, but she did not say that! I distinctly heard *take.*"

Reece regarded him in dawning comprehension. The honorable marquis chuckled throatily at his horror.

"She shall be well served, for I do believe she meant to cut a wheedle with me! She knew I would be too softhearted to refuse to escort her to that wretched place, but once there, she meant to trap me with a quagmire of her friends and her friend's friends! I cannot stand that place—everyone falling over each other to catch a title and nothing stronger on offer than warm lemonade and little stale cakes!"

The valet remained unconvinced, fingering the lapis lazulis lovingly and itching to pull off my lord's travesty of a cravat and begin again, with something rather more starched and definitely more snowy than the current pretender. But alas, it was not to be! My lord would have none of it, adjuring poor Reece to "have a very good night"—something which insulted the poor fellow no end, for how could he have a good night when my lord was jaunting about town, destroying his reputation as a valet of the foremost stature?

He did not exactly sniff, but my lord was apprised of his disapproval by the square set of his shoulders and the speaking silence with which he met these frivolous words.

The marquis chuckled. "Cheer up, Reece! I promise to keep my head down low so as to save your precious reputation. All going well, no one but her ladyship need know ought of this little exploit!"

"And will her ladyship approve?"

"Oh, undoubtedly not! *That*, my dear man, is the point!"

With these cheerful words, Reece was forced to be content. He may have been mollified to learn that the Dowager Marchioness of Rochester shared his sentiments exactly. Confronted with her son looking like a coachman rather than a gentleman of rank, she hastily waved some smelling salts about her person before moving to greet him. She was too canny a mother, however, to do more than lift her eyebrows slightly and decline a rather pungent arm.

If my lord was disappointed in this mild response, he did not reveal so, merely remarking that "since he was not dressed for Almack's, he would simply have to wait for her in the chaise," a point upon which his much-beleaguered mother could not argue. Thus it was that my lord personally drove his merry, royal blue chaise into the courtyard leading up to Almack's. When his mother descended, she refused to allow him to hand her down, for fear of soiling her ribbed gold sarcenet, acquired most especially for the occasion.

My lord grinned at her cheekily and murmured that she must not scold him, for he was feeling wicked and spoiling for a "bit of fun." Whereupon the dowager marchioness rapped him on the knuckles with her ebony fan and commented dryly that he was "an incorrigible rogue" and that she hoped he had a long and *very* boring wait ahead of him, for she intended to dance the night away and more.

The marquis sighed. Doubtless it was true, for the marchioness was *wretchedly* fashionable and boasted a *deplorably* long list of friends. They would all, he was certain, jockey for her company until it would be impossible to tell which of her delightful attributes was likely be more worn out—her slippers or her tongue.

Thankfully, the moon was full, his carriage equipped with a wonderfully newfangled gas lamp, and he'd had the foresight to bring with him a long, but edifying book. After he'd settled the horses and idly watched the procession of debutantes enter the hallowed halls, he would thank his lucky stars for the blissful reprieve and settle down snugly. *Uranometria* made interesting reading.

Miss Primrose Chartley smiled rather weakly and declined her third dance with a very handsome but sadly impecunious gentleman. Her refusal did not help her much, for just as soon as he had taken his leave, his place was usurped by *another* gentleman—not as handsome, this time, but decidedly higher in rank. Unfortunately, his pockets too, were notoriously to let.

"Am I to be surrounded by nothing but fortune hunters for the rest of the Season?" The tone held a note of amused despair.

"Beg pardon?" Lord Asterley caught her mumbled remark.

"Oh! I was talking to myself. A dreadful habit. *Do* forgive me!" She accompanied her contrite apology with such a glorious smile that poor Lord Asterley wished he were a mere youth again instead of an elderly statesman in his dotage. Miss Chartley was not hard to forgive when her eyes shone as bright as diamonds and the lights in her hair were as lustrous as copper kettles and a good deal more attractive.

"Not at all, not at all!' He bowed correctly and offered her his arm. "Captain Redding was asking after you. Shall I tell him you are on the patio?"

"Heaven forbid! I believe he is hedging his bets, for he has danced twice with Lily and at least once with Daisy. Grandfather's bequest has become quite deplorable!"

"Very irksome, I am sure." Lord Asterley did not pretend to misunderstand. The Chartley sisters were the talk of the Ton. Lord Raven had outdone himself. Undoubtedly, they would make excellent matches, but at what cost? Miss Chartley, though not precisely haggard, looked tired and a trifle out of sorts. He could not blame her in the least.

"Would you like a seat? I am certain I can procure one for you . . ."

"How kind, your lordship! But no, if I sat down I would doubtless be surrounded by a dozen impoverished peers. I do not like to sound ungrateful, but their attentions are all rather suspect and though I *do* admire poetry and sonnets I prefer them to be sincere! I have been offered Spanish coin all evening and frankly, sir, I am tired of it!"

"Shall I call up your carriage, then? You may wish to depart before the crush."

Primrose shook her head mournfully. "No, for Daisy and Lily are enjoying themselves prodigiously! Perhaps I *will* make my curtsies, though, and wait for them in the comfort of my chaise."

"Coward!" Lord Asterley took leave to tease. Primrose responded with a wide smile that reached her lovely eyes and quite transformed her often contemplative nature.

"Quite so! Lord Asterley, I bid you adieu!"

So saying, she weaved her way through the interested throng until she found Daisy and apprised her of her intentions. Then it was a quiet wait for Lady Jersey, the most distinguished of the patronesses, before she was able to plead a headache. Finally, escorted by one of the liveried staff, she was able to step into the dark, candlelit mews.

"There! It is that one, with the royal blue wheels." She was thankful that it was so close to the entrance. The coachman was nowhere to be seen. Doubtless he was partaking of his *own* jollification together with the other assorted grooms and ostlers so essential to the occasion. She opened the door with ease, for it was marvelously well oiled and waved the attendant away.

"I shall be perfectly fine, thank you! No, it is not necessary to help me up, there is a stair. See?" Deftly, she pulled down the little step and clambered in, careful not to catch her gown under her slippered feet. It was made of shimmering amber organdy and she was loath to ruin it. Though she was not vain, the color was a perfect foil to her lustrous eyes and cropped copper head that harbored just the whisper of curls. She waited as the footman lifted up the step and clicked the door shut. Then, with a wave, she turned from him and allowed her eyes to become adjusted to the relative gloom of the interior.

"Oh!" Her heart gave a lurch as she realized she was not alone. There was a *man* in the chaise, and though he was fast asleep, she could not quite ignore the broad chest and hard muscles that lay beneath his cream shirt. If he woke, she would undoubtedly be powerless, for there was a firmness about his jaw that brooked no argument. Also, his arms, reprehensibly visible in their turned-up shirtsleeves, appeared entrancingly strong. She knew a wild moment of wanting to touch them, to feel if they were *indeed* as powerful as they seemed.

Instead, she vacillated somewhere between a scream and sublime curiosity. What was he *doing* here? Surely not abducting her, when his countenance was so serene in slumber? Besides, on closer scrutiny he did not look like a gentleman at all. Rather than elegant velvet knee breeches and the obligatory clocked stockings, he was wearing a rather disgusting confection that made him appear to be a groom or a coachman at best.

"Oh!"

At last, Primrose thought she had her answer. The man *was* her coachman, taking a rather large liberty by napping in her interior. She smiled. Well, why not? He appeared exhausted.

She folded her arms and tried to ignore his presence, thinking back to the events of the evening. She *must* speak with Grandfather—his bequest was untenable. She would rather be a wallflower than suffer the attentions of a myriad of fortune hunters. She stared out the window, but it was too dark to see a thing. Strange, despite the coolness of the evening, she felt warm and her pulses were racing quite unaccountably.

She steadfastly ignored the breathing of her manservant, but when he moved, slightly, so that his hand was just touching the seam of her elegant velvet gown, she felt she had stretched forbearance to the limit. She lifted his fingers and placed them back on his chest. They were warm, ungloved, and ridiculously inviting. Primrose felt herself flush. She realized with a shock that she actually wanted to kiss them, a guilty sensation that she found as unaccountable as it was intoxicating. She resisted, of course, but the sensation lingered, causing her heart to beat quite out of pelter with her sensible thoughts.

Her eyes caught the book discarded on the floor, *Uranometria*. They widened in disbelief. *Uranometria*. The man, surely, was not *literate!* How could he be reading such an animating discourse on the universe?

She picked it up and fingered it gently. The leather smelled pleasing, and the pages were invitingly crisp. She pulled off her gloves and fingered through the book, settling, at last, for a fascinating description of the planets. Sadly, her thoughts would not settle in the disciplined manner to which they were accustomed, veering dangerously toward a certain unexpected intruder.

How shocking that she should not yet have raised an alarm! How shocking, too, that she was now searching about for her carriage blanket that she customarily kept under the squabs. It was not there. Dash it, the man must be lying on it! She leaned a little closer, then gasped as his eyes opened and she found herself caught in a vice-like grip, prone across her captor. He smiled beguilingly in the dim lamplight, then pulled her head down to his. His lips were featherlight and warm, rather more dreamy than she imagined—and she *had* imagined, though it is scandalous to reveal as much. She thought of struggling, but his arm was hard against the arch of her back and she knew a certain thrill in its obvious dominance. Struggling was out of the question. Too undignified by far. She wafted, then, in a wave of desire that made a mockery of her habitual common sense. After a whilst, she found herself reluctantly released, though there was a beguiling light in the stranger's eye as he examined his quarry in more detail.

"Whoever you are, you are certainly intriguing!" His words were amused, and held a slight hint of question. She thought his tone rather peremptory for a man of his lowly position.

She sat up as straight as she could and considered slapping his face. Then, since she could not honestly *regret* his reprehensible behavior, she thought the better of such a drastic action and raised her brows haughtily instead.

"The boot is on the other foot, my good man, for in truth though I suspect I *know* who you are, you are certainly also intriguing."

The amusement crept from striking eyes to an impossibly handsome mouth.

"It is unfair that you have the advantage of me, then. Who are *you?*"

Primrose looked cynical. It was not necessary for the coachman to feign ignorance of her identity. She hated above all things dishonesty, and so held herself a little aloof as she replied. When he didn't answer, she continued. "I am surprised you do not know me, since it is Lord Raven who pays your annual stipend. Go now, whilst my sisters are still dancing."

She mistook the incredulity in his eyes for hesitation. Her tone became more urgent, though her heart was still beating impossibly quickly and she wondered if he *realized* that his eyes were focused rather improperly on her soft, modestly cased cleavage. She blushed, for her thoughts were straying in a most immodest direction and she had it in her to wish she had chosen something more daring, like Lily. Still, he hesitated.

"I shall not betray you, for I fear my *own* behavior is equally at odds. I cannot comprehend it at all."

She sounded puzzled, which caused the gentleman to smile a little and at last volunteer a response. It was not the one Primrose was seeking, but it had the effect of causing her to tremble, a little, and close her eyes against the improper suggestion. The rogue had actually volunteered to repeat his actions. "Purely," he qualified, with a teasing glint to his observant eyes, "in the interest of comprehension."

At which Primrose regarded him sharply and asked where he had acquired the manners—if not reticence—of a gentleman born. He grinned and regarded her lips unmercifully. Miss Chartley felt her heart hammering, once again, and tried bravely to ignore it.

"You are a rogue, sir, for staring at me like that!"

"Not for kissing you?"

"Oh, undoubtedly for that! Do go away, now, you are unsettling me."

"But not frightening you?"

She regarded him in silence. Though he was behaving outrageously, had taken unspeakable liberties, and was looking very much like repeating the offense, she was *not* frightened. She must be a very unnatural sort of female, but somehow those eyes, though they spoke dangerous volumes, made her feel safe rather than the more sensible reverse.

"I shall not answer that, for my wits are singularly at odds with my senses. If you were a gentleman, you would leave at once."

"And deprive myself of kissing you yet again? You must think me a very poor sort of fellow."

"I shall scream!"

"No, you shall not, for at the slightest resistance I shall stop at once."

"Very well. Consider yourself resisted."

He looked so hurt, Primrose felt a gurgle of laughter rise to her throat.

"Oh, don't look so downcast! Do you read?" She picked up Bayer's *Uranometria* and handed it to him. He looked quizzical.

"By that I take it you mean '*can* you read?' "

She blushed. "If you like, I can teach you. *Uranometria* is rather hard-going for a beginner, but I can lend you several more suitable works."

He hid a smile. "Gothic romances?"

"Good heavens, no! I leave such nonsense to my sisters. But I have some heavenly descriptions of the new railways and the art of ballooning and horseback riding and . . ."

The gentleman wondered if she realized how animated her face had become in the lamplight. He yearned to take her in his arms again and explore the delicious crests that peeped invitingly out from the reams and reams of velvet and organdy.

"You are not paying attention!"

"Oh, but I *am!*" He eyed her impudently and chuckled as the color rose to her delicious cheeks.

"You are incorrigible. I believe I shall withdraw my offer and ask you to wait outside. You really are the strangest of servants, for none, I believe, has ever before been quite as presumptuous! Waiting *inside* my chaise indeed! You are fortunate your garments are not muddy, or my sisters would have fits."

"But not you?"

"Oh, undoubtedly me too! This gown is hideously modish—I would not have it ruined for the world."

"And there you are telling taradiddles, my dear, for I do believe it is quite dreadfully crushed and I have heard nary a murmur of complaint."

"No thanks to you! It is only my singularly good nature that saves you."

"And there, at last, I believe you speak the truth. About your singularly good nature, I mean."

Primrose blushed. She had been jesting, but the gentleman's low tones spoke of a sudden admiring sincerity. She had no patience for elegantly turned compliments and certainly, as compliments went, this was fairly stark and understated. Still, she felt a trifle breathless as her keen eyes met his.

"Spoken like a gentleman."

The marquis's eyes twinkled. "That is a relief, my angel, for I *am* one."

Five

He waited, with interest, for the effect of this pro-
nouncement. Primrose scrutinized him closely, her lips
parting just a trifle as she regarded his firm chin and
unwavering gaze. She hesitated, a little, for he did look
dreadfully heathenish in his assortment of ill-fitting garb.
Still, despite some entirely reprehensible behavior on his
part, the notion that he *was* something other than a common coachman was beginning to dawn on her rather
forcibly. She tested him gingerly. "If you are a gentleman,
what are you doing in my carriage?"

There was a moment's silence as the marquis contemplated a succinct answer. Whilst she waited, doubtful eyes
assaulted him. Then a terrible thought struck. "Good
Lord, you are not seeking to *compromise* me, are you?"

"Why should I do *that?*" He appeared interested, being
far more conversant with the reverse. One of the rather
intriguing aspects of rank was that many unscrupulous
young ladies would do anything to contrive to be alone
with him. At first, he'd suspected *this* little maiden of being unusually enterprising, but a few moments in her
company had made him revise his suspicions. Now he
listened with growing amusement.

"Oh, the same reason Sir Rory Aldershot abducted me
yesterday! You wish to gamble on the odds of my being
an heiress. But I assure you, sir, you are far off, for Grandfather is the wiliest of creatures and will no doubt change

his mind a dozen times before we are wed. Besides, if you urgently require funds, the risk is too high. I could turn out to be quite penniless!"

"That would be a tragedy." The words were serious, but the tone was too light for Primrose to be fooled.

"Don't you care?"

"Not in the slightest."

"Then why are you ruining my reputation? It seems rather a drastic step, though I must compliment you on the novelty of your idea. Did you bribe my coachman?"

His lordship regarded her with awe. She was quite the most fascinating creature he had ever come across. So self-possessed in the face of danger! He wondered, for an instant, what had become of Sir Rory. A poor sort of fellow. He would cut his heart out when next they met. Still, he had evidently not succeeded. Perhaps *he* should have bribed the coachman, wherever he was.

"My lovely one, you are suffering under a terrible misapprehension. And though I am loath to set you right, for you shall undoubtedly be mortified and quite rightly wish to strangle me for not telling you sooner, I shall take courage in my hands and tell you nonetheless." He gazed at her intently and took her adorable hands in his own. Too late she remembered she had discarded her gloves. The gentleman's hands were warm and addled her wits quite unaccountably, so that it took a great effort of will to concentrate on what he was actually saying.

". . . so you see," he concluded, "this is not *your* carriage, but mine. I am not a coachman, though I can forgive your mistaking the matter. I frightened my mother into fits when she first saw my . . . uh, enterprising garb. The truth is, I loathe Almack's."

Primrose comprehended at once. "So you dressed to be disbarred. How clever of you! Though I must say, sir, that you were excessive! All you needed to do was present yourself in riding clothes or even formal morning dress.

Without knee breeches you would never have got beyond the entrance!"

"Mmmm . . . that may be so, but I needed to be certain. My mama, you see, is wretchedly popular. I feared she would cajole the doorman into making an exception."

"Good Lord, sir! You obviously do not know the doorman!"

"Tyrant, is he?"

"Oh, frightfully so! But you say this is not my chaise?"

"No."

"But how peculiar! Ours is quite noticeable for its color. The wheels are . . ."

"Let me guess. Royal blue?"

"Oh! Yours, too?"

"I believe so. Mama likes to keep up with fashion's little foibles."

Primrose sighed. "Lily chose the color. I might have known it was in vogue."

"Lily?"

"My younger sister. There are three of us, you know. I am Primrose. We are all named for flowers."

"How romantic! What is your elder sister named?"

"Oh, *I* am the elder sister."

"Never! You are far too dewy-eyed to be the eldest anything!"

"Flummery! It is too dark for you to notice my eyes."

"Are you calling me a liar?"

"No, just a practiced flirt and as such, I had better depart immediately. Do you think we have been seen?"

"I hope so, for then I should have to marry you at once."

Gareth surprised himself. He never thought he would say those words, even in jest. He felt a moment's anxiety lest Miss Pretty Primrose should take him too earnestly, but then was chagrined, the next moment, when she did not.

Her chuckle was infectious. "You should choose your compliments more carefully, sir! You would be well served if I were to take you at your word."

He was intrigued. Most young ladies would need no further encouragement.

He frowned a little as she started fumbling with the handle of the carriage door.

"No!"

She raised her brows inquiringly.

"You can't go out. You will be ruined. Everyone knows my chaise. The crest is emblazoned on the door."

"Really? I had not noticed it."

"It was dark." He sounded impatient. "Stay awhile. Perhaps when Mama arrives she can lend you countenance."

"Lily and Daisy will be anxious if I am not waiting for them."

"They will think you have returned to the ballroom. Come, don't quibble with me. I mean to save your reputation, so let us not cross swords."

Primrose nodded. Ever sensible, she saw at *once* the logic behind the man's words. It was a pity her heart was not just as sensible. It persisted on hammering unmercifully into her rib cage. She just hoped the wild beating was not audible to the gentleman placed so uncomfortably close beside her. She moved a little and he smiled.

"Not *shy*, are you? I won't eat you, though I daresay I might be tempted to *taste* you a little more."

"No!" Alarm crossed Primrose's expressive face. Then she saw he was teasing.

"You are a horrible flirt, sir! You should mend your ways or . . ."

"Or?"

Even in the dim glow of the gas lamps she could see his eyes sparkle dangerously. Then he was moving toward

her and wrapping his sturdy arms about her so posses-
sively it felt as if he had been doing it for a lifetime. Then
his face dipped, a little, and she felt the touch of his lips
upon hers yet again. For once, Primrose's errant heart
behaved itself. It stopped its rapid beat and its loud, impossible stammering. It changed course entirely, in fact,
and appeared to come to a halt. Primrose couldn't
breathe, for time had somehow suspended itself in the
entanglement of their lips. He smelled heavenly, despite
his strange attire. So clean and crisp . . . faint dark bris-
tles pricked at her where Reece had been derelict in his
duties and not *quite* shaved as close to the skin as he
might have. But then, the marquis no doubt had grabbed
the razor impatiently and done the job himself, an act
that always *infuriated* his much-suffering valet. Somehow,
Primrose drew closer, rather than drawing back, as was
her intent.

The marquis laughed triumphantly, though his eyes
were blazing. He held her from him a little and waited
for the inevitable scold when she was restored to her
senses.

It did not come, for her tongue was occupied with shyly
exploring her softened lips as her hands went up to her
flushed cheeks.

"You must think me a wanton, sir."

"Not at all. I think you are a very wonderful lady who
has probably never before been kissed." His tone was unexpectedly gentle, and not at all flippant or teasing as
she might have expected.

"It is that obvious?" Perversely, she looked mortified.

"Only in the nicest sort of a way." He did not tell her
that his hands were clenched with the effort of not repeating the spontaneous episode. Had it not been so
painfully obvious that this *was* Miss Primrose's first encounter with the opposite sex, he might not have been
so forbearing.

"Come, there is no need to look so downcast. It was not *that* bad, was it?"

His tone took on a light, teasing note guaranteed to set her at ease.

"Now you are being absurd!" She smiled tremulously in response.

"Absurdity is my middle name. Cry friends, shall we?"

Primrose smiled. It was impossible to be ill at ease with him. "Oh, very well! But you shall have to be a little freer with your name, sir. I cannot keep calling you *nothing* the whole evening."

"It is Gareth."

It had a lovely ring to it. Primrose longed to test it out on her lips, but she had stretched impropriety far enough for one evening. "Now you are being ridiculous. You know perfectly well I cannot call you that either!"

He grinned. "First I am absurd, then I am ridiculous. There is no pleasing you, ma'am! Besides, you are being missish!"

"Not missish, just sensible. I will not call you by your first name, so don't, I beg you, even *think* it!"

"Well, *I* shall not be so nice in my proprieties! I shall call you Primrose when we are alone. And I hope, if I may say so, that *that* will be often."

His eyes lingered upon her face so that Primrose's heart fluttered like the flibberty gibberts she so abhorred. She dropped her gaze, so he would not see the confusion into which she was cast at this preposterous statement. She adopted her severest tones as she replied.

"And now you are being foolish, sir! Doubtless we shall not meet again under such irregular circumstances. And I still have not your name!"

The gentleman smiled, pleased to tease a little longer. "More is the pity, then, my sweet scolder! Absurd, ridiculous, and foolish. You should meet my mother. It will be a regular marriage of minds, for I assure you she shares your sentiments! Now don't look so cross, though I swear your features are beautiful even when you pout. No, don't grin, it spoils the effect." My lord folded his arms pleasantly and regarded Primrose with amusement. Then, taking pity on her, for she was clearly torn between a laugh and a haughty grimace of annoyance, he relented.

"Oh, very well, then, I suppose you will simply have to start 'my lording me.' Very boring, but have it your way. I am Gareth, Lord Rochester."

Primrose sat up a little straighter. "Then your mama is . . ."

"Gwenyth, the dowager marchioness. Do you know her?"

"Of course I do! She is so vivacious one would be hard-pressed *not* to know her! Besides, she is Lily's godmother."

Rochester eyed her doubtfully.

"She is?"

"Yes, although I wager she is hardly aware of the fact! She must be godmama to *dozens* of the debutantes."

"Indeed, she is. Mama seems to attract friendship wherever she goes. She had so many bosom buddies at school that poor Father quite lost track!"

"Yes, well *my* mother was one of them. Esmeralda Fincham, though it was probably such a long time ago she may hardly remember. Esmeralda married my father, Desmond Chartley, and asked the marchioness to stand godmama on Lily's birth. I believe our Lily still has the diamond pin she sent for her christening. Most unsuitable of course, and entirely too generous."

"Sounds like Mama! She is a dear creature when she is not trying to cut one of her wheedles with me. You will love her." Suddenly, it was important to Gareth that she did. He tried to figure how long he would have to sit in the carriage awaiting her arrival. There was a limit to his

patience, after all, and the temptation set before him was
rather unbearable.

He wondered what scent she used that could be so
fresh and sweet. He bent closer to breathe it once
more, then regretted that impulsive action, for the scent
was not *only* fresh and sweet, it was provocative in the
extreme, like honeysuckle or musk. He had a very masculine desire to taste of its sweetness once more, then
stopped himself with heroic forbearance. The lady obviously had no idea of the effect such a fatal scent
could have upon the senses. She looked so calm, so
peaceful, it was at odds with the erotic impulses she
was unwittingly fostering within him. Oh, how much
longer, he wondered, would he have to endure this tantalizing form of self-abnegation?

He was not left wondering long, for Lady Rochester
appeared sooner than he had dared anticipate. Her eyebrows rose markedly at the spectacle that confronted her,
but she waved the footman away languidly, rather cleverly
obscuring his view of the interior with her outrageous
ostrich feather fan. Slamming the door shut on her gay
damask shawl, she tutted a little but abandoned the thing
to its fate.

"Well, Gareth!" She chuckled a little as she viewed her
son's sudden discomfiture. She was not at all perturbed
by the presence of a lady seated comfortably on her favorite squab. Her sharp eyes detected, even in the lamplight, the crimson cheeks and the demure lashes of
copper gold that lowered, shyly, upon her scrutiny.

"You need not look so gleeful, Mama! Miss . . . good
heavens, I do not know your name!"

"Chartley." The words were chorused by both Primrose, and to her astonishment, the marchioness. Lady
Rochester chuckled and winked at Primrose, who felt she
had never been caught at such *point non plus* in her life.

"I am not *totally* a scatter wit, Gareth! Miss Chartley

is one of Esmeralda's chicks." She opened her fan then snapped it shut with a sudden click. "*Gracious,* I believe I may be your godmama!" Her smile was so infectious, Primrose lost her rigid bearing and sudden consciousness.

"No, ma'am, that is my sister Lily."

"Well, well, I knew it was one of you. And you are . . . ?

"Primrose."

"Ah, yes. Esmeralda was always quirkish." She regarded Primrose solemnly, but a little dimple fluttered on either side of her cheek. After a pause, she smiled. "The other one's a flower *too,* I believe."

Primrose nodded. "Sadly, madame, that is so. It is a sore trial to us."

The marchioness chuckled. "As I am to poor Gareth. My manners! Forgive me! It was very wrong of me to call Esmeralda quirkish." She held her hands to her face in such a delightfully flustered manner that Primrose felt her lips twitching.

"You are perfectly right, ma'am! Mama *was* quirkish, though a dear from all I recall."

"That she was. That she was." Lady Rochester's eyes misted up in sudden memory. "One day I will tell you the tricks we all got up to. But come! You have to tell me the answer to this puzzle. Did my son lure you in here or did you happen to stumble into my chaise by chance? Or"—her eyes sparkled mischievously—"can it be you have a clandestine meeting . . ."

"Mama!" Gareth brought her up sharply.

"No? But how disappointing! Gareth, I began to cherish hopes."

Primrose giggled in spite of herself. The women shared glances of amusement at his lordship's sudden discomfiture.

"He is quite terrible, you know. Takes fright at a single dance and goes to impossible lengths to shirk his duties on the dance floor. I should not have been so softhearted. I should have left him to kick his heels all night as I threatened. Still, I'm not *entirely* sorry I cut the night short. I might not have had so much as a *whisper* of this interlude if I'd not seen it myself.''

Her tone held an unmistakable interrogative that caused Gareth to explain the mistake at once. The marchioness said nothing, but glanced curiously at Primrose on occasion, especially at those times when her exasperating son's eyes sparkled dangerously clear and when his lips curled just slightly, as if at some dear, much concealed memory.

The marchioness was no fool. She knew her son would not be a Rochester born and bred if he'd not expurgated his account, somewhat. Besides, the adorable coppercurled miss was blushing furiously. She was also, she noticed, casting adoring glances Gareth's way. She hoped she would soon rid herself of the habit. It would do the marquis no good to become too puffed up in his own conceit. When they were wed, she would drop Miss Chartley a little hint.

Ah, yes! There was no doubt in the marchioness's smug, self-composed, irrepressibly matchmaking mind that her son had at last met his match. It needed no more than a few moments in the eldest Miss Chartley's company to know *that*. Too bad that meddlesome Lord Raven was making the trio the talk of the Ton. Lady Cornwallis was already letting her malicious tongue run riot and pointing to the knot of fortune hunters who were currently besieging the remaining two.

She would have to do something to quash the nonsense, of course. The future marchioness of Rochester could not be permitted to be the subject of idle gossip and speculation. And Gareth, too. She would have to work on him. A small matter, for he was already halfway gone if the darkling glances he threw Miss Chartley's way was anything to go by. The knack would be getting him to realize it.

"Mama! You are not concentrating!"

"Indeed I *am!*" The marchioness permitted her tones to sound indignant, though in truth her mind *had* been wandering. It had been exploring quite delicious avenues that had more to do with cherubic grandchildren than with getting Primrose out of her most immediate fix. Now, she fixed her attention squarely where it belonged.

"I shall return indoors with Miss Chartley. No one need know we have left the ballroom. If rumor should perchance rear its ugly head, I shall thank her profusely for accompanying me to my chaise and applying spirit of lime to my aching forehead. As far as the world knows, Lord Rochester did not attend this evening. Gareth! Climb out the chaise at once and take the coachman's seat."

"Now? It is cold!"

"Excellent! You shall be well served for serving me such a trick this evening! You dress like a coachman, you shall *be* one! What is more, I have no notion how long I shall take, for it might take *hours* before we scotch any rumors. You know what they can be like."

Gareth did know. Accordingly, he suppressed a thousand muttered oaths and the annoying suspicion that his mother was enjoying herself thoroughly, and obediently moved to the door.

"Good-bye, Miss Chartley."

Primrose felt a terrible pain that she could not quite place. Her voice was quite steady, however, when she calmly replied.

"Good-bye, Lord Rochester."

The marchioness, privy to this polite exchange, shook her head quietly. Children! How tiresome they could be at times! Gareth could have swept her off her feet and kissed her till she swooned. He could have taken the reins

reins and driven straight to Gretna. But no! He mildly says good-bye and chooses, instead, to gnash his teeth all night and shiver with cold. Gentlemen could be so dull-witted.

The marchioness shrugged her shoulders and allowed Primrose to help her with her shawl. It had got jammed in the door, somehow, and was now looking sadly crushed. Still, she had to reflect, the calamity had been worth it. She'd found Gareth a gem of a bride and he was being well punished for his earlier sins. Out of the corner of her eye, she could see his cheek twitch in the moonlight. Good! Rochester men only twitched if they were deeply moved.

Six

"Miss Chartley!" Miss Pemberton's voice was coy as she playfully wagged her gloves at Primrose. "I had not thought to see you after the second quadrille."

Primrose kept her tone light as she smiled politely and adjusted the delicate bow of her shimmering organdy.

"No?"

"No, we had all *quite* thought you otherwise occupied!" The insinuation was clear in Miss Pemberton's inquiring eyes. Primrose felt her cheeks burn, slightly, but she managed an eloquently quizzical brow as she feigned an interest in the delicacies. They were being circulated on fabulous salvers of sparkling crystal and silver. She chose a light pastry filled with salmon and a delicate pinkish cream, then bit into it slightly before formulating her response.

"How intriguing! I cannot imagine what you think might have been occupying me so mysteriously?"

"Can you not?" Miss Pemberton almost snickered, particularly as she noted a small collection of young debutantes gathering about her. Primrose felt decidedly hot, but was sufficiently self-collected to keep her back straight and her brows arched.

"How short your memory must be. If *I* were caught clambering into Gareth, Lord Rochester's chaise, I warrant *I* might have something to recall!"

"No doubt." Primrose allowed her tone to become contemptuous, causing Lavinia Pemberton's eyes to narrow at the veiled insult. She was not mollified by several giggles behind her. How *dare* Miss Chartley! Particularly as it was *she* who had been caught flagrantly disobeying society's conventions! Lavinia stifled several pangs of jealousy, for Lord Rochester was the catch of the Season besides being deliciously good-looking when he wasn't staring frostily into the middle distance and ignoring one entirely.

She decided that pointed politeness was wasted on Primrose, so she turned her back to the amber-gowned beauty and whispered something rather nasty to Miss Redding, who looked alternately amused and disbelieving. Unfortunately, the whisper was rather audible—possibly by ill-natured intent—and caught the attention of Lady Rochester, who had just been striding purposefully in Primrose's direction. Ignoring both young ladies, who scrambled to curtsy to her—she placed her arm in Primrose's and thanked her once again, in bell-like tones, for alleviating her suffering. "You really are a marvel, Miss Chartley, for I swear my headache was quite shocking before you ministered to it. How *thoughtful* of you to take me back to the quiet of my chaise, and how very solicitous. I really *must* invite you and your sisters to Rochester, sometime, for I feel certain my son Gareth would wish to meet with you and thank you personally."

She shot a mischievous look at Primrose with these words, but otherwise preserved a haughty and entirely convincing demeanor. Miss Pemberton looked sick, but never one to miss any opportunity, clapped her hands elegantly and declared that a party to Rochester would be the very *thing* to lift poor dear Primrose out of the dismals and she would talk to her mama about it at once. Whereupon Lady Rochester looked upon her with ill-disguised contempt and commented that it was not a party she had in mind, but rather a quiet country gathering of friends. She emphasized this last word rather cruelly, Primrose thought, but she would not have been human had she not rejoiced a little at the tone. Miss Pemberton deserved a hearty set-down, and in truth, she had received it, albeit in the sweetest of language and only with the very *slightest* raising of haughty brows.

In another part of Almack's entirely, Miss Lily Chartley was holding court to as lively a collection of rakes and rogues as a young lady of first Season could wish for. She was entranced by Lord Damson's desire to paint her, and torn between agreeing to sit for him, or giving the honor to Mr. Ravensbourne, a quiet-spoken man with dangerous eyes that made her shiver quite delightfully. Of course, there was always the sadly impoverished Lord Windham, but he would do nothing more daring than lavish fulsome glances her way and fetch endless supplies of lemonade. All this, of course, was thoroughly satisfactory, for Lily was a spritely creature who cared nothing for the questionable motives behind her sudden spate of popularity.

True, Grandfather *had* been rather naughty to leave his inheritance in such an equivocal fashion, but it was his, after all, and she was having the most agreeable time as a consequence. She flattered herself that the attention was not *all* due to the will, for even Lady Cowper had commented that she was in high good looks. She smoothed down the crisp white lines of her shimmering satin and glanced, for a moment, in the mirror. Yes, Primrose had been right, the simple clasp of pearls *had* been better than the diamonds she'd yearned to borrow. And how clever Daisy had been with the dewdrops! They framed her face perfectly. She was just turning to thank a gentleman in a stiff, starched collar, whose name she could not quite recall but who had just likened her dark hair to a night hallowed with the luster of moonbeams, when her eyes caught, in the mirror, a reflection that made her wide, green eyes widen just a fraction more than was usual. Just before she dropped her dark lashes in a sudden, wild, and quite stormy impulse of abandon, she felt her pulses quicken and her breathing become strangely shallow. When she looked up, the figure that had so silently assaulted her senses, had gone. Viscount Barrymore, similarly afflicted, had felt it wise to call up his horses. His situation was too desperate to take up a flirtation, however vivid, delightful, and thoroughly reprehensible the attraction. Despite Hoskin's optimism, tomorrow, he was certain, he was bound for a debtor's jail. He wondered gloomily what the pretty little snippet in the pearl white dress would say to *that*.

It was a pity, of course, that he did not stop to ask her, for Lily would undoubtedly have waved his debts aside as airily as she did those of the *other* swain who had taken up her suit. Indeed, she would have been confoundedly surprised *had* he been plump in the pocket, for so outrageously a handsome a rig as *he* was attired in must have cost a small fortune and everyone knew that gentlemen were *always* indebted to their hatters and bootmakers and the like. She sighed. She wished he had not disappeared so summarily! And now there was the clamor of people demanding the first waltz and she could not decide between them! Had it been Lord Alvaney or Mr. Campion to whom she had bestowed the honor? She wished she could remember, for both were approaching her forcefully and she rather hoped she could remember the steps. It was an age since she had practiced, and she'd never before danced the waltz at Almack's, or indeed, even in the assembly rooms at Bath. Who *was* that man? Her thoughts were most abstracted as she curtsied delightfully to both Mr. Campion *and* the Earl of Alveney.

On the west side, Daisy was fending off an almost equal share of admirers but, she, at least, had the presence of mind to remember that permissions had not yet been granted. The evening was sadly flat, for not one of the young bucks buzzing beside her bore the slightest resemblance to her dashing Barnacle Jack and that, of course, was damning enough. No one, she decided, without dark eyes and an imposing physique that was quite faultless without padding could move her in the slightest. Besides, without quizzical eyes and a slightly mocking mouth, whoever claimed her hand would undoubtedly be doomed to fail. She kept these thoughts to herself, however, as she declined the waltz very prettily and glanced around to remind Lily about the conventions.

She was nowhere to be seen, but by the buzzing of gentlemen on the east side, she was probably to be located in that direction. The orchestra was tuning up and Daisy had the most sinking of feelings that Lily was going to forget. Oh, *where* was Primrose! *She* would remember and keep Lily from disgracing herself. But no, she had retired to the carriage, of course.

Daisy hopped off her perch and tried to move toward the throng of people across the room. Her skirts were heavy, though, being trimmed with rosettes of velvet and pearls, so it was with resignation that she saw Lily place her gloved hand in that of Mr. Campion's. There was no stopping it. Lily was about to commit the most unspeakable of social solecisms and with the first notes ringing loud in *all* of their ears, there was little anyone could do about it. Miss Chartley could hardly bear to look as she saw Lady Sally Jersey bearing down upon her sister. No doubt she was going to scold her mercilessly, for the patroness's sharp tongue was positively infamous. Poor Lily!

The youngest of the sisters, quite unaware of the sensation she was causing about the room, and of the jealous twittering of feminine fans as rival debutantes waited breathlessly for her downfall, stopped a moment to gaily smell some of the crimson hothouse roses that had been cultivated for the event. When she looked up, she startled, once more, for she was face-to-face with her debonair stranger and her legs trembled unforgivably in their daring undergarments of rouched pantalets.

Lord Denver Barrymore, viscount of the realm, regarded her with amusement tinged with a hint of resignation. Trust *him* to not have bided by his instincts and called the damned horses up! But no, he *would* have to do a right turn and demand of Sally an introduction. By the looks of it, she needed it, for it was a waltz striking up and he could bet his last farthing—quite literally, as he probably did not have a guinea to his name—that the chit had not been visited with the celebrated permissions. He looked sternly at Sally, who could never, he knew, resist a gentleman of charm and address. He just prayed he had both. He obviously did, for Lady Jersey's frown lightened considerably as she applied her lorgnette to Lily and glared at poor Mr. Campion, who had the foresight to at once drop his arm and relinquish his prize.

"Ah, Miss Chartley!" Lady Jersey scrutinized Lily from top to toe until the youngest Miss Chartley would undoubtedly have squirmed in alarm had she not been fortified by a most unscrupulous wink by the dazzling gentleman at her side.

"I see Mr. Campion here was just escorting you to acquire permission to waltz. Well, permission granted, since you are a goddaughter of my very dear friend Lady Rochester and she has just rather obligingly vouched for you. You are fortunate." This last tone was dry and Lily realized at once her mistake and the lady's supreme graciousness in overlooking it. It did not occur to her to wonder how Lady Rochester—associated with her only by a prodigiously large diamond pin—should act her sponsor. She did, however, remember her manners sufficiently to bob a grateful curtsy. Mr. Campion seized her eagerly by her satin-trimmed arm. Lady Jersey froze him with a glance.

"I believe you have not yet met the Viscount Barrymore, Miss Chartley. Be warned. He is both a scoundrel and a rogue, probably in equal proportions. He has, however, the felicity of being a gentleman, so I commend you to his care and trust you enjoy the dance." With that, she deflated many a poor debutante's hopes, caused untold matchmaking mamas to seethe, and headed for the antechamber, where she could enjoy a comfortable coze with Emily Cowper and the Baroness Esterhazy. Lily, of course, did not look back.

Mr. Campion, seeing the direction of her gaze and divining, at last, that the great triumph of a waltz with Lily was not that night to be achieved, bowed perfunctorily and set his sights on the west wing, where he hoped he might make better headway with one of the *other* sisters. Again, Lily did not notice. She was blinded, in fact, by the deprecating smile of the gentleman before her, who apologized for his intervention and wondered, gazing all the time at her soft, berry red lips, whether she cared, at all, to favor him? Whereupon Lily uttered something that sounded very much like a squeal but which he obligingly took to be an affirmative. He then bowed, and led her, rather dazed, onto the floor.

Daisy felt she could breathe again. She would not have been so certain if she had noted the brooding eyes of a gentleman, darkly dressed in a frock coat trimmed with gold. He had just won a splendid, matched pair of high-stepping bays, but seemed to hold this to little account. Rather, his attention was fixed so wholly upon her shining eyes and remarkable ringlets, that he was forced to mutter an abstracted apology when he collided with Lady Dorset and her plaguey full-length hems. Fortunately, Daisy's complacency remained intact, for she had no notion of his extraordinary attention.

As the grand clock struck half past the hour, Primrose finally appeared, arm in arm with the Marchioness of

Rochester, a circumstance that caused many a knowing brow to lift. She suggested that they depart at once, for the hour was quite advanced and she was anxious to check that Lord Raven had taken his nightly regimen of syrups. The doctor had diligently prescribed them but it was a nightly battle of wills to get the obdurate earl to actually *take* them. Primrose half suspected her grandfather's recovery was due more to his anticipation of a good, down-to-earth squabble than the mixtures themselves. Still, she would not, for the world, deprive Lord Raven of his opportunity to curse and fuss and mutter quite dreadful oaths under his breath. Besides, poor Richmond would be at his wit's end. Despite all the years in his lordship's service, he *still* did not know how to manage him as successfully as the most headstrong of his granddaughters.

Daisy volunteered to search out Lily, who was in danger of disgracing herself again by ambling out into the gardens without a chaperon. When she had departed, the marchioness asked, in a mild manner, how it came to be that three such *very* lovely sisters appeared to be flouting convention and appearing in society without at least one dowager or chaperone in tow. Primrose colored, for up until now she had quite thought herself past her last prayers and old enough to escort the other two without precipitating comment. When she said as much to her ladyship, however, that lady stared at her very hard for a moment and wondered, in a rather conversational voice, whether Primrose had ever looked in front of a glass.

"Well, of course I have!"

"Then you must know, my dear, that you are very far from being past your last prayers! If you are not as popular as your sisters are proving to be, I shall own myself most surprised."

"Oh, that is only due to the ridiculous disposition of Grandfather's will. I daresay you have heard of it?"

"I have, and it sounds precisely the sort of harebrained, addlepated type of notion he is capable of! But if you think your popularity is owing only to his meddlesome nature, you mistake the matter entirely. My son, for example . . ."

"Oh, madame, *pray* say nothing about your son! I am perfectly certain he would not wish to be discussed in such a manner. He has been everything that is proper . . ."

"Has he, indeed? Well, I must say, then I am sadly mistaken in him, for I believed him to be as attractive in his own way as his dear father before him. And if he behaved with the utmost propriety in the face of such charm and undeniable beauty, he is less of a man than I gave him credit for!"

Primrose giggled. It was impossible to hold the marchioness at arm's length. Like her son, her vivacious character was infectious.

Lady Rochester's eyes twinkled. "So! It is as I suspected! You *are* in need of a chaperone! *All* of you! I shall write to Lord Raven tomorrow."

Primrose sobered at once. "Please, he is not well. I daresay he will have an apoplexy if he is forced to house some dowager or other. His temper, you know, is not what it was."

"Ha! His temper, I am certain, is *exactly* what it was! Leave him to me, my dear. I am spoiling for a good, old-fashioned fight and Lord Raven is bound to favor me with *that*, I am certain!"

On which point Miss Chartley was inclined to rather wholeheartedly concur, though if she still harbored doubts about the enterprise as a whole, she was wise enough not to say so.

Seven

"Dash it, Miles, I am smitten!" Lord Barrymore ignored the outraged protests of his dearest friend, who did not relish being woken at two in the morning for the edification of a lover's discourse.

"She had hair as black as night and a smile that seemed to light up her eyes—right behind, you know. There was just the faintest dimple behind her cheeks and oh, she had the gayest laugh. You could not help but love her if you were to see her!"

"Then it is fortunate that I won't, for Molly would undoubtedly throttle me and I would be forced to kill you, I am afraid."

Denver grinned. Miles must at last be waking, if his rapier-sharp wits were returning on form. "Do be serious! I am in the suds and have not the faintest notion what to do about it. I promised to see her again, tomorrow, but I cannot. I have that devil Raven to see."

"The earl? Is it *he* that you owe all those vast sums to?"

Barrymore nodded gloomily. "Yes, and though I have sold off the last of my brood mares, I cannot think *where* I am to procure the balance! The house is entailed and I dare not go to the cent percenters. They have *already* advanced me several hundred pounds."

"Good Lord, what did you *do* with it? Don't tell me you paid for that exquisite waistcoat, for I shall waste no sympathy on you!"

"This?" Denver dismissed his garment airily, though he *did* stop to flick a speck of dust off the impeccably embroidered seam.

"Heavens, no! I must still have the bill for this somewhere. Can't think where. Reece will know."

"Well, then? What did you do with the advance?"

"Oh! I bought a couple of coal mines."

"You kid me."

"No, indeed! Unfortunately, the wretched things are located in some ungodly place where it is practically impossible for a carriage to pass. *That*, I suppose, is how I managed to come by them so cheaply!"

"They are worth nothing, then?"

"Oh, by all accounts they are loaded! They have a very pure ore content and all that, only not a damned person can mine them!"

"How perplexing."

"And annoying."

"Yes." The two gentlemen stared at each other for a moment, before Lord Barrymore shivered, slightly, and stoked up the fire.

"I should get the housemaid to see to that."

"Wake her up at this time? Don't be so ridiculous!"

Lord Frampton—otherwise known as Miles to his intimates—narrowly avoided commenting that he wished his friend had similar qualms when it came to waking *him* up. The viscount was pacing nervously up and down the parquet flooring, though, so he desisted, for it was clear that Lord Barrymore was more troubled than he cared to admit.

"Can I not lend you the money? I daresay I can raise the wind if . . ."

Lord Barrymore shot him a dampening look. "God, Miles! I am not such a shimble-shamble fellow that I will sponge off my friends! No, tomorrow I shall see Lord Raven. If it is a debtor's jail for me, then so be it. I daresay one gets used to it. I heard if one becomes accustomed to the smell, it is almost bearable."

"That it should come to this! Is there anything I can do?"

"Will you seek out Miss Chartley for me and explain that though it is my heart's desire to renew our acquaintance, circumstance forbids it?"

"Miss Chartley? Which one?"

"Is there *more* than one?"

Miles regarded his debonair friend pityingly. "Do you know nothing, my lord? The Miss Chartleys are the talk of the Ton! There is Miss Primrose, who is serene and self-composed, Miss Daisy, who is sunny and rather too ingenuous for my tastes, and then there is Miss Lily . . ."

"Lily! That is the one! Don't you *dare* say a word against her! Oh, Miles, she is heavenly! So young and innocent! Has no notion of how to go on, you know . . ."

"Stop ranting, Barrymore! I have a plan!"

"What?"

"Offer for her! She is the very heiress you have been searching for!"

Lord Barrymore started to tell him he had *not* been searching for heiresses, but Frampton was not listening in the least.

"Perhaps you will be lucky. You have the devil's own luck, you know." Denver refrained from responding that losing half his stable, a ruby pin, facing the prospect of several months in jail did not constitute particularly good luck. Miles was continuing quite blithely, and his words made no sense at all.

"If she *is* the heiress, she will be worth an unholy fortune."

"What do you mean *if*? Do you *enjoy* talking in riddles, or is it just some unfortunate trick of fate?"

"If you read your newspapers, you would swallow your

sarcasm! Riddles, indeed. You are very behind hand not to know of Lord Raven's strange bequest."

"Lord Raven? What has *that* noxious creature got to do with it?"

"Everything, I imagine. He is Miss Chartley's grandfather. He also, by all accounts, holds the purse strings." It did not take Lord Barrymore *very* much longer to draw out the truth from his dearest friend, though he *did* threaten strangulation and death by a long sword. These inducements caused Lord Frampton to explain rather more quickly than he might otherwise have been inclined.

The odds were three to one that Lily would be the answer to Lord Barrymore's prayers. Privately, Lord Barrymore upped the ante, a little, for the stakes were higher than Lord Frampton supposed. It was *more* than mere money at stake, a complicated little twist that only gave fuel to the burning fires of a gambler born and bred. What were the chances, one might wonder, of achieving both stakes? A marriage of convenience might prove confoundedly *inconvenient* if it bore neither wealth nor mutual regard. Similarly, a financial windfall without any manner of accompanying warmth might prove sadly flat. Conversely, if he won Lily's heart but not the prize, might he not feel disgruntled? Disillusioned? Disappointed? To his astonishment, he thought not. The scales tipped heavily in his mind, reweighing the odds to his decided advantage. Miles droned on, but his voice was a mere background blur. By the time he had slipped on his superbly fitting coat, his mind was almost made up.

A very thoughtful viscount returned to Barrymore Court that night. The nightingales had given way to the early morning robins and kestrels, but sleep eluded him like a teasing wisp of curling mist. Impossible to grasp.

* * *

The earl was in fine fettle the following morning. Still wheezing, he was brandishing a calling card and rubbing his hands in eager glee. Daisy sat by his bed—for he liked to see each of his three flowers separately, though he summoned them in with a fierce voice and vowed they were nothing but a trouble to him.

"Grandfather, if you are better, let Richmond move you to the window. I have planted a scented garden beneath the eaves, so you shall smell the fragrances of jasmine and rosemary and honeysuckle as you sit. The lemons are not quite ready yet, but their leaves smell sweetly. I am certain you shall love it."

"Hmph!" Lord Raven's bushy-browed eyes softened almost perceptibly, though his tone remained a growl. "And what are you doing playing gardener, when there is a whole host of wastrel good-for-nothings I pay for the task?"

"Yes, but none that love you as much as I do!" Daisy peeped at him mischievously from under her shining, Rapunzel gold ringlets. She knew the earl would color up and be gruff, but be pleased, nonetheless.

"Ha! A tarradiddle if ever I heard one! And what do you know of love, little miss?"

Now it was Daisy's turn to color. More than Lord Raven suspected, for in truth she could not—no matter how hard she tried—rid herself of the image of Barnacle Jack. To her astonishment, the earl's lightning quick wits caught at her innermost thoughts in the most unnerving and thoroughly disconcerting manner. He lay back upon his pillows and chortled rudely.

"Ha, I warrant you yearn for a sight of that *cutpurse* you encountered upon your travels. *Yes,* I heard of that little adventure! You can't hoodwink the likes of me as well as you may your sisters! Come closer, I shall tell you a secret."

Daisy did, for there was no gainsaying the earl when

he was in a troublesome mood. Lord Raven coughed a little but waved away the nasty potion Richmond instantly held in front of his face. "Oh, go away, do! It has come to a strange pass when a gentleman cannot have a little comfortable coze with his granddaughter without the whole world standing by! And close the door!" Resignedly, Richmond caught Daisy's eye. She nodded, so he set down the glass, bowed regally—a sure sign he was affronted—and left the chamber.

"Good. A troublesome fellow, though no doubt he feels he is doing me some good. Now!" The earl's yellowing teeth glinted a little in the sunlight. He took Daisy's delicate, pink-gloved hands in his own rather bony ones.

"You are the most delicate of my flowers, but I do believe you might prove the hardiest! You shan't settle for some society beau, no matter *how* much poetry he recites! I wonder if our Lily's head shall be turned? I think not, though she stands in the gravest danger. That is the price one pays for being the youngest and most exotic! Still, I think she might surprise us yet. But come! We speak of you! If that fellow you came upon is worth half his salt, he shall find you and carry you off to his lair!"

Daisy's eyes widened, for though she knew her grandfather was talking nonsense, it was nonsense she silently dreamed of. Not *one* of the bevy of suitors claiming her hand at Almack's had turned her head so much as an inch.

"I have no notion of what you speak!"

"Have you not? Then you disappoint me vastly!" The earl looked at her hard, then chuckled. "Mr. Davenport offered for you yesterday."

"Did he?" Daisy looked rather uninterested. The earl chuckled. "He did, and though he is undoubtedly after your fortune, the scoundrel, I thought him somewhat better than Lord Quincey, who seemed uncertain whether it was you or Primrose he desired most in the world. I told him to think it over carefully before approaching me again."

Daisy giggled. "Grandfather, I do believe you are enjoying all this! You are a scoundrel!"

"That may be, but in deadly earnest nonetheless. I look to see you settled well."

Daisy withdrew her hands uncomfortably. "What if I don't *wish* to be settled well?"

"You would have to be a very unnatural sort of a female, then, or else in love with a rogue!"

Daisy squirmed uneasily, causing the earl to emit an infuriating "Ha!" in the boomy voice she detested.

She stood up and opened the window. "You are pleased to tease! Well, have your fun, Grandfather, it will do you the world of good. Can you smell my garden? When the breeze is up it should be even better. And now, since you are impossible, I shall bid you good morning!"

"Running away?" The earl laughed. "Well, I *shall* have an amusing morning. Wake me when the Viscount of Barrymore arrives."

So saying, he closed his eyes, though Daisy was not so foolish as to believe him asleep.

Lady Rochester laid her plans carefully. First, she invited the Darcy sisters to tea. No doubt, they would be in raptures over the invitation. She nibbled on her nails as she thought of other, equally provoking young ladies. There was always that spiteful Miss Pemberton . . . but no, even *she* would not inflict her upon poor Gareth. After all, if that whey-faced Miss *Simmons* did not panic him, surely a taste of Lady Susan's sharp tongue would? She would teach him a lesson for so cavalierly shifting his matrimonial choice onto her shoulders as if it were of no more consequence than a ha'penny button. When my lord was suitably appalled, she would approach him—ever so carefully, of course—about the possibilities of sponsoring the Chartley sisters. If he appeared suspicious, she would pretend it was Miss *Lily* that she deemed the most suitable. That should be enough to stir the pot to a slow, but delicious boil. If proximity with Primrose did not open his eyes to all that was desirable about a marriage, she would wash her hands of him. Still, she had hopes.

It was a very surprised Miss Darcy who opened her mail the following morning. As she exclaimed in shrieks to her mama, her pudding-faced sister, and all of the suitably awed neighbors, Lord Rochester had a fancy to her and she would have mutton's brains if *she* did not have a fancy to be a marchioness. Her joy was only clouded, slightly, by the fact that her imbecilic sibling made a similar sort of a claim. Mrs. Olivia Darcy, accustomed to the wiles of her two rather unlovely daughters, sighed and sent a reply out to the waiting groom. "The Darcy sisters would be delighted . . ." That is, if they hadn't scalped each other by the dawn of the next day.

The afternoon tea was all Lady Rochester might have hoped it would be. Except for the abominable circumstance of Gareth arriving a full two hours late and sporting a most unapologetic grin, everything was as she had hoped.

Lady Susan acidly remarked that she was unaccustomed to gentlemen being tardy, a remark that caused the marquis to raise his brows loftily and announce that it was fortunate, then, that there was no likelihood of her ever forming part of his household. At which, she turned a bright red, pinched her nostrils in slightly, and chatted, rather pointedly, with Mr. Bentley, one of the gentlemen Lady Rochester had thought it expedient to invite.

The Darcy sisters outdid themselves to monopolize his company, each talking twice as loud as any of the other invited guests, and making pointed remarks about their gentility. Their grand uncle the Viscount of Leese seemed to creep into every conversation, Davina batting her eye-lashes and Carlotta affecting a giggle that she considered rather provocative and had practiced, in private, for an age. Of course, the marquis did not share her views on the provocative nature of her rather shrill cackle. Polite-ness decreed, however, that he keep his revulsion in check.

This he did, under a curious cover of sublime but sin-gularly bored civility. He spoke largely of the weather, di-gressing here and there to mention some small matters relating to hunting—of which he had no keen interest or knowledge—and coal locomotion, which *did* interest him, but which could hardly be expected to stimulate his listeners. Still, both Misses Darcy were heroic enough to *pretend* fascination, which only served to annoy him fur-ther. At precisely half past the hour of four, his eyes met his mother's.

She actually had the temerity to stifle a small snicker, at which point, though his lips twitched in sudden amuse-ment, he felt his patience—and temper—had been tried quite long enough. He took the earliest opportunity of frog-marching her from the salon with a polite but im-placable bow to all of the guests present.

"Mama! You are incorrigible! If you wish to frighten me with this grim array of debutantes, you have suc-ceeded! Rest assured, I shall marry none of the above sampling, but I suspect, you devious old dear, that you already know that!"

Lady Rochester chuckled. "They are a dreary assort-ment, are they not? Yet Lady Susan is very eligible . . ."

"Mama!" Gareth eyed her sternly. "Cut to the quick, for though I am a splendidly patient son, my tolerance is sadly tried!"

"Very well, then. Gareth?" Lady Rochester was sud-denly not as certain of herself.

"Yes?" He eyed her keenly and gently removed a valuable crystal trinket from her hands. It was in danger of dropping, unnoticed, to the floor.

"Gareth, I have decided to sponsor the Chartley sisters into society. Lily is my goddaughter, you know. It is time I honored that commitment."

Gareth's lips lifted into a fraction of a smile, though his eyes remained stern.

"Mama, you are cutting a wheedle! If you were to sponsor every goddaughter you possessed, we should never know a moment's peace! You are up to your old tricks! You are matchmaking, again!"

Lady Rochester opened her innocent eyes wider still. "Oh, Gareth! Then there is hope? Miss Lily shall suit you perfectly!" At which, Lord Rochester, for once, was lost for words. His mama chuckled a little as she left the room. Her son was still gaping like a fish. Miss Lily indeed!

The rest of the afternoon was uneventful, for Lord Gareth disappeared entirely, allowing his poor mama to put a brave face on things and entertain her dreadful guests herself. It seemed a just punishment as she brought out tedious albums for them to gaze upon and trotted them through the gallery housing all the Rochester ancestors, past and present, for Gareth had recently sat for the obligatory oil.

Then, of course, one of the Darcy sisters—she neither knew nor cared which one—conceived the bright notion of sketching her *own* noble features. A "little token," she coyly remarked with an infuriating giggle. So Lady Rochester, always unfalteringly civil, was forced to endure a half hour at least of being cramped in a hard wooden chair with her profile to the noxious guest. Gareth, when he learned of it, only laughed *quite* unsympathetically and commented that though she was a dear, the fate was no less than she'd deserved. At which the scheming, conniving, and thoroughly irrepressible Dowager Marchioness of Rochester was forced, rather sadly, to agree.

* * *

Lord Barrymore's fate, some way away, was not much better. *He* was left waiting in Lord Raven's turquoise receiving room a lot longer than even *his* sunny temper quite liked. Across the hall, he could hear Miss Primrose play gently at the harpsichord whilst one of the sisters hummed along, a little off-key. He wondered if it was Lily, and strained his ears to catch at the notes. Oh, how he *wished* he had never set eyes on Miss Lily of the sea green eyes. He imagined her dark hair molding over her waist, falling from their clips as she sang. It *was* her, he was certain. But no! That laughter, as it broke off from song was too light, not near as sultry. Disappointed, he glanced at the beechwood clock that was preparing to chime the hour. Lord Raven was the very devil to keep him in suspense this long. He half conjectured that he could leave, his obligation met, since the earl had not had the courtesy to see him, when the door swung open.

Eight

"Grandfather will see you now!"

His back stiffened. Unmistakable. *That* was Lily, for he felt suddenly as foolish as a schoolboy, not at *all* the notorious rake he was pleased to permit the world to believe.

"Thank you, Miss Chartley." His smile was bittersweet as he made his bow.

"Oh!" Lily placed ungloved hands to flushed cheeks. She was conscious that she was only in her third best gown and that the silver green ruffles were creased. She smoothed them, but to no avail, since two of her ribbons were entangled in their lace.

"Here. Let me help you." Lord Barrymore's tones were low, his throat strangely dry as he stepped forward and disentangled the strands of satin.

"How lovely. So exactly, I am afraid, like you." Then he stepped forward, and surprised himself by taking her beautiful, headstrong chin firmly in his hands. For an instant, his eyes moved to her mouth, causing Miss Lily to emit a faint cry and close her delicious green eyes so that he saw nothing but a tangle of dark lashes. Then he set her firmly from him and watched as her eyes flew open in breathless disappointment. His pulses raced quite madly, but he did not allow himself the temptation, merely tying the ribbons firmly abut her waist as if she were no more than a schoolgirl and he a benevolent father.

"Oh!"

He raised inquiring brows.

"Are you not going to kiss me, my lord?"

"Should I?"

"It would be heavenly, I think." Lily Chartley dimpled at him blithely.

Curses! The innocent was too wild for her own good. It was not enough that he had saved her from herself last night. He was forced to do it again this moment, and that decidedly against his inclination.

"I cannot, Miss Chartley, for though I am a gentleman, I am too poor by far to be casting my sights as high as a Lily flower. That, I believe, stands heads higher than all other blooms. Too high, I am desolate to say, for me."

"How pretty! I believe that is the best compliment I have had so far! But as for being too poor, what nonsense is this? *All* my suitors are poor! *Do* say you will offer for me! I shall be much more comfortable with you than I ever would with poor Mr. Stanridge, who I fear tires me with his sonnets. Also"—she moved closer, a little confidentially—"though I do not like to believe badly of the man, I fear he borrows, at times, from Lord Byron. Have you read him, sir?"

"Byron? Ah, yes. 'She walks in beauty like the night.' I believe the quotation is apt, if *that* is what the poor fellow is spouting."

Lily blushed. "It is, and more besides. But come! You have not answered my question!"

"You appear to think I am here to offer a proposal of marriage."

"Well, of course, half Town has been in and out doing the same thing! I shall talk most earnestly to Grandfather not to guffaw at your suit."

Her eyes were so sublimely appealing that Denver, caught between the desire to laugh hysterically and cast abandon to the winds and kiss her as she deserved, had to hold himself sternly in check and do neither. Instead, he cast her gently aside and muttered that his business with Raven had precious little to do with matrimony.

"Really? Then you must *indeed* be in the suds. Gambling debt, is it?"

Denver nodded gloomily. There was no keeping the girl at arm's length!

"Grandfather is shockingly lucky, despite his gouty foot and his terrible wheeze. I don't suppose my pin money will come in handy? I bought a prodigious amount of gowns and reticules and ribbon and such like this quarter, but I believe there must be *something* left of it . . ."

The Viscount Barrymore was touched. He was more used to offering ladies expensive gifts than the other way round. But then, Lily was not in the ordinary way. Neither was she at *all* akin to the ladies to whom he traditionally tossed baubles and brooches. Lily, despite her reckless disregard for the conventions, was as pure as her name. A sweet innocent. He sighed. He wished it were otherwise. Had she been a brazen, calculating hussy, he would have had no qualms in exchanging her riches for a title. But there was the rub. She was not. Despite Hoskin's sublime confidence, fortune hunting was not as easy as it appeared.

Barrymore forced himself to laugh lightly. "You are a darling, Miss Lily! Give me your pretty, bright ribbons and I shall count myself a fortunate man!"

"What? These paltry trifles?" Lily looked down at her high-waisted gown, where the ribbons were still warm from his touch. Denver closed his eyes, trying not to see the delicate cleavage that peeped from the top of her fashionably cut bodice. She seemed quite unaware of her effect, concerned only with untying the knots that had been so firmly draped about her earlier.

"There! They are my favorite colors—wispy pearl and azure green. If Grandfather asks about them, tell him, with my compliments, that they are mine!" Her voice was defiant, for there were footsteps down the hall and their time alone seemed fleeting. Sure enough, the under butler knocked gently before making his semi-stately entrance. He stared rather fixedly at Miss Chartley, then announced that his lordship was ready—finally—to interview the honorable viscount.

At which, a whimsical smile appeared on my lord Denver's countenance. He bowed low over the youngest Miss Chartley, impulsively allowing his lips to faintly glide over her fingers as he took her hand. Lily seemed bent on saying something, but her throat was strangely choked. She smiled rather crookedly—a testament to her courageous, generous nature—and crushed the ribbons into his light, kid-gloved hands. Lord Barrymore could think of little else as he was ushered out under the disapproving eye of Lord Raven's manservant.

"Ah, Lord Barrymore! At last!"

The Earl of Raven had moved from his bed for the occasion and was seated comfortably by the window, where rain was gently tapping at thick, stained-glass encrusted panes. The viscount smiled wryly. Any "at last" to which the earl was referring must certainly have been rhetorical, for there was no "at last" about it. He had been kept waiting a full hour at the minimum.

He bowed, however, and took the seat the earl was indicating. Not quite as comfortable as the heavily brocaded wing chair, perhaps, but suitable in its own way.

"Snuff?"

"No, I thank you," Barrymore politely declined as he watched the downpour grow heavier. He shivered, for though there was a fire roaring in the grate, the ceilings were high and the chamber felt decidedly gloomy. Perhaps, though, that was simply a reflection of his mood state.

Lord Raven smiled. "Come to hand over the dibs, have

you?" The boxing cant seemed strangely out of character with the old man's regal bearing.

"I think you know that I have not." Barrymore looked him squarely in the eyes. Any moment now, he knew, he would be disgraced. The earl said nothing but raised his brows and drew out a pack of cards.

"Care to play?"

"I think you joke, my lord."

"I never jest about gambling."

"Then you will know that I never accept a game where I cannot cover the odds."

"Except for Lord Derbyshire's gaming party, I collect."

Denver Barrymore, for once, felt stricken. "Yes, except for then, though you must know, sir, I believed, at the time, that I had the wherewithal to cover it."

"How so?" The earl raised his brow quizzically.

"I own a couple of coal mines. They are manifoldly rich in ore. Unfortunately, I am advised they are imprudent to mine. The roads, I collect, are impassable."

"How very unfortunate." The earl helped himself to another pinch of snuff and watched closely as Lord Barrymore twined some ribbon about his fingers.

His answer was curt. "Yes, so it has proved."

The earl smiled. "You have nothing for me, then?"

"Nothing that will be of the least interest to you, my lord. My land is entailed and my stables are well and truly to let. It appears I am at the mercy of your goodwill." The viscount's tone was rueful as he mastered this supreme understatement.

"Not, I believe, something I am notorious for."

"No." Can he have imagined it, or was the earl smiling? God, he was enjoying himself! Barrymore's fists clenched, but he held himself back. *He* was on the back foot. The earl was entitled to laugh, if he would.

"Very well, Lord Barrymore. I shall have to ponder

upon this. Pass, I pray you, those ribbons. I have a sense I have seen them before."

"They are Miss Lily's, my lord. I have a fancy to keep them."

"Have you, by God? I should have you whipped for your impertinence."

"Very likely you should, my lord. I would endeavor to have no objections."

"But you *do* object to handing over a couple of pesky pieces of ribbon? They are of no more account than a single button on your confoundedly foppish morning coat, you know!"

The viscount ignored the aspersions cast upon his attire. He held his head up high and rose from his seat. "Yes. To such a simple matter I *do* object. They were freely given."

"*Were* they now?" The earl regarded him speculatively, a peculiar smile crossing his aging features. "Then Lily is undoubtedly a baggage, for she was wearing those ribbons this morning."

"How acute of you, my lord. I cannot deny that claim. But we are veering from the point."

"Are we? I think not. And sit down, man, I am too old to crank my head up. It might help if you stopped glaring, too."

Lord Barrymore was momentarily disconcerted. Obediently, he sat, though the hackles were still rising at the back of his neck.

The earl laughed. Unfortunately, the action precipitated a spasm, which in turn precipitated the entrance of Richmond, with a large bottle of cordial. It was lime in color, and made both gentlemen grimace in distaste.

"Take that hideous thing away, do you hear?" The earl's voice would have been a roar, had it not turned out to be something between a cough and a rather dry choke.

Richmond looked affronted, but turned tail upon the instant. If the earl was in high spirits, he was probably likely to live another hour. Consequently, he withdrew, but not without some dire mumbling beneath his breath. His gait was slow and stately, for he hoped to catch something more of the discourse. The conversation he'd overheard was taking an interesting turn.

"Now!" The earl regarded the young man before him sternly. "I wager you have heard of 'Raven's Ransom.'"

"I have, my lord. It is a confoundedly foolish notion, but appears to be captivating the attention of the haute Ton."

"And so it should. I am worth a king's ransom, Barrymore! A king's ransom, I assure you!"

"Then you should not treat your granddaughters so unkindly, my lord."

The earl spluttered. "Unkindly? Unkindly? I deny them nothing! They have every frill and furbelow a young lady could desire. All the suitors, all the courtship, they are favored everywhere!"

"And at what expense? There is not a suitor whose motive they can trust. The men who surround them like butterflies are rakes, scoundrels, and rogues!"

"Not a little unlike yourself?"

"If you were younger, my lord, I would call you to account for that! I may be a rake, but I am not a scoundrel and I am certainly not a rogue!"

"Yet you regard Lily with more than a disinterested eye."

"But not for the ransom, sir, though the notion intrigued me, a little, at first."

"And how am I to believe that?" The earl regarded his nails delicately.

"If I were fortunate enough to win both Miss Chartley *and* your confounded fortune, I would throw the latter back in your face."

"Is that a promise, sir?" There was a moment's stillness as Lord Barrymore realized the full moment of what he had just said. Then he shut his lips smartly, nodded curtly, and jammed the ribbons into the narrowly cut pocket of his superfine coat. Hoskin would have winced.

"Very well, my lord viscount, I wager, were you in such a propitious position, you would not! You would keep Miss Lily *and* her ransom."

"I told you, I do not gamble where I have nothing to stake." Barrymore's tone was stiff as he regarded the earl with distaste.

"Very well, then I shall *give* you something! I release you from your vowels to me, that you may pledge them, once again."

"They are not worth the paper they are written on. I have told you that already."

"I am not dull-witted, sir, I know that. You have coal mines positively laden with ore. I, I might tell you, have only just now procured the rights to one of the first railways in all of England. Forget about coaches and horses—they will get you nowhere. Steam and steel shall be your saving grace. You shall oversee the laying down of tracks and the commission of a suitable engine. Better than Blenkinsop's rack and pinion drive, you understand! I can't stand the man." The earl grimaced then heaved himself up off his cushions. There was a notable sparkle in his eye that might have alarmed Richmond, but he, fortunately, was not available to see it.

The Earl of Raven warmed to his theme. "I shall pay the miners and see your equipment maintained and improved. I shall swallow the bullet for all reasonable expenses, and, in return, shall expect to see my investment restored to me twofold within ten years. If it is not, the mines shall be forfeit to me along with the debts you have already incurred. Your tenure in a debtor's prison would then undoubtedly be long."

"Oh, undoubtedly." For the first time, Lord Barrymore's eyes smiled.

"Do you agree?"

There was a moment's pause. Barrymore regarded the earl closely. "What do *you* gain from it?"

Raven pursed his lips dryly. "Do not look into my motives, young man, they are more complicated than you might suspect. I like to play a deep game. Stating the obvious, however, I get a ten-year stake in the ore and fortuitously situate my railway. Your mines will be leasing the tracks for decades to come!"

"*If* they are successful."

The earl smiled and inclined his head.

"It is a gamble, my Lord Raven."

"It would not interest me in the slightest were it *not*, my Lord Barrymore."

"I should have to have full decision-making authority. Also, I shall have to be free to employ whatever experts I deem necessary. I am fairly well acquainted with Richard Trevithick of Cornwall. He runs a steam locomotive in Wales."

"Ah, yes. The Welsh Pendarran Railroad. A milksop! What about William Hedley? *He* builds a locomotive with guts! Last I heard, his engine was hauling ten coal wagons at a rate of five miles an hour. Now *that* is what you need, boy!"

"Possibly, but I should like to make that decision myself."

"Hah!" The earl snorted and looked about for his *Morning Post.* "Spare me the details, boy. Just get the best design you can find. That Stephenson fellow might do the trick. He is completing some newfangled design with six wheels and a multitubular boiler. Talk to him."

Lord Barrymore bit his tongue. He would *not* ask the earl who that "Stephenson" fellow was. Doubtless he would find out for himself in due course. Now, he pressed his point home.

"Then you will cede the authority?"

His lordship waved his hand testily. There was a cough, then a grudgingly whispered, "Naturally."

Barrymore sighed inaudibly before taking the next hurdle. "For the duration of the intervening ten years I would have to draw on a working wage. Say, twenty thousand pounds."

"Ten. The rents from your lands will keep you in your confounded waistcoats!"

The whisper of a dimple could be detected in my lord's firm, decidedly rakish jaw. He held his own.

"Fifteen, or I could not countenance the undertaking. The risks are too great."

"Nonsense! Where is your bottom, sir? Without this arrangement, you would be in debtor's jail *now!*"

"Yes, but out in the next quarter. If I sink myself as deep in debt as you suggest, I might rot in prison forevermore!"

"True." The earl's eyes gleamed. He always enjoyed a game with high stakes.

"Very well, you shall have your fifteen thousand pounds. You may draw on my banker tomorrow. Grafton-Everest in Caversham. And not a penny more, mind!"

There was a moment of silence. Lord Barrymore pulled the ribbons out and twisted them about so that Lily, had she seen him, would have protested loudly. Then he laughed. "I believe I shall take you on, sir! Ten years. Once you are repaid, I shall keep title to the mines and all of their contents."

The earl inclined his head slowly. "You drive a hard bargain. It is good. I cannot abide namby-pamby milksops who cannot take a horse by the bit upon occasion."

Lord Barrymore bowed. He was just congratulating himself on a magnificent escape—Hoskin was right, he *did* have the luck of the devil—when the earl regarded him from under magnificently bushy brows that had not yet quite been tamed by his illness or age.

"And *now*, my lord," he said, with a wicked, rather self-satisfied smile upon his face, "I believe you have the necessary collateral to make the greater wager."

Lord Barrymore understood him perfectly. He did, however, take a moment to raise his brows in a suitably inquiring manner.

"Would you, if you win Lily *and* my ransom, return one to keep the other? I wager not."

"And I, my dear sir, wager *so.*" The earl gazed, for an instant, at the younger man. He seemed hideously full of vitality and energy. A reflection, in truth, of *himself* at that age. He sighed. Lily would no doubt like him that way.

"Then it is agreed."

"Just a moment, my lord, two small questions."

"The first?"

"May I have Miss Lily's hand in marriage?"

"Would you care if I say no?"

Barrymore grinned. "Not overmuch."

"Hmmph!" The earl glared, but there was a glint of youthful appreciation in his baleful eyes. Barrymore would not be the man he thought him if he quailed at the first obstacle.

"You are honest, if not polite. Very well, if you can tame her, you can have her."

"Perhaps I do not *want* her tame."

"More fool you, but have it your way. What is the second question? I grow fatigued." The earl did not *look* fatigued, but Barrymore decided not to press him upon this point.

"What are *you* staking on this wager?"

"Audacious pup!" The earl's eyes gleamed. Then he grinned as if he were but eighteen, and not a wizened old man, held out a bony hand to Denver, and whispered something into his left ear.

Richmond, straining his ears behind the partition to hear, could have kicked himself that he did not. He sidled away in deep disgust. All he had heard—and that muttered with a frightful guffaw of laughter—was something that sounded very much like a "haven's dancem." He would have been astonished to know how close he was to the truth.

Nine

Lord Armand Valmont whistled through his teeth as he allowed his prize bay mare to be saddled. He had spent a splendid morning, outfitting himself in such an outrageous rig that he dared not don it in front of the groomsman, for fear of being carted off to Bedlam. Still, he could feel the gay bandanna—an interesting confection of crimson shot with yellow—deep in his pocket.

Under his sensible greatcoat, he had on a dark cape lined with a delightfully gaudy flamingo satin. It was trimmed with black fur to match his immaculate hessians. His sword presented something of a problem, for it was hard to tuck it into his faultless buckskins without having it noticed. Likewise, he could not mount his horse *wielding* the wretched thing—half his staff would have an apoplexy, fearing, for certain, an impending duel. He thanked the Lord his well-balanced pistols presented no problem. They were nicely hidden—thanks to a saddlebag more accustomed to carrying grouse than deadly weapons. Still, it served the purpose well, so it was now only the matter of the ruby-encrusted sword to worry about.

Lord Valmont was inclined to replace it upon the mantelpiece of his ancestral home, where he had lifted it down earlier that morning. A stubborn voice told him, however, that a certain Miss Daisy would be far happier if he brandished it in a suitably villainous manner. Swords, he had it on the best authority, were romantically superior to common pistols. They also had the decided advantage of being Gothic.

His lordship stepped up to the darker side of the stable, where he had set it down upon a bale of hay. Looking at it with whimsical resignation, he picked the sheath up nonchalantly and returned to his horse.

"Oh, don't stare, Jackson! I am not about to murder somebody!"

"No, my lord."

"And I am not going to kill myself in a duel either, so you can take that tragic look off your face!"

"Yes, my lord. Begging my lord's pardon . . ."

"Yes?"

"What are you going to *do* with that thing?"

"*Do* with it?" Lord Valmont looked suddenly jaunty astride his bay.

"Why, Jackson, how odd of you to ask! Is it not perfectly obvious? I am going to cut purses and hold up carriages!"

Whilst poor old Jackson was spluttering a bewildered reply, his lord and master kicked his knees in and cantered off at such a rate that there was no remonstrating with him. As he later told Brunhilda, the scullery maid, "There is just no telling with gentry folk!"

My lord was not so devious as to keep to his word, for though he might have enjoyed the novelty attendant on such unsavory escapades, there was simply no telling when Miss Chartley might be pleased to either take a lonely stroll, carrying her reticule, or call her carriage up. Though ardent, he harbored no burning desire to lie in wait in his spectacular costume for hours on end. He was therefore forced, sadly, to dream up a simpler scheme. One that he hoped, nonetheless, would cause violent tremors in the heart of the lovely Miss Chartley and convince her forever of his perfidy.

Or, at the very least, he reasoned, cause her to fall into his arms with wild abandon and pronounce him more heroic than Gawain or Lancelot or any other hero she might have filled her darling, ringleted little head with.

At precisely midnight—though he could not exactly tell, for it was too dark to consult his fob despite an obliging moon—my lord dropped down from a plum tree, where he had tethered his horse—and into the grounds of Lord Raven's estate. He crept to the back of the imposing house, lit only, he noticed, by wax tapers, and regarded each window carefully. It was impossible to tell which might be Daisy's, for they all seemed quite dreadfully alike. Nevertheless, my lord put his trust in faith. If the third sister was anything like the two he had already met, there was nothing, surely, to worry about. He put a leather-gloved hand to a masked mouth and yelled in a low, but eerie tone.

"Miss Daisy, Miss Daisy, I have come as I promised! Miss Daisy, by the light of the moon, I pledge you my troth!"

Nothing happened, and my lord wrapped the cloak about him closer, wishing that the whole of it were furlined, not just the elegant edges. He began again, feeling rather more foolish than he had at the beginning of the whole escapade. What if she did not come? What if he were arrested by the watch and taken up before a magistrate? Oh, fie on such traitorous thoughts.

"Daisy, Daisy!"

A window flew open and a lamp flared. So! Lord Raven *did* use gas, after all!

"Hush!"

Not Daisy, though there was a glimmer of her smile behind the admonishing eyes.

"You shall wake up the household."

A vision of beauty confronted him, with lashes dark and thick and dreamy. More sultry than Daisy, but perfection, nonetheless. My lord sighed. How *sad* that his heart was already lost, else he might well have tarried awhile . . .

"You must be Miss Chartley the third."

"And you must be the cutpurse, or that splendid bandanna is sadly wasted!"

"Do I not cast fear into your heart?"

Lily giggled. "Should you? I believe you are too handsome, sir!"

"And *I* believe you are a baggage! Is your sister within?"

"Who, Primrose?"

My lord's mouth trembled on the brink of an appreciative smile. "Are you a scatterwit, then, Miss Chartley?"

Lily laughed. "I have been told so, on occasion! But if it is *Daisy* you want, you are depressingly out of luck. She is snoring quite dreadfully and I fear I shall not wake her."

"Try, then, for this sword is prodigious heavy and I should like to lay it down, soon."

"Very well, but you must stand still, for if you move about too much you shall wake the dogs. They bark quite fearfully and you will be discovered in a matter of moments."

"How comforting! Hurry, can you?"

My lord was rewarded with an impish grin before the head disappeared from the window and a brighter flame seemed to light the chamber within. It seemed an age before he heard anything more, and he was just wondering whether the confounded girl had gone back to sleep, when he heard a rustling sound at the curtains. Then an infectious giggle. He cleared his throat and began his rather out-of-tune chant once more.

"Miss Daisy, dream Daisy, I yearn for thee at moonlight, at starlight, at midnight . . ."

A head popped out of the window. The right one, this time. It was delightfully tousled, the color of moonbeams, ringlets all helter pelter and cascading about wide, cornflower blue eyes. True, my lord could not exactly *see* the color in the darkness, but what sight was short on, imagination made up for amply. A closer sight of her and he damned his imagination to perdition, for she was wearing nothing but a thin shift with a couple of modest flounces that did nothing more than inflame desire further than it was already inflamed.

"Barnacle Jack!" Her face lit up with such patent joy that my lord was gratified.

He bowed outrageously low and flourished the sword so that the rubies gleamed red against the brilliant gold.

"You kept your word!"

"To call out your name on a moonlit night? I am doomed, Miss Daisy! Doomed to moan it forever!"

Miss Chartley, far from being sympathetic to this sad fate, clapped her hands with delight and declared herself well pleased. Whereupon my lord cursed the distance between them—a mere matter of two stories—and begged his little flower to consider herself kissed. Despite the darkness, he could see her blush at these words, but since she did not slam the window shut, call out the guard, or indeed, do anything more than part her wide lips and swallow hesitantly, my lord was moved to believe that the little darling had actually done his bidding. He laughed in triumph and was just about to inquire whether his kisses—even imaginary ones—improved with age—when another familiar face peeped at him from an adjoining curtain. It was rather more disapproving than the first, but my lord endeavored not to quail with fright.

"Miss Primrose! Well met, though I fear you interrupt a very pretty interlude between myself and my loved one."

"Nonsense, sir! I would wager my last hatpin you fear *nothing!*" Though her voice was familiarly tart, he could sense her laughter.

"True, madam! Barnacle Jack is as fearless as the night itself! Does your sister love me a little, do you think?"

There was a gasp from Daisy and a chuckle from Primrose. "Very likely, for she was always a featherheaded widgeon!"

"Well, *do* you?" Armand kept his voice as soft as silk as he gazed up at the middle Miss Chartley. Though he found the heroics amusing, he was unusually serious as he awaited the reply. Little Miss Chartley, it appeared, had crept into his heart when he was least expecting it. She was so warm, so unreserved, so unutterably charming, that he felt himself defenseless against the great tide of tenderness that welled up when he saw her. It was unaccountable, really, for it was *Primrose's* sense of the ridiculous that more nearly matched his own. Still, Daisy's round eyes and childlike naïvete appealed to some deeper, more primitive part of himself that had, until now, remained untamed.

"I hardly *know* you, sir!"

"What does that matter? Time marches not with the soul. Does your spine tingle when you see me?"

"Don't answer that, Daisy, it would be unseemly." Primrose's voice was sharp.

But Daisy was nodding, slowly. The eldest of the trio sighed and removed her head from the window. She stared hard, for a moment, at the cutpurse's outrageous attire and his equally outrageous profile, for it was far too handsome for his own good. Then, smiling a little, she made up her mind. She disappeared into the shadows and indicated Lily to do the same. Much encouraged, Lord Valmont continued.

"A little?"

"Prodigiously."

"Ah, truthful one! I would you are *ever* so endearingly forthright." There was a slight pause, then Lord Armand began his questioning again, this time with a tiny smile creeping up the corners of his delectable lips.

"Have you dreamed of me, dear heart?"

Again, the bobbing bright ringlets and wide, slightly shy eyes.

"Then you know me well enough."

"Do I?"

"Would you prefer to wait to know your own mind?"

"No! I know it."

The future Earl of Westenbury allowed the smile to widen a fraction. He was suffering from a cricked neck and decidedly frozen feet, but he could not have cared less. Only one more hurdle to cross and the maiden of his dreams would truly be his pledged. Strangely, he was more nervous about the question he was about to ask than about any of the others before it. He fiddled with the cape so that the flamingo satin breezed back a little. It was too dark, now, for Daisy to see, but she sensed a certain restiveness.

"Would you mind terribly if I turned out to be a gentleman and only a rogue on weekends?" He set down the sword, ruby side up, upon the wet grass. The gold was as heavy as lead.

Daisy's eyes widened. She was silent a little, considering. "I should like you, I think, even if it were the other way round—a rogue on weekdays and a gentleman on Sunday." My lord's eyes gleamed appreciatively.

"What if I were to wed you for the Raven's Ransom?" There was a moment's silence. Then Daisy, ever truthful, swallowed hard.

"You would likely be disappointed, sir. Primmy is always luckier than I."

"Ah, but I would have *you* to console me!"

"I am not very rich, sir. As a matter of fact, I have only my pin money to sustain me."

"But it is a prodigiously generous sum, is it not?"

"Yes . . ." Daisy sounded doubtful. A man who could

sport a sword like *he* was doing, would likely consider her prodigious allowance a paltry affair.

He understood her hesitation and smiled. "If it is not, I could always rob some coaches."

"You could get killed."

"I shall be careful."

"Will you spare the elderly and people who are particularly frightened?"

"Cross my heart. I shall scrutinize all my victims carefully. In certain instances, I shall interview each one and take care to rob only those who are fierce, mean, and cowardly."

Daisy stared at him with suspicion. Though it was too dark to see the laughter lines about his mouth, she caught some of the irony of his tone.

"You are not telling me Banbury stories, sir?"

"On my honor! When next I choose to rob a passing barouche, all passengers who show the *slightest* inclination toward heroism shall be spared."

"And the elderly and sick?"

"Oh, undoubtedly them, too, if you will it. I shall reserve my talents purely for the spineless and the selfish."

"Very well, then, sir, I am satisfied."

"Excellent! Then, Miss Daisy, delight, I shall make haste to steal you from all chance suitors and wed you out of hand. There is no time to waste, I believe, with a ransom as rich as Raven's on your pretty angel head."

"Oh!"

"That does not please you?"

"It does, oh, it does! But . . ."

"There are buts?" Lord Valmont's face clouded momentarily. Miss Daisy, he had noticed, did not want for suitors. Perhaps he should not have rushed his fences. . . .

"I have not a thing to wear!"

The cloud vanished. "I like what you have on."

"Oh!" Daisy realized how flimsy her shift was and

flushed quite delightfully. A little of the lamplight fell on her face so that Armand could just glimpse the delicate pink before her countenance was shadowed, once more.

"You are teasing, sir! I cannot possibly present myself to be married in a shift." Armand wanted to murmur that he could hardly think of any garment more suitable, but he manfully held his tongue.

"Then I shall suffer agonies and return for you at sunset, tomorrow."

Daisy's eyes sparkled. "This is exactly like a fairy tale! Grandfather will be spitting mad!"

"You sound pleased. Is he such an ogre, Lord Raven?"

"No, he only pretends to be one. He can growl quite prodigiously, but he is the greatest honey that ever lived."

"Yet you are pleased that he shall be angry."

Miss Chartley waved her hands airily. "Oh, naturally! Grandfather's favorite activity is gnashing his teeth and growling about something or other. It keeps his wits sharp. This shall keep him amused for an age!"

Lord Armand Valmont pondered, for a moment, whether he really, truly wanted to be a source of such questionable happiness.

Deciding he did, he nevertheless could not resist asking a fairly natural question, under the circumstances.

"I suppose it amuses him enormously to partake in duels, and suchlike?"

"When he was young, he ran two people through with the tip of his rapier. He can tell some frightful tales!"

Lord Valmont sighed, resigned to his hideous fate. "How fascinating. I must swap anecdotes, sometime."

Daisy's eyes sparkled. Lord Armand Valmont, heir to the seventh earldom of Westenbury, could not help noticing that they widened, too. He felt his pulses race in a most ungentlemanly fashion and did nothing whatsoever to stop them. The sensation, he found, was worth the small trouble he might have convincing Lord Raven that he was something more than a common felon. He considered, for a moment, informing Daisy, too, but feared that would be a mistake. He might fall too dramatically in her estimation to make a suitable recovery before sunset the following night.

"You must have some fearful tales to tell."

"You will shiver in your shoes."

Lord Valmont refrained from reflecting that the most fearsome tale he had yet to tell was the time he acted as an intrepid second to young Viscount Rigsby, who had rather foolishly challenged Lord Ashburn to a duel while in his cups. The outcome had had hilarious consequences, but none, he feared, that would appeal to Daisy's rather bloodthirsty imagination. He would have a fine time dreaming up satisfactory heroics to please his bride. Still, the effort, he felt, was worth it.

The night was growing subtly lighter, but the cold still bit into him sharply.

"Alas, my Daisy, the dawn is breaking. I must be swift as the wind, or a horrible fate awaits me."

"Hanging?" Daisy shuddered uncomfortably. Horrible deaths were all very well in Gothic romances. She had a rather nasty suspicion that she wanted them to stay between the pages.

Lord Armand watched her as closely as he could from two stories below. He hoped he noted a glimmer of doubt in her soulful eyes. It would be very trying indeed to get himself hanged, drawn, and quartered for her ghoulish edification. He rather hoped that her tender nature, for all its love of the dramatic, would prevail.

It did.

"Fly at once. I shall not sleep a wink until I know you are safe. Oh, please, *please*, kind sir, can you not give up this wandering life? I shall live in daily dread, else, and that would be horridly uncomfortable, I am sure."

His lordship had difficulty choking back a delighted

chuckle. "Horridly uncomfortable" was just the type of understatement that endeared her to him. He was just relieved that she was not going to expect a caped rider for a spouse except, perhaps, on special occasions. Life, otherwise, might prove awkward. He could not immediately think of a precedent for coach-robbing earls clad in powder black.

"For you, my love, I shall forsake all! Henceforth, I shall no longer be a highwayman and I shall bestow my name upon some other, less fortunate villain. Barnacle Jack shall disappear forever, vanquished only by a lady with an impossible twinkle in cornflower eyes!"

Daisy clasped her hands to her exceptionally delightful breast. My lord was not yet sufficiently reformed to avert his gaze as possibly he should have done. On the contrary, his stare became so fixed that poor Miss Daisy was cast, once again, into a pretty confusion that arrested my lord still further. Sunset tomorrow could not come, in his estimation, soon enough.

"What shall I call you, then?" Her voice was suddenly shy.

"I?" His voice deepened, for he could not playact on a matter of such inscrutable importance. "You shall call me Armand."

"Armand?" She tested it on her tongue. "It is romantic!"

"That is fortunate, for it is my birth name." He refrained from telling her it was only one of a string of several more boring Christian names. He felt that Henry, Mortimer, James Garcia, eighth Viscount Valmont and heir to the seventh earldom of Westenbury lost something in the telling. His mother, French by origin, had insisted firmly that "Armand" be tacked on *somewhere* in this litany, and in truth, it had been as "Armand" he had become known all through his boyhood.

"What shall you do, if you give up this wild life?"

"I shall spend my days loving and adoring you."

Daisy dimpled. "Silly man! Perhaps you shall have the Raven's Ransom."

"Perhaps." His reply was noncommittal. He wanted to shout "To the devil with the Raven's Ransom," but he did not dare.

"I must go. It is late. Do not worry your pretty little head about me. Raven's ransom or not, you shall be mine. And Armand—*this* Armand—looks after his own"

Then, with a swagger, and a suitable flash of rubies, he turned his back.

Daisy sighed as she watched him, the bandanna once again over his extraordinary features. His cape billowed over him with a flourish of flamingo pink, the dawn just offering sufficient light to perceive the brilliant color. She wanted to call him back, then desisted.

He waited for the window to click shut above him, before untethering his mount. If he had known what was next to ensue, he might have taken care to be quieter.

Ten

It started with a faint bark, somewhere invisibly behind the house. The Viscount Valmont's horse, faintly restive from the wait, flared its aquiline nostrils and tapped the ground faintly with delicate hooves. Armand stifled an oath and murmured to it softly in French, a language he'd always found soothing. Perhaps it was because his mama still used it at times, when she was tenderhearted, or much moved. Either way, the horse did not appear to be impressed, for she whinnied uneasily and refused to obey the viscount's expert tugs at the rein. In a moment, he knew why.

Four great hounds were unleashed and bounding toward him in the faint dawn light, growing fearfully larger—and louder—with every stride.

Behind them, a sleepy sentry—much startled—was giving chase. He gasped as he took note of the quality of the trespasser and bade the dogs be silent. Sadly, they paid him no heed at all, so Armand was forced to hope his horse would prove her mettle and not bolt, as he himself very much wished to do.

He folded his arms and remained perfectly still, however, as the hounds wheeled all about him, alternately gnashing their teeth and panting at their exertions. After a moment or so, he felt inclined to stretch out his arm and pat the closest of the four. My lord, it must be said, presented a very strange sight with his cape outstretched dramatically. It was a commanding spectacle, though, and one that must have appealed to the dogs, for they stopped their dramatics and frolicked about him in a less menacing fashion.

The sentry stared at him in awe. "Ye 'ave a right way wiv yer, guv! Them 'ounds be real terrors in the general way!"

"I'll warrant." The heir to Westenbury allowed a faint dryness to creep into his tone. Unfortunately, it was lost on Potts, who was staring at him as if he had two noses or several heads. The viscount, surmising his turn of thought, removed the bandanna from his chiseled features and stifled a sudden grin.

"You must think me mad."

"Not so mad as the last guv wot cut up a lark, me lord! 'E decided to be a coachman, wot wiv his 'at and boots an all. 'Ad it off Simmons the postboy, I did. There be strange goin's-on, I tell yer. Strange goin's-on."

"Really?"

"Oh, aye. Ever since the lord an' master 'ad Master Anchorage up from Lunnon, things 'ave not bin the same around 'ere, oh, no, they 'ave not!"

Lord Valmont might have enjoyed spending a few more moments in idle—but informative—gossip with the sentry, but his trusty steed seemed to have another opinion on the matter. When two of the hounds sniffed curiously around her fetlocks, she took exception and whinnied on two hooves, causing all four of the beasts to scatter cautiously, though not before baring their teeth and emitting decidedly menacing noises from their throats.

"If you will pardon me, I must be on my way."

Lord Valmont exuded an elegant poise that was somewhat at odds with his position. Still, he was a gentleman, and even in the direst of straits, gentlemen did not grow fainthearted and canter away without so much as a backward glance.

"Beg pardon, me lord, but that be precisely what I canna be doin'."

The viscount lifted an eyebrow in surprise. He hoped it was sufficiently haughty.

"And why not, pray?"

"On account of 'is lordship orderin' me to keep an eye out for all them shenanigans wot might arise. Seems 'e was expectin' a few 'igh larks."

"Was he, by George? Well. I should be loath to disappoint him. You may tell your lord and master I shall call on him tomorrow first thing."

To the honorable viscount's profound surprise and annoyance, this bland statement—whilst perfectly true—did not seem to satisfy the minion. What is more, out of the corner of his eye, he could see two of the hounds creeping closer. His thoroughbred flared her regal nostrils and in deference to her, he threw aside caution, sighed profoundly, and announced that his fate was undoubtedly in the sentry's hands. Whereupon that gentleman—if such he could be termed—grinned a wide, toothy, rather happy smile—and wagered his rather grimy nickle that there would be a handsome outcome to all this.

Lord Valmont snorted. "Possibly, my good man, but if there is, it shall not be from me! I hope for your sake Lord Raven is as generous as he is mad."

Whereupon the sentry nodded doubtfully and commented vaguely that "Me lord was not allus the terror wot 'e seemed." And with this happy assurance, the Honorable Henry, Mortimer, James Armand Garcia, eighth Viscount Valmont and heir to the seventh earldom of Westenbury, was taken into a polite but very firm custody. He wondered whether his alter ego, the enigmatic cutpurse, would have been quite so sanguine at his prospects.

* * *

The dawn broke pink across the sky. Daisy, in high fidgets, wondered whether to confide in her sisters. It was not in her nature to keep anything from them, but oh! Would they not count it as passing strange that she should fall in love so completely with a stranger not a week of her acquaintance? Worse, an impoverished one with felonious ties and a warrant upon his head? If it was *Lily* up to such tricks, she would undoubtedly scold her for a featherhead.

Daisy sighed and allowed her thoughts to roam to that evening, when his dark head would return, once more, to below the eaves. Would she go with him? She trembled to think it. Then she trembled again, to think not.

Across the hall in a delightful canary yellow chamber, Primrose nibbled at her elegant nails. How happy she was that Daisy's gentleman had returned! Daisy deserved happiness and gaiety and a little adventure in her life. Even if he proved *not* to be a highwayman—and Primrose— practical Primrose—counted, no, *relied* on this being the case—he still had a zest for life, a sparkle, and a sufficiently pliable sense of humor to suit her Daisy very well indeed. She wondered how much the Raven's Ransom would influence any decision he made. She hoped not *too* much, though with gentlemen it was always hard to tell. He might, after all, have engineered their whole meeting upon the moors. But no! He had no notion that they would be fleeing from Sir Rory Aldershot, or that their wheel would be needing mending.

Or had he? Primrose shivered and pushed the thought away. Grandfather's reprehensible ransom was causing her to be jumpy and overly suspicious. She tried very hard to keep her thoughts on Daisy, but they kept veering toward her *own* rather unmaidenly conduct the night of the ball. Oh, *what* a cake she had made of herself, clambering into Lord Rochester's chaise! And how providential, for surely if she had searched the earth, she could

not have found a man more complimentary to her spirit
than he. Her lips tilted upward, for a moment, for Primrose, though dreamy, was always scrupulously honest with
herself. In truth, it was not just to her *spirit* that he was
uplifting. He had the most wanton effect upon her sensible person and frankly, though she was appalled that
she should feel quite so brazen, she would not forgo the
sensation for all the decorum in England.

Lord Rochester was a man she could grow to trust and
depend on. He had already very ably managed to keep
her out of *one* unholy, unforgivable scrape. It was his cool-
headedness, after all, that had stopped her dashing from
his chaise and positively *proclaiming* to the world that she
had been compromised. Oh, but how unsettling it all was!
Lord Rochester, whilst no doubt enjoying the interlude—
Primrose was not so coy as to imagine it had only been
her senses so rivetingly engaged—would, sadly, consider it
just that. A pleasant interlude. He was a seasoned bachelor and the foremost catch of the Season. It was unlikely
that a prosaic, rather sensible society miss past her first
Season was likely to ensnare him. Especially not when her
sisters were both so much more beautiful and lively, and
it was a guinea for a groat she had no fortune to sweeten
any dowry he might require. Primrose avoided thinking
of the embarrassing "Raven's Ransom" that hung over
her head, for she was certain that such a thing would not
weigh with a man of Rochester's stature. If anything, it
was an annoyance, for it was causing her name to be ban-
died about town in a manner she could only deem unseemly.

Oh, curse Grandfather! She wished, for once, his keen
mind was not as convoluted as it undoubtedly was. *Now*
she was saddled with a bag of undesirable suitors and a
dream that was beyond fulfilling, a circumstance far worse
than her amiable spinsterhood of a few days before.

Primrose looked upon her slender fingers. Her nails

were now rather shorter than they had been, for she'd been absently nibbling for several minutes. Fortunately, she was a rather tidy sort of a person, so the damage did not appear quite as bad as it might have, had it been Lily, or even Daisy, committing a similar offense.

The mug of hot coffee steamed in Lord Armand Valmont's hands. He had to admit that though he was undoubtedly a prisoner, he was certainly a very well-treated one. The poor sentry had been running circles around him all evening and Mrs. Bartlett's partridge pie tasted uncommonly good at dawn. He felt a little foolish in his spectacular garb, but since none of the house servants seemed to bat an eyelash at his outrageous rig, he relaxed a little and turned the pages of yesterday's *Morning Post* which one of the scullery hands had been so obliging as to save. He wondered what Daisy would say if she knew he had spent the night in captivity in Lord Raven's own kitchen.

He smiled a little, for doubtless it would be rather tame to her compared with the type of trial she might imagine him facing as a common felon of the road. Still, by all accounts, the interview in store for him with the eccentric Lord Raven would be trial enough, so he cast aside the society column and waited with a growing impatience that was not detectable in his cheery smile and polite compliments to cook and chambermaid.

Both, it might be said, thought him a prodigiously handsome fellow and felt many a flutter of the heartstrings at his wayward gaze. The stable hands were occupying themselves in wagering all manner of things concerning him. Whether his boots shone from champagne or beeswax, whether the rest of his stable matched the fine mare they had groomed for him as he dozed a little by the kitchen fire, and most importantly, whether

Lord Raven would send him the rightabout as he had done many a suitor before him. Many whispered that it would be a pity, for such good looks were a rarity, and "the gennelman was powerful 'andsome."

The scullery maids crept closer to have a quick glimpse at his features and Richmond, privy to the cozy scene, shook his head disapprovingly and muttered that my lord must be "dicked in the nob" to countenance criminals in his noble home. At which he was shouted down with indignation, for it was plain as a pikestaff that the gentleman was "gentry, like and up to some 'igh larks wot is not our place to unnerstand." They nearly came to fisticuffs over the issue, but as dawn broke sultry and leisurely and pink across the cobblestones, my lord was pleased to put an end to all comment by announcing that undoubtedly the illustrious Earl of Raven must be wakened.

"Certainly not!" Richmond glared at the intruder, who stared back politely, but with unyielding fortitude.

"Then, my good man, I shall have to either cut my way out of here with my sword"—he patted the golden object with intent—"or find my own way to his chambers. Much as I have enjoyed your delightful society—and Mrs. Bartlett, this pigeon pie was exceptional—my compliments— I find I have other matters to attend to. I believe, up until now, I have been remarkably patient."

"Aye, for a villain!"

"Say you so?" The heir to Westenbury's mouth creased into an amused grin. "Then try not my tolerance further, for *this* villain is quick of feet and minded to test his steel."

"Potts, you are a half-wit to have left him with his sword."

"But it is gold, sir. And crusted with rubies, like. I couldna take such a thing off 'im. Besides, 'e promised to be'ave, gennelman's 'onor!"

"A pox on gentleman's honor! The man is a cutpurse."

"Aye, but if he is Miss *Daisy's* cutpurse it be different, like."

There was a silence about the kitchens as everyone regarded the prisoner with renewed interest. My lord was given to understand that Miss Daisy was much beloved of Lord Raven's household staff, no matter how he himself was viewed.

He spent quite some moments agreeing pleasantly with Miss Ainsley's shy commendations of her dear mistress's person until Richmond himself lost patience and declared that Lord Raven needed to be informed about the intruder's impertinence.

Whereupon Lord Valmont managed to infuriate him further by agreeing, sweetly. When he murmured that that was precisely what he had demanded in the first place, Richmond looked daggers at him and turned on his heel. There was no arguing with such irrational logic, so Lord Raven's noble valet salved his bruised ego by wondering, wickedly, what his employer would do about the odious man's presence.

He smiled to himself as he nimbly took the carpeted stairs up to the main hall. Raven, at least, could be relied upon to give the masquerading jackanapes a regular boot in the rear end. Even with his gout, the earl would doubtless be up to such an exertion. Maybe he would even hand the conceited young rascal over to the law. Either way, the excitement would doubtless do his noble employer a power of good.

In this he was correct, for Lord Raven was in high fidgets, waiting to be dressed and shaved and pacing about above stairs in a fit of the morning dismals.

When Richmond apprised him of the criminal awaiting his pleasure in the kitchens, his eyes assumed an interested gleam, but there was something in him that was vaguely disappointed, though he could not fathom it himself.

"Trussed up, is he?"

"No, sir. As meek as milk and being fed up like a prize pigeon." The disgust was evident in Richmond's tone.

"Mmm . . . now why would that be, I wonder?"

"Fellow seems to *want* to see you. Had the temerity to order me to awaken you!"

"And you instantly obeyed his directive."

"I?" Richmond puffed himself out indignantly. "I should say *not*, my lord!"

"Then why are you bandying the tale about at this ungodly hour?" The earl's eyes, for once, twinkled. Richmond said nothing, but gave a disapproving sniff.

"Speechless, are you? An excellent thing. It shall stand to this varmint's credit. *What* did you say his name was?"

"I didn't. And you cannot mean to see him! He is an intruder and a cutpurse. By the looks of him he would not stop at highway robbery either!"

"Yet you are all alive in my kitchens, I infer."

"Oh, alive, yes! The fellow could charm the hide off a donkey, I don't wonder."

"Then let him try it with me. I believe my hide to be suitably thick."

"He threatened to cut his way out of here with his sword."

"Did he, by God!" The earl's eyes gleamed appreciatively. "Now that is more like it! Tie him up and tell him he may try it."

"*Me*, my lord?"

"Of course you, or shall I do it myself?"

Richmond wavered. There were times he worried for the sanity of his noble employer.

"Chicken-hearted, are you?"

"My lord!"

"Oh, stop my lording me. Fetch me my stick. I shall

see him in the kitchens myself. Doubtless there is some of that plum tart lurking about somewhere. I shall fetch myself a piece."

This startling proposition at once confirmed Richmond's sudden alarm. My lord *was* mad.

"The kitchens are four flights of stairs, my lord, and the tart is laced with rum."

"I know it is, you blockhead. That is why I retain Mrs. Bartlett on such an excellent salary. And as for four flights, do you think I don't know the disposition of my own home? I believe it is four flights and one small stairway off the landing besides. There, you see, I am in the right of it. I'm not in my dotage, yet. Now move out of my way."

"No!"

"No?" My lord's tone was cold.

"I shall fetch the scurvy knave up to you, rather."

"Hah! Too late, Richmond, I'm of a mind to shake the cobwebs out of this old white head. Now fetch me my stick, will you, before I collect it myself and break it over your back!"

This threat did not move his valet in the least. Collecting all his dignity, he shook out the coverlets and remarked that the weather looked to be pleasant, all things considered. Whereupon the earl glared at him and grabbed at his stick, muttering that it would serve Richmond right if he one day *were* to beat the living daylights out of his disobedient person.

Whereupon Richmond eyed him calmly and remarked that he was duly terrified, but that if the earl was *bent* on killing himself by going below stairs, he might just as well do it shaved.

Lord Raven grumbled a little about interfering, do-gooding jackanapeses, but allowed himself to be steered toward the great, gilded mirror, beneath which Richmond had prepared the blades and his soaps and the chafing

dish of warm water and hibiscus soap. Then he was settled, with some comfort, into a buttoned leather wing
chair, still muttering oaths and issuing commands for the
confinement of their interesting—and rather dashing—
prisoner.

He had not long to mutter, for the prisoner himself
had grown fed up with the waiting. Demanding of the
second housemaid—sword drawn most fearsomely, as she
was later to relate—the direction of my lord's private
suites, he lost no time in grappling with the house's ge-
ography and locating the necessary interior. He would,
quite probably have knocked, but the door was still ajar
from Richmond's indignant entrance and the old man's
reflection was visible for all to see in the seventeenth cen-
tury looking glass at opposite ends of the paneled wall
from where he sat.

"Beware, Lord Raven, lest your man's blade is as sharp
as mine!"

The valet whirled round in consternation, but the cut-
throat did not make any sinister advances into the room.
Rather, he adopted a merry—and annoyingly arrogant—
stance as he lingered, cape and all, in the door frame.

Richmond seethed. "Hear you, my lord, the villain
threatens you in your own home!"

For an instant, there was a pause. Lord Raven swallowed a faint glimmer of recognition. Though he scowled
fiercely, the manner in which he folded his arms held a
certain smug satisfaction. Fortunately, this was hidden to
both Richmond and the young, lithe man who eyed him
a trifle curiously.

"Hold your tongue, Richmond. *That* is no threat. It
would be a thousandfold more devilish if he wished your
blade to be as *blunt* as his. Good God, if you were to
shave me with a razor as lamentably unsharpened as *that*
one, I daresay you would do me *untold* damage. Just look
at the thing. It is a disgrace."

"I see your eyesight is as good as ever, Raven."

"And you are as impertinent as always, my intriguing pup. Now put down that sword. It is a hazard."

"Never say it. You were used to be fearless."

"And still am. I was referring to its gilded glare. The thing is so gaudy it would *blind* a man before it smote him."

For an instant, a glimmer of amusement crossed Armand's face.

"There have been times I have thought so myself. But come, sir, you bandy words."

"And you play with your health. Set the thing down and have a care for your elegant—if decidedly ill-clad—back. The stupid thing weighs a ton, if I recall."

"Oh, I am sure you do. Vividly."

There was a meaning behind the tone Richmond could not quite fathom.

The Earl of Raven's eyes became hooded.

"That was all a long time since. I was young and feckless then. And yes, upon reflection, steel *would* have been a better choice. I am glad I had it not, though, for your father would surely have come off the worst."

Armand raised his brows a trifle enigmatically. He let the comment pass, however, and fingered one of the jewels encrusted in the unsheathed sword.

"Instead of which, you neatly pinked him and presented him with the back of your golden blade."

"Whimsy, my boy, sheer whimsy."

The earl yawned.

"But come! I grow fatigued with this conversation. My youthful indiscretions are so far in the past as to be wearisome."

"Then forgive me for boring you. But you must allow, my lord, that I have some provocation. But for Mrs. Bartlett's pigeon pie, it has been a tedious night."

"Has it? That is not what *I* believe."

"And what do *you* believe, my good lord?"

"I believe that being caught like a veritable sneak thief in the night must have held excitements of its own."

"Ergo, the night was not tedious. I concede you the point, Raven."

The twinkle reappeared in Armand's deep, honey hazel eyes. For an instant, they were reflected in the older man's avid gaze. He shook his head, however, and frowned.

"You deliberately misunderstand me, Valmont. There were *other* excitements, were there not?"

"Indeed."

"Ha! So we come to the very heart of it. Which one of my rapscallion granddaughters is pleased to captivate your attention?"

"They are *all* captivating, my lord."

"You deny a preference?"

"I do not."

"Then speak, before I lose patience with you and call in the watch."

"At sunset, sir, I elope with Daisy."

"Moonshine! Daisy would never be so undutiful!"

"Care to place a wager?"

The viscount smiled sweetly and the earl signaled to Richmond to continue lathering his chin. There was a long silence as the valet, used to Raven's unpredictable ways, took up the razor and began his careful work. When it was done, the earl surveyed the viscount with grim amusement.

"Done!"

"I shall call on you in the morning, sir."

"With your bride?" The earl sounded disbelieving. Armand's eyes glittered. He nodded and ignored Richmond's choking protests.

"With my bride." His tone was firm.

"*Hah!* An elopement is never such if it has a guardian's permission. *Then* it becomes merely a swift termination to a speedy betrothal. I therefore grant you my good wishes and full consent, you impertinent young pup."

For once, Lord Valmont was speechless. He set down the sword—which indeed *did* look rather ludicrous in his elegant hand—and took a step closer toward his father's sworn enemy.

"Are you serious?"

"Never more. Daisy was ever a featherheaded chit with no notion of what was good for her! She has the pick of London's beaus and here she chooses a fanciful fribble like you! Still, you are not, I trust, a dullard, and notwithstanding your father's blood—which I must needs abhor—you shall make a tolerable spouse if all I hear about this godforsaken town is true."

Lord Valmont's features relaxed into a slow smile. "The rumors are veracious, then. The lion that roars with fury is no fiercer, in his own home, than a pussycat. Daisy warned me."

Lord Raven bridled with rage at this most dire of insults.

"Nonsense! Do you think it is *altruism* that spurs me? Pah! A thousand times, pah! No, my dear fellow, far from it. I consent to this nonsense merely because in so doing, I win my wager. You shall *not* elope at sunset, for you marry with my knowledge and prior approval. Thus, my dear man, technically speaking, you are not eloping. So sad, but you lose your wager and stand indebted."

The noble Lord Valmont bent his knee in humility. Though the eagle-eyed Raven thought he was flippant, the sincerity of his words were hard to misconstrue.

"So be it, then, Raven. For the gift of Daisy I shall consider myself *ever* in your debt. Take your sword back. It has come full circle and served a certain purpose. My father, who is nothing if not appreciative of irony, shall doubtless smile if he ever comes to hear of the matter."

"Which I trust he shall not."

Armand shrugged. Then, whilst Raven was still wrestling with his golden gift—it had been thrust unceremoniously into his lap and lather was dripping down onto the rubies—Armand quixotically took his leave.

Eleven

He was too pleased with his morning's endeavor to notice the open door to the morning room, where Lily, the picture of innocence, sat upon a rocking chair delicately embroidered in shades of pale pinks and greens.

There was a slight flush upon her perfect cheeks, but apart from this, there was nothing to show she was thinking quite sinful thoughts, cross as crabs that she had not managed to eavesdrop on the earl's conversation with Denver, Lord Barrymore.

She had fared rather better with *Daisy*, unashamedly catching little wisps of her conversation with the cutpurse highwayman, who had so obligingly chosen *her* window to attract Daisy's attention. Oh, how romantic it was! How *lucky* Daisy was to have found such true love! She would not care two pins for the fact that her young man was not a gentleman save, of course, for the cost of her gowns. Still, Daisy did not, in the general way, care a toss for such matters, so Lily waved the point away airily.

Besides, there was always Grandfather. He might be a regular old tartar, but beneath the baleful eyes and scraggy brows lay a kind heart, though he would have a fit if she accused him of it. He would never let Daisy starve and she could, after all, have all her castoffs. Especially the ones with the silver trim, they were so flattering to her guinea gold locks. Then there was always the Raven's ransom. . . .

Daisy thus satisfactorily disposed of, Lily allowed her thoughts to wander once more to a certain Lord Barry-more. Oh, he was so elegant! She did not think she had ever before seen anyone with such perfectly molded shirt points, or such impeccably tied cravats. As for his coats, so tight across his chest, nipped so skillfully at the slender waist, oh . . . she was certain he did not use padding for his shoulders or well-muscled thighs!

She giggled a little, for she had gleaned her certainty during the waltz, where she had touched those hard, velvet-hosed thighs several times during the rather fast dance's execution. Oh, *quite* accidentally, of course! She wondered whether Barrymore had noticed, and smiled secretly. She thought he had. Why, oh why would he not offer for her? Half of London was doing so, thanks to Grandfather's crazy scheme. But she was not interested in half of London! She was interested only in a silly man, too handsome for his own particular good, who was too proud to kiss her as undoubtedly he should!

Indignation welled up in Lily. She was the dearest creature, but rather spoiled, since she was the baby of the family and undoubtedly the most breathtaking of the Chartley girls. Consequently, it was rather hard for her to be patient and she was just devising cunning schemes to force a certain Lord Denver Barrymore to come to his senses and whisk her away in the most romantic of fashions, when her reverie was disturbed by the upper housemaid.

"Oh, Miss Lily! You are to dress at once! Lord Raven wishes to see you immediately!"

"Now? Before breakfast?"

"Yes, ma'am! And in a rare taking he is! Laughing 'is 'ead off and poor Richmond at sixes an' sevens wiv 'im an' all!"

Lily's eyes twinkled as she allowed her hair to be brushed vigorously, so that it shone in the early sunlight and cascaded abundantly over her shoulders and down the length of her back. Annie the maid marveled, as she always did, at the beautiful sight. She was learning to be a dresser and Lily, always tenderhearted, had offered herself as practice. Her *real* dresser, a rather stiff-rumped sort of person, had taken immediate affront, but Lily was not to be shaken. Thus it was that on all days where there was not some event requiring the rather more expert services of Grantley, Annie was permitted to play with the shining black tresses and choose from the wardrobes of modish dresses and bonnets and ribbons and gloves and half boots and hats. Sometimes, Lily would chuckle at her choice and gaily reselect, but most times, little Annie's taste was exactly in synchrony with her own. Now she chose a saffron gown trimmed with gay green ribbons that exactly matched her eyes and pale kid gloves with Grecian sandals strapped merrily to her perfectly well-turned ankles. Lily looked so young and innocent when she entered the earl's room, that he smiled a little, before reverting to his usual lordly glare.

"Good morning, Grandfather!"

"Don't good morning me, madame! The sun is too bright and my chilblains hurt fiercely. Come a little closer. I can't expect to hold a decent conversation when I am bellowing across a room."

Lily stepped closer gingerly. Her sarcenet gown was not more than a week old, and she was loath to have lemonade or cordial or that vile concoction that Grandfather swallowed cast upon her person. This had happened before, of course, so she stepped forward warily.

"Now, Grandfather, you are not to plague me! I can see in your eyes you are about to read me a lecture and I would rather, if you please, kiss your forehead and read to you instead."

Lord Raven grunted. Lily, ever hopeful, took this for assent, kissed him saucily, and weaved her way to the bookshelf. "What musty old books! You must have some of mine! I am certain you shall like Sir Horace Walpole, for he writes quite thrillingly and there are not quite so many volumes as there are in *some* of my novels! Shall I fetch it?"

The Earl of Raven wheezed a little, and gestured to her with a bony hand.

Reluctantly, Lily drew closer. "I suppose you are determined?"

The earl chuckled. "But naturally. And what do *you* think I shall be scolding you about?"

"That is not fair!" Lily sounded indignant. "If I guess, I may be mistaken and then I shall be scolded for something you knew nothing about!"

The earl again hid his amusement. He adored characters with spunk and little Lily, though decidedly naughty and more than a little vain, was exactly to his liking.

"You shall have to risk it, my dear."

"Just remember, I am too old to spank!"

He looked fierce. "Really? I shall have to consult Primrose about that. *She* will know."

"Grandfather, you are teasing me! You *know* I haven't been spanked for an age!"

"Mmm, more's the pity. I had the latest bills from Madame Endicott's."

"The milliner? Oh, Grandfather, were they frightful? I always lose track about such things. She is so horridly persuasive and I always seem to come home with heaps of vile confections that I wouldn't even pass on to *Annie!* I really am dreadfully sorry. You can take the amount out of my next quarter."

"Be sure I shall, you minx! Now come here, I have something important to discuss with you."

"Are they marriage proposals?" Lily sounded suddenly hopeful.

"Indeed they are. Lord Wainsborough offered yester-

day, and Sir Archibald Trafford, too. No, I mistake. That
was for Primrose. Or was it Daisy? I shall have to check."
He clicked his hands for a list and Richmond, hovering
close by, obliged. My lord searched about for his spectacles. Then, with a quivering hand, he applied them to
his ears and squinted at the page. "Ah, yes. Suitors for
Lily. Ten, I believe, not counting Waring, who is entirely
ineligible and Barrymore, of course."

"Barrymore?" Lily jumped up and snatched the paper
from his lordship's hand.

"Tut-tut, young lady! You are not to grab. Very uncivil
of you, I am sure!"

Lily did not hear. Her eyes scanned the paper eagerly.
"But, Grandfather, you have not written the viscount
down anywhere!"

"He is not suitable. Now Mollington . . ."

"Mollington is a great baby, Grandfather!"

"Well, then, Wainsborough. . . ."

". . . cares only about restoring his coffers. If Primmy
or Daisy get your wretched bequest, he would likely have
an apoplexy and die on the spot."

"How convenient."

Lily grinned. "Yes, very, but I should prefer to not have
the bother. What if *I* got your wretched ransom? I should
be saddled with him for life!"

"You would be a countess."

"Tsha! A pox on countesses!"

The earl smothered a laugh and coughed convincingly
instead. Barrymore, as he had suspected, would be perfect for Lily, but it would be over his dead body that he
admitted it. Lily was such a troublesome creature, if she
caught a whiff of approval, she would turn tail and run
a mile.

"I will thank you to remember that your dear *grand-
mama* was a countess, young lady!"

"Well, one in the family is sufficient, then! Besides, let

Primrose be a countess! I am sure she will be perfect for the part."

"Mmm . . . excellent advice. Might I ask if you had anyone in *particular* in mind?"

Lily blushed, though she was glad to have turned the earl's wrath from herself. "Nooo . . . and Primrose would eat Wainsborough for breakfast! I shall ponder the matter and report back to you directly."

"How thoughtful." Raven's sardonic tone was quite lost on Lily, who nodded her head gravely and set her mind at *once* to the weighty matter of Primrose's suitors. She was chagrined, therefore, to find that Raven had not lost the thread of their former discussion. His next sentence made her heart sink into her pretty little sandals.

". . . In the meanwhile, you might consider the list. The only man I forbid is Barrymore, for he is a gambler and a rake."

Lily's eyes flashed, her chin tilted stubbornly and her beautiful gloves reached an indignant waist.

"How unfair, Grandfather, when you might *just* as well be describing yourself!"

"Impudent! I am handsomer than he!"

Lily giggled, in spite of her annoyance. No one—however fond they might be—could describe the Earl of Raven as "handsome." His brows were too bushy, his complexion too sallow, and age and ill usage had taken their toll upon his rather scraggy features. Lord Barrymore, on the other hand, was the very pink of health, with the liveliest of eyes and a dreamy curve to his lips that made them quite enchanting to most young ladies and one in particular.

"Giggle all you like, little madame! I tell you, in my day I was a veritable Adonis! Ask Richmond, if he can cast his mind that far back. But we wander from the point. I forbid you to marry Barrymore."

"That is unfair!"

"He is only after the Raven's Ransom."

"And whose fault is that? You know perfectly well you have dangled it as a carrot in front of every suitor we have ever had. Well, I tell you, Grandfather, I don't care the snap of a finger for your silly ransom!"

"And Barrymore? I'll double your allowance if he can say the same."

Lily looked disdainful. "I won't gamble when the odds are heaped against me. Of *course* he cares about the money! He would be an addlepate if he did not! *All* my suitors care about the money, though it is only my *eyes* that they write sonnets about! They are passing pretty, I believe." Lily could not help that comment as she caught a glimpse of herself in the glass. In truth, her sea green eyes *were* truly magnificent, encased as they were by fronds of deep, dark lashes.

"Baggage! I believe I shall buy you a looking glass for a wedding gift."

"Then I may marry Barrymore?" Lily's voice was surprisingly eager. The earl nearly relented, then considered he would be needlessly depriving himself of a great deal of fun. The little chit would doubtless dream up *something* outrageous to keep him entertained if he forbade her her way. The Chartley sisters were spirited things, if nothing else. He had no doubt, however, that in the end, all of them would marry well. If Lily became the Viscountess Barrymore, he would not complain. Or he would, of course, but purely as a matter of form.

Now that he had suitably provided an income for the viscount—and one that he had no doubt would bear fruit, for Lord Barrymore was more acute than many gave him credit for—there was certainly no rhyme or reason why his dearest little granddaughter should not become his bride. There was no reason to tell *her* that, though. He beetled his brow menacingly and glared in what he hoped was a suitably fierce manner.

"Certainly not! You may review my list and decide from there. If you have not made your decision in three days, I shall wrest the matter from your hands and decide for you."

Lily squealed. "Grandfather! You *cannot* be so curmudgeonly!"

"Can I not?"

"No!" But Lily knew Lord Raven could. He was notorious for his sharp tongue, malicious temper, and stubborn turn of thought. That he had always been singularly kind to his orphaned grandchildren did not weigh with her in the least. Kind he may have been, but quarrelsome, too! She tilted her chin in a manner he secretly adored, and glared at him stare for stare.

"Grandfather, if you persist in your stubbornness, I shall not answer for the consequences."

Lord Raven inclined his head regally, though his stomach hurt with the effort to force down a spate of rumbling laughter.

He nodded regally, and waved her away with a great sweep of his bony fingers.

"Just remember, Miss Lily, you are never quite too old to be taken over my knee. I may be in my dotage, but I believe I am still *quite* capable of making a derriere smart."

"Oh!" Speechless, the youngest Miss Chartley turned on her heels and fled.

It was perhaps an hour later that her indignation had subsided enough to locate an inkpot in the jumble on her chamber desk and pen a rather daring—and hasty—note to Denver, Lord Barrymore. It was underscored several times and was *precisely* the type of letter that would have incurred the rather rigorous punishment outlined by the earl earlier.

Nevertheless, Lily was nothing, if not brave, and decided that since her life would be worthless without at least making a *push* to engage Lord Barrymore's fabulous attentions, the risk was minimal next to the gain.

Sad to say, there was no excusing such forwardness in a female, even in one as vivacious and ingenuous as she. Had Primrose—or even Daisy—discovered her intent, they would undoubtedly have advised her against this shocking venture and burned the billets-doux in the flickering grate. As it was, they were both strangely wrapped in thoughts of their own—it was as if a fever was about the place—and hardly noticed Lily's prolonged absence. Thus it was that with the help of Annie—a most romantic, if rather *foolish* maid, the note managed to pass the beady scrutiny of the Raven under butler and make its way, via two grooms, a footman, and a rather curious valet—to Lord Barrymore himself.

What this eminent personage said or thought when he read the note was anyone's guess, but it was observed by several people in his household—Mrs. Quivers not the least of them—that he was rather more cheerful at tea, partaking of at least two portions of her grouse and perigord pie, and recommending the rest of the staff to do the same.

When he left, not soon after, he was brandishing one of his finer canes and whistling something rather jaunty. Hoskin sighed. He was glad his lordship was in spirits, once more, but he did so wish he could remember his position. Viscounts ought never, upon any occasion, so far forget their lofty rank as to emit anything but a regal hum at most.

Twelve

"Gareth, be a dear, will you, and ride over to Lord Raven's residence? I have just finished inscribing an invitation to the Chartley sisters, and have missed the mail."

The Marquis of Rochester's heart missed a beat. He eyed his mama narrowly, for in truth his thoughts had been wandering to the matter of the Chartley sisters—or one in particular—all morning. Lady Rochester had *not* missed the mail, for there was a stack of cream-colored wafers upon the mantelpiece, all neatly embossed in red with the wax seal of the Dowager Marchioness of Rochester. If she had looked closely enough, she would have seen there was another, upon the stack. That was his own, in slightly darker paper, and franked with an equally heraldic crest.

"Mama, you may be the most wonderful mother in existence, but you are also a brass-faced liar! Don't cozen me into believing you've missed the mail, for I shall simply not believe you!"

The marchioness grimaced. "Sometimes, Gareth, you are just like your father! I could never cut a wheedle with him, no matter *how* hard I tried."

"It is fortunate, then, that he was so besotted with you that you always got your own way anyway!"

The marchioness's eyes misted over. "Oh, Gareth, I miss him!"

"I, too, Mama." There was a moment's shared silence, as Lord Rochester closed his book and ambled up to the fireplace. He placed his hands behind his ample, rather muscular back and contemplated the flames for a moment.

"Mama?"

"Yes?"

"Perhaps you are right. It is time I set up a nursery."

Lady Rochester refrained from jumping from her seat and throwing her arms about her wayward son. No need to frighten him into fits! Gently does it . . .

She picked up a tapestry—some paltry thing she despised, but it was simple enough—and sewed a few stitches. She could always throw the horrible thing away later, or give it to one of the housemaids.

"Really, Gareth? Do you have a young lady in mind, or shall I just pick for you, as we have agreed upon? Miss Lambert is well enough, though I fear she has something of a temper. Still, you do not want too meek a wife, or I could suggest Miss Tilbert . . ."

Gareth's eyes lit up in sudden amusement. "Mama, I thought we had agreed you cannot cut a wheedle with me! You know perfectly well none of those young ladies interest me in the slightest!"

"But Miss Chartley does?"

"Miss Chartley does."

Lady Rochester breathed a long sigh of satisfaction and eyed Gareth closely. Should she mention Primrose, or would that be too precipitant? Too precipitant, she thought.

"Miss Lily Chartley shall be perfect for you! Such a beauty, with her wild, black locks and exotic countenance! You shall doubtless be the talk of the Ton for you, Gareth, are uncommon handsome yourself!"

For a moment, Lord Rochester stared at his mother in blank incomprehension. Miss Lily? Surely she did not

think he would fall for an ingenuous youngster several
times his junior, who, whilst undoubtedly beautiful, had
none of Primrose's ready wit and steady poise? He
stared at her closer. There were laughter lines about
her mouth. Little minx! She was bamming him! Well,
two could play at that game! He smiled sweetly and
announced that undeniably, Miss Lily was supremely
well favored.

Lady Rochester seemed taken aback for a moment,
which made him whistle, happily, between his teeth.

"Shall I take the invitations over now? I shall speak to
Lord Raven upon the subject myself. I will need to fix
my interest at *once* if I am to have a chance. Half of England has designs on her already."

"Fix your interest?" Lady Rochester dithered. Though
she had a burning desire to see the marquis wed, she
only hoped Gareth was not about to tumble into some
terrible mistake. Lily was undoubtedly beautiful but she
was hen-witted and rather vain—oh, not copiously so, but
just sufficient to try the patience a little. Lady Rochester
had a feeling Gareth's patience did not need trying at
this stage of his manhood.

"Is that really necessary? Lord Raven would have to be
madder than I give him credit for if he does not hedge
all his bets and wait for the greatest prize. And you,
Gareth, without wishing to turn your head, must surely
rank as *that!*"

Lord Rochester lifted his shoulders eloquently. "Mama,
you are a doting parent!"

"Nonsense! Unless the Chartleys are being courted by
princes and dukes—and if they are, Emily Cowper would
have been bound to tell me—you have the decided advantage of rank!"

"Not to mention fortune . . ."

"Precisely."

"And good looks . . ."

"Now, Gareth, you are teasing me. I know perfectly well that though you are *passing* handsome, you care nothing for such matters. Poor Reece, how he puts up with you, I cannot conceive!"

"Reece is contented enough, when I don't have a fancy to be a coachman. But Mama, we stray from the point."

"That you need to make an offer? It is a nonsense! Bring the girls out and see how they do. You may look them *all* over if that is your wish."

"Aha!" Gareth chuckled.

"What?" Lady Rochester sounded pettish, but Gareth only smiled provokingly. If his mama did not want the older and more judicious *Primrose* for a daughter, he would eat his elegant beaver. Since he was reasonably certain he would not have to resort to such drastic measures, he retrieved it from the occasional table where it had lain, and thrust it, rather, upon his head. It looked singularly debonair, a fact that was not lost on his eagle-eyed mama.

"You will not do anything rash?"

He regarded her innocently, but she was in no way reassured, for a telltale dimple had appeared on his chin. The boy was so like his father, he was impossible to scold.

"My lord?" The butler interrupted their conversation with a murmured apology.

"There is a gentleman below stairs who desires speech with you. I informed him you were not at home to visitors, but . . ." The butler shrugged his shoulders in as expressive a way as he was able, for he was not a man not given to excessive displays of emotion.

"Does he have a name, this mysterious personage?"

"Ah, yes! I would not have bothered you else. It is the Viscount of Barrymore, my lord."

"How intriguing! Show him up, if you please! Though I have pressing business"—he glanced teasingly

at his mama—"I believe it can wait." So saying, his lordship stuffed three beautifully gilded invitations into his
perfectly fitting morning coat of emerald superfine.
Had Reece, his redoubtable valet, witnessed this spectacle, he would surely have fainted. Thankfully he did
not, for the act was followed by something equally unforgivable—the removal of his beaver, which was flung
rather unceremoniously onto a hat rack. Sadly, it
missed.

"The proposition is fascinating. Is your backer reliable?"

"Impeccable."

Lord Rochester raised his brows slightly. He would *have*
to be, given the scale of the project Barrymore was out-
lining. Despite the fact that he and the viscount tended
to move in different circles, he found he rather *liked* the
man. Denver, Lord Barrymore, was a neck or nothing
kind of man. A gambler, undoubtedly, but a whimsical
one at that. Rochester was one of the few to suspect him
of not taking his attire nearly as seriously as his fame
suggested. He had that slightly satirical look about him
that Gareth suspected was a kind of mocking salutation
to society and its foibles. Though fastidious, his eyes
gleamed with a certain wry amusement that belied outward appearance. Now, he toyed with a wineglass, fingering the rim so that it emitted a high, rather soprano note.
He grinned and set it down.

"Oh, don't look so superior, Gareth! I may call you
that, may I not?"

The marquis surprised himself by nodding amiably.

"My backer is no other than Lord Raven himself."

Gareth's eyes sharpened. He made no comment as he
reached for the crystal decanter and poured himself another glass of smooth, amber-shaded liquid.

"Lord Raven? Now why would he be interesting himself in newfangled nonsense like railways?"

"It is *not* newfangled nonsense! Raven has a Midas touch and a positively indecent knack for sensing where there is money to be made. *He* doesn't believe it beneath him to be making money on anything but rents from his land."

"No, but there are many among us who do."

"Then we must look to our laurels, for it will be the merchants and the industrialists who take over the power of England, you mark my words!"

"You have a point. I have often thought we are an archaic bunch."

Lord Barrymore, for once, was serious. "It is you and I, Gareth, as peers of the realm, who can make a difference. Let us blacken our hands a little with hard work—what of it—we shall see the rewards tenfold in wealth, but in more than that—in being at the forefront of a great new dawn, where man is limited not by the number of his horses, but by the power, only, of his imagination."

"That is a very sweeping comment."

"It can be substantiated. Only think! If we can develop a steam-driven engine with the power of forty horses, coal can be extracted and carried into British homes at so much less time and cost. It will mean even the poorest tenant can have fires in their grates, and warmth in their homes. God! It can mean that *other* steam-based engines can be designed, for there will be the coal to fuel them."

"And you own the mines." Lord Rochester's tone was dry, but there was a sympathetic crease to his brow that reassured Barrymore, a little.

"True, though Raven will get the most out of the venture, I suspect."

"A king's ransom, in fact."

Barrymore grinned. "Better than a *Raven's* ransom!"

Lord Rochester swallowed and allowed the light to filter into his glass, causing his spirits to sparkle, for a moment. Raven's Ransom. That is what he might have when he married Primrose. He pushed the thought from his mind. It was unworthy of him, for his attraction, he knew, had little to do with Lord Raven's ridiculous offer. He squinted at Barrymore, who looked more susceptible to such a prize. Would not a gambler by nature be drawn, inexorably, to such a tantalizing prospect? He liked Denver, the young Viscount Barrymore, but he could not set aside the suspicion.

"Let us talk of the ransom for a moment. Half of London is doing it, why should not we?"

"What shall we say?" A militant sparkle suddenly entered the viscount's eye.

"Shall we say that the Chartley sisters are worthy of such largesse?"

"We can, but if your implications are as insulting as I infer, I would have to run you through with a sword."

"And why, pray?"

"Because one of them is imminently to become my betrothed."

Lord Rochester felt as though he had been kicked in the pit of his stomach. He stood up and walked away from the table, for had he remained, the Huntingdale crystal would undoubtedly have splintered on his superb marble floor.

"By Lord Raven's honorable consent, I presume?"

"What else?" Barrymore shrugged his shoulders in an engaging fashion, but the marquis was not in a humor to be mollified.

"May I ask which one?"

"Oh, the fairest diamond of them all. But come, let us not bandy lady's names about. It is not my custom."

The fairest diamond. Then he *did* mean Primrose! Oh, *why* had he chosen to tease his mama and delay fixing her interest the very moment he knew he was smitten? Lord Raven, surely, would have chosen him above some trumped-up popinjay who took more account of his waistcoats then he did of his pockets. Barrymore was notoriously in debt, despite owning, as he claimed, some of the wealthiest mines on English shores. And look at him now! He had some strange, faraway smirk on his damnably handsome countenance that caused the usually mild Lord Rochester to want to throttle him. He kept his voice steady, however, and snapped his fingers to have the dishes removed. A lackey stepped forward at once, though it was not generally the marquis's custom to treat him so.

"I shall help you with your little project, Barrymore, if you grant me one small request."

"Anything." The viscount felt a slight tingling about his pulses.

If the marquis joined forces with him, the project would not fail. Everyone who knew anything knew that Lord Rochester had a passion for science. It was he who, for a wager, had put up the blunt for Matthew Murray's steam locomotive that had so inspired Richard Trevithick. He had also, some time past, traveled to the colonies to see Oliver Evan's noncondensing high-pressure engine. That same year, Oliver had built a steam-powered boat, the first of its kind. Lord Rochester had been one of the first to venture upon it. His rank and indisputable knowledge lent credence to any venture that might otherwise appear ramshackle. If Rochester endorsed it, one might be sure the whole of the *bon* Ton would. Now he was asking a small favor, and Denver felt certain that whatever it was, he could offer it.

"Anything? Excellent. Then we are agreed. I shall write to my acquaintance, George Stephenson, at once. I shall also procure for you all the expert knowledge you might require for an enterprise of this scale. Though you may not use Hedley's design, he shall be consulted on the project, for I believe his ideas are sound. In return, you shall drop your claim to Miss Chartley. I believe that with the revenue from this enterprise, you shall make the Raven's Ransom look paltry. You don't need it, Barrymore, drop it."

There was a moment's silence as the viscount digested this stipulation. On the one hand, he saw Lily, smiling, intriguing, adorably merry, tantalizing in the extreme, and extraordinarily—quite extraordinarily beautiful. Truth to tell, in respect to her, he had almost forgotten the Raven's Ransom, for Raven's wager was a two-edged sword. He knew that by honorably claiming one, he could not expect the other. How *dare* the man! Without thinking that in some respects Lord Rochester was correct, Lily's fortune *had* been a lure to him from the outset, he could only see the great insult that besmirched his very real feelings for the irrepressible Miss Lily. He kept his tone even as he looked Gareth, Lord Rochester, squarely in the eye. There was no vestige of the amicable accord that had been evident earlier.

"You jest, surely."

"I have never been more serious. I wager you have not approached Miss *Chartley* for her hand."

"No, and I do not intend to."

Lord Rochester breathed easier and walked back to the table. He was just congratulating himself on his quick thinking, when Lord Barrymore continued.

"I intend to abduct her, you see." A smile lurked about his eyes. No doubt Lily would deem that *very* good sport!

"You cur! I shall foil you, be warned."

"My private life is none of your business, Rochester!"

"Maybe I shall *make* it so, if it impinges on mine."

The viscount stared at him in astonishment. "Jumping Jupiter, Gareth! You don't mean to tell me *you* are after the Raven's Ransom?"

Gareth looked at him in distaste. "Hardly." He wanted to grind Lord Barrymore's handsome nose into the butter dish, but good manners and a lifetime of calm civility prevented such a hasty recourse.

"Oh, then it matters not what I do with my Miss Chartley! At all events, she shall be the Viscountess Barrymore, soon, and quite above reproach! If it eases your conscience a little, I swear she shall not be despoiled before she is wed. It might interest you to know, my lord Rochester, that this is not simply a question of the ransom. My feelings, in this matter, are really very much engaged. Quite unaccountable, really, for a bachelor life has always seemed rather advantageous to one of my free spirit."

"I'm sure it *has.*" Civil as he was, my lord Rochester could not keep the irony from his tone as he surveyed his rival. What a damnable pity he actually *liked* the man, for otherwise he might surely be forgiven for booting him from his home. It would do his immaculate cream buckskins the world of good, no doubt, to have boot polish applied to the posterior seams.

Barrymore grinned, ignoring entirely the sarcastic tone. "Well, I suspect it is a parson's mousetrap for *everyone* at some stage, and at least the chit is pretty!"

"The 'chit,' as you call her, is about to be sponsored by my mother! She shall doubtless be residing in my town house for the rest of the Season, so your plans, sir, shall have to be revised."

Barrymore frowned, then swiftly did as the urbane Lord Rochester had sarcastically suggested. He revised his plans. He would carry Lily off immediately. Tonight, if that was possible, for he had no desire to cause a scandal by breaching the lovely Lady Rochester's private gardens. If *she* were Lily's chaperone, he would be doomed to an endless spate of morning calls and perhaps, at best, a trip to Astley's circus. He shuddered, a little, at the thought.

"Very well, I shall do as you suggest. Now come off your high ropes, if you please. I had no *notion* you could be so stiff-rumped! Cry friends, shall we?"

Gareth, accosted by appealing blue eyes and a light-hearted lilt of the lips, melted a degree, reminding himself sternly to look to his laurels if he wanted to secure Primrose's future not as the Viscountess Barrymore, but as the eminently more preferable—to himself, of course—Marchioness of Rochester. He hoped his suit would not be too irksome to Primrose, who thus far had appeared to display a gratifying degree of affection for himself. Still, there was no accounting for young ladies' tastes, especially as the rascal he was now shaking hands with so civilly had the face of an angel, with deplorably romantic locks that glinted a little with gold.

For the first time, Gareth, Lord Rochester, questioned his dark, aristocratic countenance. There was a whisper of silver creeping into his luxurious, ebony hair that spoke of substance and maturity rather than Grecian gods endowed with eternal youth. He sighed a little, then handed Barrymore his stylish cane. Barrymore had the confounded impudence to wink as he took it, and Gareth found himself smiling, a little, in response.

"I shall write to Trevithic and Stephenson today."

"Thank you. I am anxious to set the business in motion. This color is splendid, do you mind?"

Gareth had no time to reply, for Denver had whisked one of his mother's prime blooms from her vase and was inserting it, jauntily, into his buttonhole.

Drat the man! He *did* have the advantage of a certain spontaneous style.

Lord Rochester wondered which elements would appeal to Primrose more, then pushed the gloomy thought from his mind. The lady would undoubtedly decide. He hoped it was sooner, rather than later.

Thirteen

Three men laid careful plans. Two of them were wise enough to procure special licenses. The third, rather less precipitant, had armed himself merely with an enormous bunch of hothouse roses and a basket of oranges that were as sweet as they were unseasonable. A merchant in London's seedier south side was even now congratulating himself on his enterprising venture, for the rather regal gentleman, dressed impeccably in doeskin breeches and a morning coat of enviable azure blue, had paid him handsomely for his trouble.

He would know him again, that one, for his mount was a perfect Arabian of ice white, blessed with a proud stance and a high stepper to boot. It would not, he knew regretfully, be for sale. Matthew Bludgewick of Trentham Place, as he liked to rather royally describe his habitation, was a keen man for horseflesh. He also knew the gentry when he saw it. This man, though neither stiff-rumped nor too high in the instep, was undoubtedly that. With a small shrug, he watched him trot off across the cobbles, the delectable fruit adding a little color to the saddlebag.

Lord Rochester hoped that the oranges would find favor. He felt a little foolish, arriving unannounced at Lord Raven's residence with a bouquet that obscured his skillfully tied neckerchief and a basket of citrus that, however sweet, should certainly rather have been delivered. The butler would probably send him around to the servants' entrance! The thought made him smile, a little, as he waited for his imperious knock upon the ornate brass door knocker to be answered.

He did not have to wait long, for the under butler was becoming used to the ebb and tide of morning corners that seemed to perpetually be thronging to Lord Raven's door. Each asked after him respectfully, but there could be no doubt, of course, that it was the *Chartley* sisters that was the attraction. Now, Lord Raven's manservant raised his eyes a little at the sight confronting him. He stepped back, a tad, to receive the flowers, then stopped in surprise.

"My lord Rochester!"

"Ah, you know me. I was just about to produce a card."

The under butler, still new to his job, snickered at what he regarded as a very fine joke. Not know him indeed! The Marquis of Rochester, the very pink of the Ton!

"May I see Lord Raven, if you please?"

"Lord Raven?" The man was struck dumb. He was certain his lordship would be after Miss Primrose or Daisy or Miss Lily at the very least. And they were all in such high good looks today, too! It was a shame.

"Very well, your lordship. I shall see how he does. He has been rather ill, you understand."

Lord Rochester's eyes twinkled as he announced that he understood perfectly. Raven's tempers were as famous as his disagreeable, ill-conceived ransom.

The under butler bowed and made his suddenly stately way out of the room, just stopping, for a moment, in the kitchens, to announce what a "prodigious agreeable gentleman the marquis" was before handing his message over to a disapproving Richmond.

"His lordship is not to be excited."

"What? What?" came bellowing from the bed. "Come in here, you rag-mannered fellow! Did you say there was someone to see me? Barrymore, eh?"

"No, sir."

"Ah, then it must be another proposal. Fetch me my walking stick, Richmond. This shall be lively."

"My lord, you have had far too much excitement for one day. The doctor . . ."

". . . is an old pie-faced, chicken-hearted, lily-livered woman! Get me my neckerchief, Richmond, before I throw this nasty concoction out the window. Are those flowers for *me*?"

"Flowers?" The under butler, in his confusion at the spectacle, had forgotten about the precious red blooms.

"I suppose so, my lord. The marquis did not say."

The earl's eyes gleamed. "Marquis, eh? Ah, *now* we are talking! Fetch me my diamond pin, Richmond. And my snuff."

With a sharp look at his employer, who truth to tell, *did* look rather animated, despite his bony fingers and frail countenance, Richmond bowed and set about doing his bidding. The under butler, perceiving that this meant an affirmative reply for the visitor below stairs, *also* made his bow. He was waved away with an impatient hand, so it was not long before he was taking the steps two at a time and praying that the toffee-nosed butler would not catch him at it.

"My lord!"

"Yes?" The marquis turned from the portrait he was studying and smiled.

"The earl will see you now."

"Ah, excellent."

"Mama, I am bringing home the loveliest creature. I am certain, with your kindly heart, that you shall love her always."

"Mais oui, chéri?" The Countess of Westenbury smiled prettily upon her only son. "But zees is exciting! I shall

guess this sweet creaturrre!" She rolled her *r*'s with greater stress than normal, for she was excited.

The viscount smiled. "You can *try!*"

"It is zee 'orse?"

"No, Mama! You have enough of those!" The countess pouted a little, but her eyes twinkled.

"It is zee moonkey?"

"Monkey? Nonsense, Mother! A monkey would be very trying. It would hang from your chandeliers and cause havoc with your silk drapes."

"It is not, zen, zee elephant?"

Lord Armand Valmont laughed. It was a deep, throaty laugh that womankind seemed to dote upon and his mother loved in particular.

"No, I would *not* describe her as an elephant."

"But aha! It is a 'er, then? 'Ow very intriguing!"

"Very."

"But, Armand, you would not bring one of zose opera dancers—what do you call zem? 'Igh kickers? To meet me?"

"High steppers. And, Mama! How shocking!"

"Yes?" She peeped at him with a smile.

"Yes." Armand was firm. Though he was very well acquainted with the ladybird set, he would certainly not entertain the notion of bringing one of them home. The idea was appalling.

"I geeve up, *ma chéri*. What is zees fascinating creature?"

"It is a girl, Mama. I am meant to carry her off into the sunset tonight."

"A girl? But, Armand, you are so young!"

"Young? I am eight-and-twenty!"

"Is she preety, zees girl?"

"Oh, she is just like the little porcelain doll you brought from France."

"*Foi!* No girl can be *so* preety!"

"Miss Chartley can. She is livelier than your doll, though. She sparkles as she talks, and oh! Her imagination! You will love her, Mama, for she lives in a dream-world, just like you."

"Zat is very good, for I cannot abide girls who look at you *so*"—she pulled a rather toffee-nosed grimace—"when one talks of zee dragons and dungeons and peexie dust."

"I can assure you, my Daisy will be quite wide-eyed in fascination."

"Then breeng 'er to me!"

"I shall, for I am meant to carry her off into the sunset tonight, and I'll be *damned* if I will spend three uncomfortable nights in an ill-sprung chaise to get to Gretna, when with the special license I procured today, we can be married charmingly from home!"

"Armand, you are not worthy of such a one! A 'eroine *yearns* for a leetle discomfort!"

Armand chuckled.

"True, but I shall tell her I am escaping the Bow Street Runners. That shall be discomfort enough. She thinks, you see, that I am a highwayman."

"A 'ighwayman? And the little one still wishes to marry you?"

"Fervently, I hope!" The countess clapped her hands. "I theenk I love 'er already. Bring 'er 'ome by all means. But you, *ma cher*, you must stay away."

"Stay away?" Armand looked blank.

"It would not be feeting. Until she is your bride, it would be a scandal if you stayed."

"But . . ."

"Armand . . ." The countess's expressive face looked suddenly stubbornly forbidding.

"Oh, very well, Mama! Unless I have actually married her, I shall return to town upon the instant, though the horses will not thank me for it. It is pitch dark upon the roads, now that the moon is no more than a sliver of a crescent."

Lady Valmont appeared to have little sympathy for such a paltry matter. She waved it away, in fact, with an airy gesture that did justice to her long, elegant fingers.

"Eet is good. So! If I love this . . . this . . . cornflower?"

"Daisy."

"Daisy. You shall be married tomorrow. I *weesh* your father was not so far away!"

"The earl? He is not as romantic as you, Mama. The King's business must come first. He will be pleased, I think, at the prospect of an heir."

"Oh, Armand! He is not so cold as you think."

Lord Valmont smiled. "If he chose you, Mama, he *must* have fire somewhere beneath his icy reserve!"

"Indeed! *Ma foi!* Just look how he challenged Raven when the man tried to . . . to . . ."

"Mama, you are blushing! And Raven paid dearly for that kiss, for he lost his golden sword."

"True, but it was better than 'is life."

"It was *Papa's* life that was threatened."

"So! Eet is long ago, now."

"Yes. Mama?"

"*Mais, oui?*"

"Daisy is his granddaughter."

"The Raven's?"

"The very same."

There was a long silence. Armand swallowed and felt his chest tighten in sudden concern. Surely his mama would not object . . . ?

A tinkle of infectious laughter lightened the tension. "So! Eet comes a full circle. Your father shall see the 'umor."

"I hope so, Mama, I hope so. Tonight I shall ride off

into the sunset with my bride, and you shall see how well I have chosen."

"You shall ride with your back to the sun, *chéri*. You are traveling *east* to Westenbury."

"Mama!" Armand sounded genuinely shocked. "How *can* you be so prosaic! I have a good mind not to include you in this escapade at all."

At which, the incorrigible Countess Westenbury rolled her eyes in the most uncountesslike of fashions, and called for her smelling salts.

"Lord Rochester. What a singular surprise! I knew your mother. Chirpy little thing. Might have married her myself, but for a silly scandal and a temptingly pretty widgeon called . . . good grief, I forget her name, but she is the Countess of Westenbury now."

Lord Rochester had heard of the scandal, but he was too polite to refer to it. Instead, he withdrew a pinch of excellent snuff and offered the same to Lord Raven.

"No, by God, won't touch the stuff unless I have mixed it myself. Now where was I? Oh, your dear mama. I trust she is still a beauty, though time must have wrought some damage. Even *I* am not as handsome as I once was." He gave a bark of sudden laughter. "Your father cut me out neatly, I fear, though I blame it entirely on his tailor. If he hadn't been wearing one of those *dashed* military style coats by Scott . . ." The earl sighed. "Your mother had eyes for no one else after that."

Gareth refrained from mentioning how relieved he was that this was the case. Instead, he inclined his eyebrows, murmuring a polite "Really? I do not believe she ever mentioned the circumstance of your being acquainted."

Raven gave a bark of slightly bitter laughter. "No, I don't suppose she has. Probably took me for some doting old fool. I was much older than she was, you understand."

Gareth thought he did, so his nod was perfunctory, for he did not wish to appear pitying.

The old man grunted. "Madeira?"

"Thanks." Civilities accorded, his lordship took a seat by the window and inspected his elegantly manicured hands. Despite his credentials, he was suddenly strangely unsure of himself. Certainly, it was hard to begin, especially if Raven had already accorded the honor he was about to ask for to that trumped-up sprig Barrymore.

The earl regarded him closely. If there was a slight, mischievous smile behind his eagle eyes, Lord Rochester was too overset to notice it.

"I suspect you know why I am here."

"No, I am intrigued. Doubtless you shall tell me."

"I have come to offer for Miss Chartley. If she agrees to do me the honor of becoming my wife, I shall own myself the happiest of men."

Lord Raven regarded him with sudden animation. Ha, if that wasn't one for the pot! He had rather hoped for Barrymore, but had not raised his thoughts so high as a marquis. He schooled his hands to be still, for they were itching to rub together with glee. Instead, he rather mildly—for one of his temperament—inquired *which* Miss Chartley Lord Rochester referred to, for he assumed he must have some kind of preference in this matter.

"Oh!" Lord Rochester stared at him in some surprise. "Miss *Primrose* Chartley, of course."

"No 'of course' about it, my boy. I have had suitors begging for all three on at least two occasions. One, however, had the unmitigated gall to tabulate which he desired in order of perceived merit."

"But that is frightful!"

"Precisely." Lord Raven watched the younger man in amusement. Secretly, he was as pleased as the punch Richmond brewed at his specification. He had caught Primmy—ever his favorite—a catch beyond even *his* hopes. But the bait, the bait! Surely Lord Rochester's coffers were not so far depleted that they needed restoring from the ransom? But why else would he offer for Primrose? He hardly knew her! He decided to prod, a little. It was all part of his fun, after all.

"The happiest of men, eh? Doubtless you will be happier still if Primrose's name was picked from out my tricorne."

"Your tricorne, sir, is of no concern to me. Keep it upon your head, I beg. It is almost certainly of more use there."

"What? What?" Lord Raven almost bellowed at this calm, rather mild reproof. Still, that was ever his way. Beneath the gruff exterior, his rather kind heart was rejoicing. If this young man could play fast and loose with his fortune, he didn't need it. Lord Rochester, marvelously, unaccountably, was offering for Primrose out of sounder motives than he had feared.

Lord Rochester cut into his private thoughts. "You hear me, Raven! The wretched ransom—and yes, I call it that—is of more nuisance than consequence. Allow me Primrose, and I shall be satisfied with the *real* treasure."

"You shall, shall you?" The gruff voice, in spite of itself, was more mellow.

"Oh, undoubtedly."

"The minx! She said nothing of meeting you at all."

The marquis felt a sudden stab of pain.

"Nothing at all?"

The earl, for the first time in forty years, actually grinned.

"Nothing at all. That means, my dear, glum-looking greenhorn, that in the contrary way of females, you have made a conquest. Shall I ask you how this came to pass?"

"I think not." Lord Rochester's lips twitched a little, though his voice remained pleasingly firm.

"Bother! I think it would make the most intriguing tale

yet. Despite her calm exterior, Primrose has always struck me as a dark horse, rousable to passion."

"Quite possibly, but it is a tale that I *assure* you, my lord, shall remain untold. I take it you are amenable to my offer, despite any or all prior claims?"

The Earl of Raven shrugged. It would not do to appear too eager.

"Suit yourself."

"Oh, I shall, my lord. I shall. By the by, I have a missive here from my mother. How remiss of me not to have handed it to you earlier."

"The marchioness? May I have it?" If the earl appeared a little eager, Rochester appeared not to notice. He rather pitied the old man, really, for there was nothing in the missive that was likely to bring hope to his cheeks or a sparkle to the heavy, black eyes.

He was wrong. His lordship ripped open the contents and snorted, a *decided* glimmer in his world-weary eyes.

"Ha!" He said. "Ha! So your mother thinks she can whisk away my granddaughters in the twinkle of an eyelash, does she? Well, there she is very much mistaken! Lily may be her goddaughter, but by god, blood is thicker than water any day! She shall not 'sponsor' them, if you please! As if the Chartley sisters need sponsoring! Why, their blood is all as blue as you please, their lineage unimpeachable, as granddaughters to the Earl of Raven!"

Rochester was gentle. "That may be so, sir, but they are still in need of chaperonage. Why, Primrose believes she is old enough to play that part! She as good as told me so!"

"Stuff and nonsense! Primmy is a diamond of the first water; she is not to be regarded as a miserable, maudlin, meddling old . . ."

"Ah"—Rochester's eyes lit with sudden amusement— "I take it you do not hold chaperones in high regard?"

"No I do not! Crabby old spinsters! And if you have

the impertinence, sir, of suggesting that my Primrose falls into that category, why, I shall . . . I shall . . ."

"Withdraw all consent?"

"Precisely. And stop smirking, sir! You are liable to choke! Though what in tarnation I should care . . . Good God, I feel another spasm coming on. . . ." Lord Raven put old, gnarled hands to his chest. Alarmed, Gareth rang the bell hard and stepped forward. Lord Raven appeared short of breath, but recovered sufficiently to wave the younger man away irritably with his cane.

"I am not dead yet, Rochester, so you needn't look so grim. And don't think to slumguzzle me with your kindness merely because I apparently have a foot in the grave. There is fight in the Raven yet, and I give you fair warning."

Brave words, but they failed to have the desired impact on his guest. Lord Rochester refused to continue the argument, despite various taunts from his host. Instead, he rather solicitously handed the earl some water—for which he was not thanked—and waited quietly for a manservant to arrive.

He took heart when Lord Raven revived sufficiently to remark that if Lady Rochester *did* take them on, she would best have her wits about her, for his granddaughters were nothing, if not hen-hearted, and would undoubtedly lead her a merry dance. By which Lord Rochester inferred that grudging consent had been given, and privately rejoiced.

Sadly, the marquis, though burning with sudden impatience, did *not* speak with Primrose that day, for by the time his singular interview with Raven was brought to a close, the sisters had left the house, headed, with just a groom and a footman, for Hookhams and the London Museum. He was not alone in his regret, for Lily, too, was sighing at this rather unexciting agenda. She wondered whether Barrymore had received the note she'd

penned, and more importantly, what he would do about
it. Surely, *surely*, he would not be so hard-hearted as to
ignore it?

Perhaps she ought to have stayed at home in case he
called. Better still, she ought really have sneaked out of
the house and called up a hack. She had no patience
with young ladies who sat around in hope when they
could have been devising ingenious ways of shaping their
own fate. True, she could be ruined, but oh, at such a
very tender age, the specter of such a thing seemed too
far away to contemplate. Besides, she had *not* imagined
the blaze kindling in Lord Barrymore's eye. She wanted
nothing more than to kindle it again, detestable Raven's
Ransom or no.

She was still deliberating over her next rather uncir-
cumspect course of action, should Lord Barrymore fail
her, when her eyes alighted on a rather old-fashioned
landau. Despite the fact that the wheels were not as well
sprung as they might have been, the carriage was smart,
all up to the rig with a fresh coat of paint. It drew to a
halting stop some small way up Marlborough Street. None
of the sisters hurried, for the chaise was unknown to
them, but something in the bearing of the sole passenger
sent delicious warning tingles up the youngest Miss Chartley's spine.

Fourteen

"Good afternoon, ladies!"

"Good afternoon, my lord!" Primrose answered, for Lily, though a wreath of sudden smiles, was suddenly, uncustomarily, tongue-tied. My lord—for indeed, it was undoubtedly Lord Barrymore within—did not appear to notice. Rather, he grinned and politely remarked that the weather was crisp, for that time of year. At which both Primrose and Daisy agreed heartily.

Lily, however, was silent, for she was gazing quite shamelessly at the gentleman in the debonair morning coat of ruby red superfine. She appeared mesmerized by his epaulettes, which indeed *were* rather handsome, being trimmed in gold braid and adding a military style to his jaunty ensemble. Still, my lord could wish that the full force of her deep emerald eyes could be cast a little higher, perhaps, to match his own. In this wish he had to be patient, for Lily—ever resourceful even in tongue-tied crises such as these—was now scheming to consult him alone. She thus did not needlessly waste her energies on trifles like looking up. The amused, rather twinkling blue eyes that watched her were doomed to disappointment.

"Would it be daring, Miss Primrose, to offer to convey you all to wherever your destination might be?"

His gaze turned from Lily with reluctance and alighted, once again, upon the remaining sisters.

"I am afraid, so, my lord." Her eyes stared at him levelly.

Daisy dug her parasol into the elder Miss Chartley's ribs, but she need not have bothered. Dear Primmy was merely having fun at his lordship's expense.

"It would be daring, sir, for I do not believe that your elegant chaise would house more than two extras at most, and we have five between us, counting Horsley our footman and Standish, the groom."

Both men shuffled uncomfortably under the viscount's sudden scrutiny.

"True, Miss Chartley! How very maladroit of me not to have perceived the problem instantly. Shall I send for a larger chaise?"

"On no accounts, my lord, for Daisy and I were merely stepping into Hookhams and that, as you can see, is not so very far at all."

"Ah. And Miss Lily? Was she not going to select a book for herself?" My lord addressed himself very properly to the *elder* Miss Chartley, but it was clear by the direction of his smile that it was the *younger* Miss Chartley that maintained his interest. She answered, now, before Primrose could dream up a plausible reply.

"No, for I still have *Evalina* to get through and the heroine is so tedious it takes her *pages* to do anything!"

"How very inconsiderate! I am certain that if *you* were the heroine, your readers would not have the substance to make a similar complaint."

"No, for I should not weep into my pillow and pray for miracles. I would take action upon the instant."

"Like writing clandestinely to the hero and demanding immediate rescue?"

Lily shifted uncomfortably in her pastel walking boots of powder blue. She shot a glance at her sisters, but they seemed satisfyingly unaware of the innuendo that was passing between them. So, gathering her courage, she took a deep breath, and looked, at last, boldly into the handsome face.

He quirked an eyebrow that nearly caused her to choke. Pointedly, she ignored him, as she replied, with some emphasis, "*Exactly* like that, my lord."

"Ah."

He smiled noncommitally but Lily was not deceived. She no longer wondered whether he had received her note, or how to ask him in so public a place with the sharp ears of her sisters about her. They were dears, of course, but she knew she had been horribly naughty in demanding an assignation with the frivolous likes of Denver, Lord Barrymore. *Especially* when Grandfather had so expressly forbidden it. Primmy was bound to have scruples. Daisy, too, though her soft heart would feel earnestly for her. Better they knew nothing of it. Now, she waited for Barrymore's next move. Not anxiously, for by the set of his shoulders he was bound to have thought up *something*. One did not have such delectably compelling shoulders if one was not a man of firm resolve. Lily, for all her youth, was determined about this.

"Shall *you* step into my carriage, then?"

"Said the spider to the fly?" Primrose's tone was light, but the words were curt and interrogatory.

"With the groom up front, of course. Stanley, was it?"

"Standish. And *that*, of course, makes all perfectly acceptable." Primrose allowed him a glimmer of a smile. My lord responded in kind, though he cursed poor Standish to the devil.

"Standish?"

The groom made an inarticulate gesture, being a man of fewer words than stable talents—and hoisted himself, pillionlike, upon Lord Barrymore's finest beast. This was not nearly so fine as Lord Raven's, being one of the few the viscount had not sold off to recoup his debts, but it was admirable nonetheless. Standish made a huffing murmur into his throat and subsided back into habitual silence.

"And now, Miss Lily?"

Lord Barrymore stared hard at his beloved. She gazed at him in trusting triumph and tried desperately to still the sudden beating of her heart. Surely a man brazen enough to whisk her out from under the elder Miss Chartleys' noses must care? Or did he merely wish to privately—and decidedly—decline her rash offer of herself and the gamble that necessarily came with it? At either possibility, Mistress Chartley's heart felt quite entitled to hammer ceaselessly in her chest, and did so with unrelenting vigor. As she climbed into the landau and waved her sisters away with an airy brush of her satin-gloved hand, she could hardly hear herself think. She wondered whether her thoughts were as transparent to Lord Barrymore and she winced. Oh, if only he were not *quite* as debonair! *Or* quite as much in need of funds!

She was very quiet as the horses settled into a pattern and clip-clopped against the cobbles in a soothing, if rather monotonous rhythm. The viscount's groomsman must have known his destination, for his lordship saw no need to issue any altered commands to the first postilion. Rather, he concentrated all his energy on *not* kissing the adorable Miss Lily full on the lips, an act he was perfectly certain she would approve, but one he was equally certain society would not. So he laid his cane upon his knees and settled for watching the breeze play havoc with her neat, rather elegantly turned chignon. Lily said nothing.

"Excellent weather, is it not?"

She peeped at him. Her eyes were wider than he remembered, and more green. Behind her, England was turning from cobble to lane. She scarcely noticed, for his voice was a luxurious tone she had not before encountered. Still, she was not the type of lady to agree without question to everything a gentleman—however personable—might say, so she turned her mind to the question and pulled her bonnet down hard.

"*If* you are partial to great gusts of wind and icy squalls, my lord."

"Icy squalls? You exaggerate. But here, if you are cold, you may have my traveling rug."

For the first time, Lily blushed. The rug was warm from his knees and the intoxicating thighs one tried so hard not to notice. Or at least to *peep* at without being observed. So annoying that Barrymore seemed to be a mind reader, for he obligingly revealed his legs, shockingly clad in buckskins that had not the shadow of a crease upon them, and stretched them—and himself—luxuriously, so she could see both the buckskins and the broad expanse of his impeccable chest.

When she blushed again, he merely chuckled and cocked his head annoyingly in her direction.

"Where are we going, my lord? Should we not be turning back?" The first question was asked idly, to turn his mind from his coxcomb thoughts. Also, to introduce a safe topic of conversation. It was about time, Lily thought, that she conversed. She would not like Lord Barrymore to think she was deficient in turning out a common phrase. The second question came rather more sharply, for she had just noticed, from the pastoral scenery, that they were well beyond the boundaries of fashionable London.

The viscount grinned and wrapped the traveling rug snugly abut her person.

"Turn back? After all the trouble I've been to to abduct you? It is not easy to do such a thing, you know, in the very heart of London! I was forced to bribe your under butler into divulging your direction, and that, you know, goes against the grain with me!"

"*What?*" Lily gazed at him in a turmoil of confusion.

"Do I infer this is not to your liking? I felt perfectly

certain, after the note I received, that this was your most earnest desire! I have had my team tooling up and down the streets all morning, hoping for a glimpse of your lovely self."

"My nose is red from the cold. I cannot be lovely at all."

"True. That is why I propose we marry at once and have a delectable wedding feast by a cozy fire. That way, your nose will soon be restored to its former glory."

"Oh, you are horrid! There is nothing wrong with my nose. You trifle with me, sir, and I cannot say I like it!"

"No? Then I shall have to make amends. I assure you, madame, that when next I trifle with you, you shall like it enormously."

Lily blushed. "You are a coxcomb, sir, and I should scream!"

"Oh, undoubtedly. That would certainly be the *correct* thing to do in such a circumstance."

Lily looked at him doubtfully. Was he teasing her? Certainly, there seemed to be a frivolous ring in the deliriously fine lilt of his tone. If only he would stop looking at her, then perhaps she would be able to think! She averted her gaze and Lord Barrymore very kindly suggested that he order the landau to stop.

"Why, my lord? That we may turn back?" Lily felt a most unaccountable stab of disappointment.

"No, don't be so absurd, my chicken, we are not turning back. I merely meant so that you can scream. Stanley shall not hear you if the horses are trotting at this pace and the breeze is howling behind us."

As he spoke, a great gust of wind flung the remains of Lily's walking bonnet skyward. Her grown-up chignon came adrift in seconds, causing a squeal of dismay.

"There, that is a start, but I cannot help but mention a better attempt ought to be made. That sounded more like a squeak than a gusty shriek. Stanridge has not so much as heard you."

"Standish. And that was not a scream. That was merely annoyance at the loss of my bonnet. I fear it cost Lord Raven a fortune."

"And shall undoubtedly cost *me* an equal one in its replacement. Forget the bonnet, I despise the things anyway. Your hair is much better as it is. It is flowing like a witch."

"What a horrible thing to say!"

The Viscount Barrymore grinned. "Then get used to it, for I shall *always* call you a witch. If you didn't have green eyes that entranced me quite sinfully, I should not now be making a cake of myself by marrying you!"

"Not even for the Raven's Ransom?"

"Oh, quite possibly for *that,* but I cannot be certain."

He was teasing again, but Lily could not help wishing he had not answered as lightly. *Was* he abducting her purely for yet another gamble? For a chance at the riches Lord Raven dangled so skillfully before him? Suddenly, despite all her earlier protests, it mattered to her. Yet is was the one question, in all earnestness, that she feared asking. So she accepted his flippant answer with a toss of her head that sent such sparks flying between them that Lord Barrymore thanked the heavens that he had a special license in his pocket. There were certain limits to a gentleman's patience, after all! Lily certainly raised him to those limits faster than even the first serving wench he had bedded as a boy.

In front of them, Standish was growing restless. It was not his place to question the gentry, but Lily was a high-spirited thing and if she took a notion into her pretty little noggin there was nothing anyone could do about it. Nothing, of course, save the *butler,* who would probably take a switch to his shoulders before dismissing him out of hand. Miserable, poor Standish could only glance in dismay at the first postilion—a gentleman very firmly entrenched in the viscount's household—who seemed to see nothing amiss in an unscheduled trip into the country.

"Stanborough seems restless."

Lily giggled. "*Standish,* you horrid fellow! And I don't wonder he is restless, for Grandfather shall have spasms when he finds out."

"Then you agree to relinquish your pretty name of Chartley and take up the hideously sober appellation of Barrymore?"

"You have not yet asked, my lord."

"One never proposes when one is abducting. It is not *comme il faut.* All the textbooks agree."

"Now you are being nonsensical!"

"And *you* are avoiding my query."

"Oh, very well, then, I shall be Lady Barrymore. But I warn you, my lord, if we are headed for Gretna I shall be chilled to the bone and *quite* unable to speak my vows. I've heard the journey takes days and I have not even a feathered muff."

"How improvident! One should always dress to be abducted. It is the first law of any decent ladies' seminary. I am surprised your education is so deficient."

"And *I* am surprised you know so much about young ladies!"

"Are you? Don't be. I am rather knowledgeable on that score."

Lily felt a sudden lump in her throat. She cast her eyes downward, so that he would not get a glimpse of her maudlin tears.

"Yes, a rake and a fortune hunter. I had heard that."

Barrymore's tone was suddenly hard. "Do not be deceived by all you hear, Miss Lily." He relented as he caught the glimmer of a shimmering tear. It had fallen from downcast eyes and stained elegant pastel-colored gloves. "Oh, *do* look up! *I* shall try not to eat you if *you* try not to sniff! We are not traveling to Gretna, but we have several miles more to traverse in this unsatisfactory traveling rig. Yes, you are perfectly correct, I *should* have brought a closed chaise, but sadly, being at *points non plus,* I sold it!"

This served only to make Lily cry the more, for now she was perfectly certain that his lordship meant only to marry her to restore his fortunes. Or at least to *gamble* on such an event. Gamblers, she had heard, were always optimistic. What if Lord Raven and his horrid tricorne hat picked Primrose or Daisy? He would be ruined! And it would be all her doing for begging him to abduct her. Or if not abduct her precisely, then marry her out of hand, which was practically the same thing! A little sob escaped her despite her best intentions.

Lord Barrymore deemed it necessary to place his arms about her and tuck her a little closer to his handsome frame. Their knees were now touching and his arms felt delectable about her waist. Mid sob, Lily opened her mouth in astonished delight. Lord Barrymore definitely felt that a kiss was in order. Unfortunately, he was all too aware of Standish, who was fumbling with the reins and causing his excellent bay mare—acquired at great cost— to stumble slightly. He sighed, and sat back regretfully.

"If Stanford hears you sobbing he shall run my man through with a knife and doubtless me as well. *That,* I fear, would be tedious."

A glimmer of a smile appeared in the wide, green eyes.

"Standish, my lord. And I doubt he carries a knife. But a blow to your head might suffice just as admirably." She tilted her chin cheekily. He *did* care! She could *swear* he did!

"Baggage!" Lord Barrymore scowled, but his laughter made a mockery of the frown. Lily thought she had never gazed upon anyone more handsome or peculiarly wonderful in all her life. She swallowed a little breathlessly, pushed back several strands of long, ebony hair that the wind had caught on her lips, and sighed.

"It is what you really want, my lord?"

"Can you doubt me?" His tone assumed a slightly mocking twist before he took a long breath. In the pause, Lily's heart ached, for she was suddenly very fearful of what he might say next. My lord sensed that, for he took her hand, caressing her fingers a little so that they burned through their gloves. Mockery changed to a gentleness that sat uneasily upon a rake's shoulders. Still, he surprised himself.

"It is what I really want." Deep blue eyes bored into hers and she felt a tremor, whether at their strong sincerity or at something more basic that stirred within her, she knew not. What she *did* know, was that there was to be no turning back with this man, adventurer or not.

She closed her eyes to the sensuous blue that was assaulting her senses. Her breath caught in her throat and her lips opened oh, so invitingly. My lord touched them with his finger, and truly, the sensation was more erotic than had he done the same with his mouth. Lily's eyes flew open instantly, but the damage was done. Her bodice felt tight against her chest, and strange, intoxicating warmths seemed to whisper to her of pleasures to come. Amused, Barrymore watched her innocent surprise and wondered at his own response. They would suit, he and the Lady Lily. He was certain of it.

The moment passed as the carriage stumbled, a little, upon a hole in the path. The second mare whinnied, but continued on with admirable speed.

Lily watched as Barrymore gestured to his postilions. Her breathing was no easier, but somewhere at the back of her mind her thoughts were jolted into a more proper direction. Somehow, she really ought to alert her sisters that she was well. They would be troubled if she didn't return within the hour. Being a kindhearted soul, she pondered the problem for an instant until her eyes flicked back to the viscount. Her brow, puckered in thought, smoothed at once, a naughty grin mischievously taking its place.

Really! She was being abducted, one could not possibly arrange for every particular. When she was married, she would demand to return at once to Raven Place and oh, how astonished everyone would be! And she, the youngest sister, married—quite respectably, she thought—first. When she chuckled a little and voiced the thought out loud, Barrymore regarded her strangely, so that she felt hot and flustered once more.

"Yes, dearest," he murmured, but there was a lazy, teasing smile playing across the curves of his lips. "But first, don't you think, we might withdraw to our wedding chamber? Much as I *adore* being a guest at Raven Place"—here his tone became disturbingly dry—"I believe I would much rather postpone that particular pleasure in favor of other more . . . uh . . . well, yes, shall I say it? More *particular* pleasures. Unless you object?"

Under his gaze—which was not *quite* as lazy as he would have her believe, Lily colored, felt shamelessly wanton, blushed delightfully, and muttered that no, she could not find it in herself to object to so delightful an agenda. At which her husband-to-be laughed out loud, patted her fondly, and remarked that indeed, she would have no cause to regret this bold course.

The rest of the journey was a haze for Lily, who shivered under the traveling rug but welcomed the cold that bit into her shoulders and caused her fingers to freeze in their gloves. It convinced her that she was not the victim of some impossible dream, about to be wakened by the sound of the breakfast gong or curtains rustling open in her chamber. No, *such* a dream would doubtless be perfect. Certainly, it would not be so prosaic as to allow considerations of inclement weather and aching, stiff limbs to spoil the heartwarming effect of being about to become the Honorable Viscountess Barrymore.

It was not until their turreted destination was finally reached, the warmth of chimneys spiraling promisingly into the afternoon sky, that she realized that his lordship's words, whilst charming, had nevertheless still been ambiguous. It might, after all, have been the Raven's Ransom that he wanted with such an earnest sincerity.

Standish dismounted quicker than usual and opened the landau with fumbling vigor.

"Lawks a mercy, Miss Lily, you bin givin' an old gennelman like me a nasty fright jauntering about the countryside without so much as a by-your-leave! And what will 'is lor'ship say, I wunner? Turn me off without a character 'e will, you see an' he won't!"

"Then you shall have to take up employment in my stables, my good man. Her ladyship will be needing a groom when she is my wife."

"Your wife?" Standish stared at him suspiciously.

"Been I ain't knowin' nothin' about *that*, pleasin' your honor! An' it is more than me life is worth to be allowing Miss Lily 'ere into that there inn, no matter *how* gentrified it is!"

"Good man! You restore my faith in your common sense. I shall expect such excellent perspicacity when you are her personal groomsman. For now, however, let me remove that suspicious glare from your countenance and ask you to act witness to the ceremony. I trust you can *then* have no objection to her partaking of an excellent repast in this very fine—if I may say so—posting inn?"

From the beam on poor old Standish's face—now wreathed in toothless smiles—my lord inferred there was no further objection. Which was just as well, for the archbishop had been pacing about the private drawing room for well on an hour, and was at that moment *again* consulting his excellent fob. Lord Barrymore had been distressingly vague about the time in which he desired the ceremony to be performed. Still, his donation had been prodigious. . . . The archbishop patted his waistcoat and settled for a further intrusion on his time.

He had not long to wait, for the couple entered very soon after that. The bride, he thought, was in high good looks despite her gown being a rather frivolous confection for the taking of solemn vows. Still, even a hardy old soul like the archbishop could see that she was a dazzling beauty and for that, one could make a few allowances. Especially as she seemed suddenly becomingly shy.

Lord Barrymore bowed politely, exchanged a few perfunctory but civil words with him, then gestured for the rites to take place. And so, Miss Lily Chartley, frozen, dazed, tired, and stiff, became, but a few enchanting moments later, her very grand Ladyship, Lily, Viscountess of Barrymore.

Fifteen

The archbishop nodded pleasantly as he gestured for his carriage to be brought round. He breathed in deep of the fresh country air and picked a blossom idly as he waited. He'd waved away the footman and come down himself. It was not often he had a chance to collect his thoughts and just for today he thought he might dispense with a little ceremony. After all, the couple he had just left *behind* him had.

He did not generally make a habit of marrying peers of the realm in strange country inns, but by and large he was pleased that he had bent the rules a little. The couple—both gently born—no trouble about that— looked like April and May, a pleasing contrast to some of the very proper arranged marriages he'd had to attend to recently. He patted his waistcoat, rather pleased, too, with the repast he'd discovered awaiting him. It was not *all* inns that employed French cooks, nor many lords who thought to order him up dinner. Lord Barrymore, for all his sorry reputation, was no skinflint. Neither, by the looks of it, was he stony broke, as he'd heard whispered. He smiled benignly on the pair, blessed them unctuously, and departed.

He did not see, as he turned into the gardens, that there was a chaise harnessed and ready for travel. In it, was a shifty-looking gentleman who eyed him impatiently and called out a curse under his breath. It was not precisely drunken, but it had a definite lilt that would have alarmed the cautious archbishop had he heard it. Fortunately for him, he did not, being much occupied with thoughts of spending the bounty his morning work had yielded. Barrymore had been generous. Church windows warred with chiseled ceilings in his mind. There was much to be said for both, but alas, a choice must be made.

As he considered, the dark carriage horses of the lone stranger began their paces in the courtyard. They were not to be changed, despite half a morning's gallop across the Westenbury plains. Sir Rory Aldershot within, regretted this fact, for he believed he had something of an eye for horseflesh and considered it annoying that he had to treat his beasts in this careless manner. Still, as he told himself, caution would not serve him now. Only brazen impudence and a heedless disregard for the sweating animals.

Once his aim was accomplished, they could rest so long as they pleased in the paddocks near Quimby. And Quimby, at last, would have a chance to be restored to its former glory. *If* he could keep his cool, that is. He peered around through the inn's entrance, ignoring the inquiring eyes of the overbold innkeeper's wife. Instead, he threw a penny at a nearby urchin and beckoned him closer.

"Another where that comes from if you can keep the viscount at his dinner for an hour or more." The boy looked puzzled, so he concluded that Barrymore might be traveling under a false name. After all, if it was abduction the viscount intended, he would hardly wish to advertise his whereabouts to all and sundry.

He tried again, this time with a more accurate description of Barrymore.

"Oh, the swell, you mean? Right yer are, guv. I'll keep 'im at table right enough! I can pilfer me a swag of the innkeeper's finest. *That* always slows 'em down, I can tell yer!" The boy grinned.

"Have a care if it doesn't!" Aldershot's tone was threatening, so the grin turned to a sulky scowl. Aldershot flashed the coin in front of his face and the lad grabbed at it.

"Not so fast! If you want it keep a clear head on your shoulders and do my bidding. If the viscount so much as steps foot out of the dining parlor you can kiss it good-bye."

" 'E won't, guv. And 'is lady, like?"

"You never saw a lady."

The boy stared. "Bein' as I'm not blind, yer honor, I saw a lady as sure as I am standin' on two feet."

"Then perhaps I shall have to plant you a facer so that you are *not* standing on two feet."

"Huh?" The boy glared suspiciously and more than a little fearfully.

"Oh, scat, there is no talking to you; your comprehension does a half-wit credit. Just keep your mouth shut or you will be sorry."

Now *these* were words the boy could understand. He pocketed his penny and nodded knowingly. "Cross me 'eart, I won't blabber a mort."

"Good, or you shall regret it. Now scram."

The boy complied with suitable haste as Aldershot descended from his chaise and snapped his fingers imperiously at the innkeeper's wife.

"My good woman, I wish to speak immediately with the lady within. There has been a carriage accident and her sisters, sad to say, lie in dire need of succor."

"Laws a mercy, and she just arrived and travel weary and all. My lord has just asked for the sheets to be aired and the beds turned down."

"I'll *wager* he has," thought the man grimly. He said nothing, however, but the woman hesitated with a slight query upon her face. Taking stock of her type in an instant, Sir Rory drew her close and muttered something confidentially in her ear. Her face changed to outraged fury.

"Well, fancy that! And this an honest hestablishment! I would never have said it from the look of 'is face."

"Ah, mistress, handsome is as handsome does and there are many a rogue blessed with a lying countenance." Sir Rory Aldershot did not tell her that he was one of them. Rather, he contrived to look sad and admonishing at one and the same time.

The innkeeper's wife wiped her hands on her apron and shook her head. "Ah, that be true, that be true. And the lady's sisters, me lord?"

"Overturned the carriage in their haste to stop these clandestine meetings. They shall all be ruined if the story were to come out."

"Mercy me! I shall get the lady right away and save her from her own folly. Mayhap she will bless me in time to come."

"Mayhap she will." Sir Rory nodded benignly and hid the smirk that threatened to show itself. Good! If the wench seemed reluctant, the innkeeper's wife would not be suspicious. Rather, she would be more zealous in saving Miss Chartley's virtue and delivering her into the waiting arms of Sir Rory Aldershot, Esquire. He grinned and fleetingly wondered whether the wares were as worth sampling as they seemed.

Soon enough he'd know. Soon enough. There would be no escaping him a second time.

"You may leave us now, Stanwick."

"Very good, me lord. And may I wish you and the missus a plentiful life blessed with little wee lordlings and . . ."

"Yes . . . yes." Lord Barrymore's eyes never left her ladyship's face, but at this passing remark the gleam intensified in the deep, intoxicating sky blue.

"Lordlings? Well, well, there might be something in that, Stanmore. Close the door, will you, and take yourself off to the kitchens. Belike there will be a tankard of ale and a hot stew awaiting you for this day's work."

Standish bowed, murmured a confused thanks, and shut the door. It would be right pleasant, he thought, to share a crust with the first postilion.

Her ladyship endeavored to ignore the intoxicating gaze which held her in its thrall. Instead, she took up cudgels with her lord, for if she did not, she would most like disgrace herself by swooning from the alarming desire that was captivating her senses.

"You are a wretch! You know perfectly well his name is Standish!"

"Is it?" Barrymore's lips quirked.

"*Yes*, as you well know, though you have called him a dozen other names this morning! It is not fair to tease your underlings so!"

"But he is such good game, my love. I could swear I saw his lips twitch when I called him Stanmore, a few moments ago."

"Indeed they did! They twitched to *correct* you, my lord . . ."

"Denver."

"Denver . . ." Lily blushed, especially as Lord Barrymore kissed her fingers at her demure acquiescence. She pulled them away quickly.

"You are not listening!"

"Oh, but I am! You were saying that Stanfop's lips twitched to correct me, but I must remind you, my little one, that they did no such thing." He returned her fingers firmly to their place in his warm hands. Then he was monstrous enough to occupy himself with removing her gloves, an act that made Lily curiously weak and quite unable to resist, despite a sudden desire to cross words with him. He kissed each ungloved finger gently, though his tongue lingered sufficiently upon each to leave his lady wife tingling in burning anticipation of more of the same. My lord, seeing her reaction, laughed a little and dropped her hands. My lord was pleased to tease and Lily scowled, for she was unused to the mysterious warmth that was creeping over her person and causing her limbs to quiver like one of Mrs. Bartlett's jellies.

When Barrymore was so unfeeling as to laugh, she drew her skirts about her, determined at once not to be swayed from her path. To no avail! Barrymore saw the opportunity, whilst her hands were busy with the hems, to sweep her up in his arms and plant a kiss upon her creamy neck. Lily wriggled a little, and managed a faint retort, but it was silenced by that wondrous mouth again. This time, soft as a butterfly upon her rosy lips.

"Oh!" He smiled at her response and set her down again, the better to work at the high lacing about her bodice. Lily thought it was time to argue, once again, for if she did not, she would be most shamefully lost to all the proprieties.

"He did not correct you, my lord . . . Denver . . . because . . ." She blushed rosily and removed his hands from her lacing, for in truth, they were engaged in the most excruciatingly sweet activities and she could not be expected to think—let alone argue under such circumstances—"Stanfop . . . Standish! . . . is so well trained! It would not be fitting for him to correct you and thus he does not. Shame on you to take advantage of him so!"

Barrymore raised his brows and released her, though his body was a full inch closer than it strictly ought to have been. He inclined his head solemnly, though the twinkle lurking in those hypnotic eyes remained.

"And thus I am admonished, fair shrew. Standish he shall be hereafter. You see, I am already under your foot."

"You are *not* under my foot!"

"No? Then perhaps we shall repair upstairs swiftly to rectify the matter. There is much I yearn to show you, lady wife."

Lily felt a flush of color steal over her. Barrymore was looking at her so intently, with such a delectably wicked smile playing about the corners of his mouth, that her courage, for an instant, failed her. Now he had drawn closer so that the curve of his thigh was just brushing her gown and she was forced to tilt her head to save herself, pressing her lips into an abdomen that was hard and covered only by a lawn shirt that seemed indecent in its fit.

My lord groaned, a little, a sound that surprised her and caused her mouth to part in query. She was lost, then, of course, for Denver Barrymore was far from saintly and it was too much to expect forbearance from a rake.

His lips were touchingly sweet, yet when she yielded to them wonderingly, she was not deceived by their seeming softness. Beneath the gentleness lay a strength she was willing to explore, though she feared a little as well. Despite her sauciness, she was yet an innocent and matters of the flesh like these, though tempting and heavenly, were still unknown and daring and wickedly forbidden. This, despite the vows she had only recently exchanged. Barrymore stopped for an instant, and pulled his thigh back from her gown, so that she felt she would faint from the loss of it. Instinctively, she reached out and pulled it back, a state of affairs that caused Barrymore to curse the tardiness of the maid, who was still preparing their chamber upstairs. When he obliged by not only returning his thigh to her, but also by cupping his hands about her loosened bodice, she gasped a little, then chuckled throa-

tily, her eyes still wide—*heavenly* wide and green glittering
as emeralds in the sunlight.

"So *this* is what all the fuss is about. I have always wondered."

Barrymore's eyes gleamed. It was not so hard to be an
adventurer after all, though in truth the Raven's Ransom
was not now the thought uppermost in his mind.

"*Have* you, naughty puss? And what exactly have you
wondered?"

Lily, who found she quite liked her new position, encased in my lord's arms and having the tips of her delicate
pink breasts rubbed in the most shockingly lascivious
manner, pushed herself a little closer, causing my lord to
forget his question entirely and forget, too, their lowly
surrounds in the innkeeper's private parlor. Lily, pleased
to be bold, matched kiss for kiss with an eagerness that
was gratifying to the viscount, who found that his bride
was just as beautiful as he had conceived on the instant
he'd first caught sight of her. She was just giving herself
up to his sweet caresses, melting passionately into his excellent frame, when the innkeeper's wife appeared.

"Well!"

Barrymore ignored her, but Lily remembered herself
enough to lift her head guiltily and push back her bodice,
which had loosened itself outrageously in this exchange.
Though she wore demure pastel colors, with her dark
hair flowing and her cheeks flushed a rosy red, she looked
positively wanton. The innkeeper's wife eyed her full, well-
kissed lips in disdain.

Then an image came to her mind of her husband the
innkeeper, and she had it in her to feel a sudden, mortifying pang of envy. For Lord Barrymore, wicked rake
that he was, was the type of man a woman took note of.
From the muscular calves, hardly hidden in those insuf-
ferable buckskins, to the crest of his golden head, he was
the type one lusted after in dreams and never thought

to see in the flesh. But there he was, godlike, mocking, and not altogether decent, for his neckerchief was loose and his tight breeches were swollen in parts a maiden had no business to notice. But the innkeeper's wife noticed, and the sight added to her virtuous fury.

"Well, I say!" Hands pressed to hips, she looked so outraged that Barrymore was inclined to laugh, rather than order her out imperiously, as he might otherwise have done. Lily, younger, and conscious of a multitude of sinful thoughts, looked more abashed. The woman seized her opportunity and pointed a finger in her direction.

"Come with me, missy, I must 'ave words with yer!"

Barrymore restrained Lily's step. His expression hardened. "The viscountess is going nowhere. If you have something to say, say it now and then begone."

The woman stopped midsentence. Viscountess? Laws a mercy, were they married, then? Then she looked at Lily's flushed cheeks and knew that it was more likely she was flinging herself into clandestine company with a rake. Her resolve hardened.

"Bein' it be private business about Missy's sisters . . ." She stressed the word "missy" defiantly above Lily's head. Barrymore was about to protest, but Lily had darted to the woman without warning.

"My sisters?"

"Aye, they be hurt, miss, and no thanks to ye! Thinkin' you bein' ravished an all, they gave chase and 'ave now come to a sad and 'orrible end."

The innkeeper meant in a ditch, but Lily went as white as a sheet, hearing her last words and putting the worst possible construction on them.

"Oh! Take me at once!"

"Don't be ridiculous, little featherhead!"

Lily's eyes flashed dangerously, but her immaculate bridegroom failed to notice. In truth, he was about to

tell her about the note he had left Lord Raven. This was
designed to set the aging earl's mind at rest *entirely* regarding Miss Chartley's wedded state—for which Barrymore already very properly had tacit permission. Sad to
say, though, it was penned a might saucily, for Barrymore
took pleasure in being one step ahead of the earl. He
had no fancy to be Raven's puppet and the note, a declaration of tacit war, was designed to declare it. His eyes
creased a little as he remembered the wording. Raven's
notorious feathers would be ruffled, no doubt about it.
But as to sending Daisy and Primrose scampering over
the countryside after him? Not likely.

He wondered how to explain this to Lily, but he was
too late. In a heedless dash, she had followed the innkeeper's wife to the kitchens, and was gone. Shrugging,
Lord Barrymore snatched up his beaver and was about
to follow, when he was waylaid by a little urchin carrying
the best bottle of burgundy he had laid eyes on since the
war.

"Pleasin' your honor, the innkeeper sent this up wiv
his best compliments, me lord."

"Did he, by God? Then he knows that I am not a lascivious rake, but a beleaguered bridegroom instead!"

The boy did not understand a word of the well-modu-
lated tones, but bethought him of his penny and bobbed
an "Aye."

"Then he has told his lady wife the same?"

Again, the bob.

Lord Barrymore laughed. "And *was* there a carriage
accident, little varmint, or was that all my lady's fancy?"

Now *this* the boy understood. Not the bit about lady's
fancies, but the plain English part about carriage accidents.

"Pleasin' yer honor, there be no carriage accident from
'ere to Fairfields."

"No? And how can you be so certain, little sprig?"

"Acause of what if there was, I would be sent scampering to the smith and the wheelwright and old Dr. Farley wot is a dab hand with the leeches and all."

"Mmm . . . and has none of these pleasant tasks been assigned to you?" My lord's eyes crinkled with sudden amusement.

"No, pleasin' yer 'onor. I 'ave only to scrub the basement floors and melt the candle wax back into tapers." The boy sounded gloomy at the prospect.

"How dull!" Lord Barrymore stretched his hand out for the burgundy. Lily, no doubt, would be back in a few moments. Her sisters were safe. The innkeeper's wife had merely been overzealous in her efforts to save the inn from disreputable goings-on. He hoped the innkeeper would give her a regular scold for her sanctimonious interference. She ought to be *whipped* for interrupting such a promising interlude. Still, it was afternoon yet. There was time enough later for a *multitude* of disreputable goings-on.

Lord Barrymore smiled as he dismissed the boy with a penny. The child gasped, for he could not believe his good luck. Then, thrusting it into his grubby pocket, he ran, before the fine gentleman could think better of his charity.

Sixteen

"You!" Lily looked at Sir Rory Aldershot with undisguised loathing. She was not permitted to say more, for Sir Rory pulled her into the chaise and sprung the horses without so much as a backward glance. Lily screamed, but the pounding of the hooves muffled her voice and the pace they set was such a spanking rate that there was no chance of anyone within hearing her. A cloud of dust was behind them, so there was no looking back. Sir Rory did not seemed perturbed by the volume of her yells, but rather settled back into the hard seats with a satisfied smile.

"So! I have plucked myself a bloom. And which one are you? Rose, Hawthorne, Daffodil? No, too exotic a countenance, I fear. Perhaps I shall call you Passion. There is a flower in the east that bears that name. You suit it well, little Passion. And you may stop pummeling me. It shall not do you the smallest token of good and may yet anger me. *That,* I fear, shall bode no good for you."

There was sudden menace in the voice of the slim, nondescript man beside her. He was wearing cream breeches and a tan jacket that, though modish, was slightly too large for his frame. His cravat was tied *à la mathematique,* but somehow it lacked the élan with which Barrymore carried the selfsame style. Perhaps because the shade was buttercup yellow and rather unflattering to the pale features.

Blue eyes protruded not unpleasantly from a lean, masculine face, but Lily noticed that they slanted slyly and she shivered. She would have held him for no account but for the fact that his wrists were sinewy and held hers in an unpleasant vice. She noticed, too, the flash of steel as they were jolted in their seats. He carried a weapon, then.

He noticed the direction of her glance and released his grip on her hands.

"Yes, it would be foolish to flee. Sit down, rather, and see if we can finish this."

Lily gasped at his implication, for his intent was unmistakable.

"You cur!"

"Yes, I have been called that by some." The man's tone was complacent rather than annoyed.

"I shall be missed."

"Shall you? Then they shall call *Barrymore* out, I fear. It is he, after all, who abducted you first. In the full sight of witnesses. I might add there were *several*. I was but one."

"Yes, but . . ."

"Ah, I see. Your tastes run to that type, do they? Your blood runs hot for him, does it? Well, it can be so with me. Indeed, you may count yourself fortunate. And do not *glare* at me so. If you behave, I shall wed you. Let me not repeat myself too often. It is no small thing being the wife of Sir Rory Aldershot. I have estates in Quimby. You shall reign there supreme, my little passion flower."

Raven Place was in an uproar. My lord had received a note from Lord Barrymore, and it had left him with a spasm such that Richmond could do nothing for him and was forced to hold up his hands in righteous despair. The earl seemed to veer from outrage—wherein could be

heard a series of very lusty oaths—and amusement, for
he would bang the counterpane with his fist and chortle
intermittently. By and large, his valet was satisfied that no
lasting harm would come to him, for his demeanor,
though volatile, seemed generally in keeping with a good
humor, though only those who knew him well would
guess it.

"The rascal!" he would say, crushing the heavy brocade
within his fingers. Then he would take out his spectacles
and read the missive again, such that Richmond was
tempted to prise it from his hands and read it himself,
so great was his curiosity. Still, despite his desire to account for the earl's latest start, he remembered his station
and resisted the temptation. The note lay crumpled beside the earl's bed, ready to be reread in a sudden fit of
anger and amusement yet again.

"Impudent dog!" my lord chortled yet again then
frowned when he saw the long-suffering Richmond hovering nearby.

"Well, don't just stand there! Fetch me a glass of my
best porter. And the French stuff, mind. I don't doubt
that there will be excise men after my head for it, but
there is nothing better, you know, than the smuggled
ware, and it will be the best today, Richmond, or I will
have your explanation!"

Richmond toyed with the idea of mentioning that the
doctor had not prescribed so heady a draft then thought
better of it. The earl was glaring at him sternly, though
an odd twinkle of pleasure lurked behind his bushy, gray
brows.

"I am a trial, am I not, Richmond? Well, I shall make
it up to you by offering you a glass of the same. Good
for the digestion, mind, and will take those silly furrows
off your forehead. Go to it!"

Richmond, more than honored by this offhanded gesture, made no further complaint. He was confirmed in

his opinion that the Earl of Raven, though mad, was nonetheless an exemplary employer if you could overlook his bluff manners. And Richmond could.

Below stairs, the Misses Chartleys were removing their pelisses and sensible gloves. Both were dreaming unmaidenly thoughts, but neither revealed as much to the other, for such maundering was unfitting and quite unlike their usual, cheerful selves. Daisy was wondering, with a quiver of her heart, whether Armand—her heart fluttered as she thought of that seductive, all-intrusive name— would truly be back for her that night. Primrose, rather less dramatic, felt a faint wistfulness as she imagined Lord Rochester's bold dark eyes raking her over. She wondered if she could possibly maintain her composure when next they encountered one another. She thought not.

"Good morning, Mistress Bartlett! Has Lily arrived back, yet?"

"Miss Lily? No, dear! Was she not with you girls? I feel certain I laid out her walking boots same as you, like."

"Yes, you did, but she was taken up in Lord Barrymore's chaise. She should have returned by now." A frown creased Primrose's brow, and a copper curl fell across her brow, only to be pushed back by an impatient hand.

Daisy frowned. "Should we have let her go, I wonder? Lord Barrymore is a fortune hunter. I had it off Meg."

"And Meg talks too much! I find Lord Barrymore's manners impeccable. Besides, there is Standish." Primrose spoke almost to reassure herself, for in truth, though she would not own it, she was worried.

"Perhaps Lily has twisted the poor man's arm and forced him to take her to Astley's! She has been pining to see the circus."

"Very likely." Primrose did not allow doubt to creep into her tone. Daisy, though a dear, was easily alarmed. She turned to the housekeeper. "We shall be in the cellars when she returns. I have a mind to still some of that cherry wine. The sediment, I hear, is excellent for a fever. If it is so, I shall have a great quantity of it made up and sent on to the estates. It will be a chill winter, I fear."

Mrs. Bartlett murmured assent. "What if Miss Lily does not return?"

"Oh, she will. If she does not within the hour, however, best call me. How is Grandfather today?"

"Swearing ten to the dozen and calling for porter." Mrs. Bartlett could not hide a wry smile.

"Excellent. Then he is recovering! Water down the porter, will you? It is not good for him."

"Mercy me! Water it down? That I shall not, miss, for I value my life!"

Daisy chuckled. "She is not wrong, Primmy! If you water it down, take it in yourself and make very certain you are not wearing your best gown! As a matter of fact, wear that hideous emerald, for he is sure to throw it at you and the muslin could bear discarding."

"Nonsense, it is still perfectly good. All I have to do is remove Lily's tiresome rosettes and the thing will be quite wearable. Very well, Mrs. Bartlett, have it your way. Give him the porter if it will please him so! Perhaps I shall go up and talk to him myself. Daisy, you go down to the cellars. I shall be with you directly."

"No! I shall withdraw to my chamber, if you have no objection." Daisy blushed, for how could she say she wished to choose out a wedding gown for herself? Primrose would doubtless laugh at her pretension, for who was to say that her romantic hero would in truth return to whisk her away as promised? It was all too much like a work of fiction to be real or true. She sighed with relief as Primrose nodded, her mind too filled with misgiving for Lily and concern for the earl to be at all suspicious.

As Daisy crossed the long gallery that led to the west wing, Primrose checked the hall clock absently and ascended the great stairs. If she was anxious about either of the Miss Chartley siblings, she made no further comment.

An unsettling five minutes with Raven made her startlingly aware that something was amiss. He was brandishing a paper in her face then snatching it away as she tried to read it.

"Go away, miss, and leave a gentleman to enjoy his porter in peace!"

"Sir, you are being mysterious. What is that piece of parchment you flutter in my face?"

"Ha, would you not like to know!" He wagged his finger in her face and chortled. "Your sister, brazen hussy, is to wed this day."

Primrose at once thought of Daisy and wondered however the earl had come to divine her secret. Ever since her midnight tryst with the mysterious gentleman, she had come to suspect as much. Daisy was in high fidgets today, forever touching her luxurious bright curls in front of the glass and showing, by her curious lack of interest in the offerings of Hookhams, an abstracted air that had left the quick-witted Primrose wondering. Still, since she felt a liking for Barnacle Jack—or whoever else he happened to be when he was not masquerading as such—she did not react to the news with the requisite hysterics. Instead, she calmly filled the earl's tumbler with water and remarked that she guessed as much.

Of course, Lord Raven was referring to *Lily*, who had just scampishly defied him—as he knew she would—and eloped with Barrymore. My lord was not a fool. He knew that though the viscount had impudently termed it an abduction, his adorable scamp of a granddaughter would have been a *most* willing participant in the matter.

"*Did* you, by God!" The earl's eyes gleamed with amusement, but Primrose made no comment. Rather, she drew back his curtains a little, allowing soft sunlight to stream into the ill-lit room. My lord made no comment, so she took courage into her hands and handed him the drink. He eyed her with scowling dislike and there was a moment when Primrose wished she had changed into the emerald. Then Lord Raven stared at her hard, laughed a little, and tossed it down without a murmur. Primrose was so surprised she could have fallen over backward.

"Ah, little Miss Prim and Proper! You are a dark horse, I swear, for a strange little bird tells me that it shall be *you* who is next."

Miss Chartley, unaware that Lord Raven had the advantage over her, and had recently engaged in an extremely profitable interview with a certain eligible marquis, disclaimed a little hotly and muttered that the earl was raving.

"Ha! Raving indeed! You see if wedding bells are not in the air, ere long, my little Miss Marchioness! You see!"

To placate him, Primrose nodded and allowed that she would do just that. The earl regarded her from under his brows and muttered that he would give a ransom to know the sum total of Primrose's activities. Primmy blushed, for Raven was the last person in the world she cared to confide her secrets to. Heavens, mistaking a peer of the realm for her own coachman! She could scarce credit it herself; she certainly was not going to lay the matter open to the *earl's* lusty speculation. She colored just *thinking* on the circumstance, for certainly for a young lady of her sensible, orderly, and unimpeachable virtue, the night at Almack's had been a strange diversion indeed. A telltale smile hovered on her lips at the very memory and the earl settled back with grim satisfaction. He loved his granddaughter dearly, but could never resist the impulse to tease the life out of her. "So!" he said. "Daisy and Lily are not the *only* naughty pusses in my household."

"Lily?" Primrose was diverted for a moment, for she

could have sworn the earl knew nothing of Lily. They had talked only of Daisy.

"Aye. But I am sore beset by the lot of you! Leave me now, that I may brood my misfortunes in peace." Primrose wisely chose not to push him further, for the old man was looking suddenly tired, despite the excited lights gleaming behind his sagging eyelids.

"Very well, Grandfather. I shall not disturb you further." Raven grunted, so Primrose stole closer to him and placed a light, butterfly kiss upon his forehead. At this, he glared, but the eldest Miss Chartley did not allow this to concern her. She would have been more perturbed by far had he smiled.

"Lily back yet?"

"Not a sign of her, Miss Primrose! I took the liberty of sending a footman round to Lord Barrymore's residence. She will be ruined if he took her there, but perhaps the groom will know what my lord's intentions were."

Primrose's heart stood still, for a moment. Mrs. Bartlett was right. Lily *would* be ruined if Barrymore was careless of her honor. What if she had misjudged him? If he was nothing but an unscrupulous adventurer who sought to abduct her for the ransom? Lord knows, they were fair game to half the world now that the whole of London knew the extent of the fortune Raven had placed on their heads.

She shivered and determined to go at once to Upper Grosvenor Square herself. If Lily needed help, she was duty-bound to provide it, however difficult the venture. It was she, after all, who had permitted Lily to be taken up by the viscount. If she had been mistaken in his intentions . . . she thought hurriedly. Night must not be permitted to fall without Lily safe back home. The consequences would be dire and very hard to quash, since

London had taken them up as their pets. Bother, bother, and botheration! She thought, for an instant, of seeking out Lord Rochester then realized there would be no time to await an answer.

After a moment's hesitation, however, she penned a quick note to him—no time to be squeamish about the niceties of imperious missives to unattached gentlemen—and sealed it with a determined fist. She signed it a simple "Miss Chartley," for though Lord Rochester had made free with her name once before, she was not so lost to propriety as to presume on that previous familiarity. As it was, she was already beyond the bounds. She trusted the marquis would overlook the offense. She was very certain, somehow, that he would at least stand friend. Her heart fluttered for a moment, for she was beginning to doubt her instincts. Then she scolded herself for a fool and handed the letter up to the butler, who was hovering solicitously nearby.

"See to it, if you please, that all haste is made to the Marquis of Rochester. Wait for a reply. It may be that his lordship follows you out. If he does, obey him in all things, for he acts for me. Go now!" Primrose waved her hand. The butler did not mention that such tasks were for errand boys. He saw genuine distress in Primrose's lovely eyes. Even her clipped tones and imperious commands spoke of an emergency, for in all things she was tranquil and courteous. He bowed, instead, and made haste to do her bidding.

Primrose took the steps two at a time and flung off her gown, which by good fortune was not one of those fashionable rigs with a thousand tiny fastenings at the back. Such was more Lily's style. This morning gown of copper-colored organza was waisted high at the bust and required only a deft twist of satin and lace to loosen the overgarment. This was flung over Primrose's head, the serviceable brown underskirt meeting the same fate in just seconds. Stripped to her shift, Primrose shivered slightly and knelt before an old chest that had not been opened in donkeys' years, but which contained, she prayed, a jerkin and knee breeches and a crisp white shirt that was probably faded by now. In truth, she was right, for these were the playthings of her childhood and the boys' garments had been used in all plays and pageants for time immemorial until they were pronounced young ladies. *Then* they had been told sternly to put away such unsuitable playthings and act fairy princesses and Gothic maidens if they still needed an outlet for youthful exuberance. Never as much fun, of course.

Now Primrose eyed the doublet doubtfully, for she had grown in places since she had last pushed her slender frame into the attire. She threw off her shift and firmly wriggled into the linen shirt. It fitted, but would not fool sharp eyes long. She dared not think of discovery, so she followed the shirt with the knee breeches and pulled on a pair of boots that were also tucked away neatly in the chest. Hopelessly in need of a shine, of course, and tight so they pinched—Primrose had not realized quite how much they'd all grown—but they'd serve.

Her copper curls glinted in the sunlight, and she eyed them with misgiving. Though cut short, the curls were altogether too feminine to be deceptive. She tucked them away under the brim of a beaver and hoped her disguise did not have to endure long. It would be sufficient, she thought, to pass unmolested through Bond Street, where she would need to take a couple of rights and a single left again into Upper Grosvenor. If she walked briskly—the chaise was too damnably identifiable—she should make it. Certainly, she had a greater chance of arriving undetected than if she walked unaccompanied through these streets as a woman. Even calling up a hackney cab as a young lady

would be asking for too much trouble. Primrose was
nothing, if not cautious, though her current actions
seemed to belie this. She hesitated, a moment, over
whether to tell Daisy her concerns.

No! Grandfather had all but said Daisy was to wed. By
his demeanor and his description of her as an impudent
hussy, she inferred that he *knew* she was planning to
elope. Let Daisy have her happiness.

If she returned with Lily, there would be no cause for
alarm. If she did not . . . Daisy must not be burdened
with the knowledge. There would be time enough after.
Let her enjoy, at least, her wedding vows free of frowns
and sighs and lamentations. There would be enough of
those after.

Primrose pulled herself up shortly. Nonsense! Like as
not she was enacting a Cheltenham tragedy and Lily—
naughty Lily had simply lost track of the time. Lord
knows, Lord Barrymore was as handsome as the devil
himself. If he was wooing her with soft words and whis-
pers, hours might easily seem as minutes. Even now, she
was probably eating cream puffs at Gunther's and waving
to all of her acquaintance.

Primrose prayed Standish was still on their track and
had had the sense to remain entirely visible. The world
would delight in an *on-dit* such as that. She grabbed a
walking stick from the hall and hastened down the steps.
If she was to save Lily—either from *her* folly or from Barrymore's, there was no time to waste.

Daisy she left in the kitchens, merrily stilling cherry
wine to her angel heart's content. The bright-eyed
minx's thoughts were dreamy, romantic, and altogether
far away as she tammied the precious mixture through
cloth. Armand, Armand . . . she sighed the name out
loud so two scullery maids, divining the improper direction of her thoughts, giggled. Daisy, dream Daisy, did
not hear. She was engaged in the extraction of soothing

sediment, quite unconscious that her most dear and sensible sister was embarking on an adventure all of her own.

Seventeen

Lord Rochester's door was slightly ajar, for he was expecting Fothing, the jeweller, at any moment. When his butler coughed politely at the entrance, he laid down his papers and smiled. "Ah, I was expecting you. Will you seat the gentleman in the library? I shall be with him shortly."

"My lord, it is not the jeweller who has called, but a linkboy sent round from Lord Raven. I have a missive directed to you. I believe there is some urgency attached to the matter, but like as not the linkboy was exaggerating." The butler coughed uncertainly, for in truth he was not certain he had done the correct thing. No doubt the note would have kept.

To his relief, my lord did not seem angered by the interruption, rather he thanked him mildly and extended his hand. The butler delivered up the crisp, freshly sealed wafer and withdrew with a silence that owed as much to his station as to his shining, soft-heeled shoes.

Rochester ripped open the message with interest. A woman's hand, he thought. This was confirmed on reading.

My lord,
   Forgive my intrusion. I suspect the Viscount Barrymore of abducting my sister, though I hope and pray I am incorrect in this assessment. If you feel able, I would much ap-

*preciate your help in this matter and trust your discretion
entirely.*

Yours,
Miss Chartley

Miss Chartley. Lord Rochester did not stop to think
which Miss Chartley was the author of this missive. Rather,
his mind conjured up hideous visions of the only Miss
Chartley he cared about being carried away by a golden-
headed devil-like Barrymore. Gareth's heart stopped. The
blackguard! The viscount had warned him of his interest
in Primrose, but he had taken no heed and left the matter
too late. He would cut his heart out with a sword and
throw it to the dogs. He would . . . but already Gareth
had swung into action. He opened his mahogany drawer
and took out a dueling pistol. Swords were very fine, but
from a distance a shot was more effective.

If he had harmed a hair on Primrose's head . . . he
could not bear thinking of it. He did not waste time calling for a stable hand, but rather ran nimbly down to the
stables himself. He would have chosen his black Arab, for
that would have been swifter, but stopped a moment, and
selected a well-sprung barouche. A closed carriage was
what he needed, for he would return Primrose to her
household with her reputation unstained if it was the last
thing he did. Then he would secure a special license and
marry her out of hand the very next day. Such assurances
were necessary thoughts to him as he tapped on the
coach door and gestured the horses to go faster. Sadly,
for they were traversing down congested London streets,
where cobbles, hacks, gigs, and hawkers all conspired
against him, they could not put up any more of a spanking pace than they already were setting.

Primrose, hurrying down Bond Street and Burlington,
caught a whisper of his carriage wheels as he made a
turn. She did not know for certain they were his, though,

so she carried on quickly, her feet making greater progress than the carriage, for she had the advantage of nimbleness of gait and the ability to duck through crowds.

"Hoy there!"

Primrose did not stop, but her heart beat a little faster. There was a small crowd of street urchins across the way. She hoped they would let her pass in peace.

"Penny for the crossing." Ridiculous! One did not have to part with a penny to cross a simple road in broad daylight! It was not as if they were street sweepers or linkboys. She pressed on, her heart beating faster yet. The boys, sensing easy game, tagged her and set up a chorus of cant words that she took as menacing, though she understood nothing of the sense. If she had a penny, she would have gladly parted with it, for she had no desire for trouble and every need of speed.

Sadly, of course, she did not. Her golden guineas—Lord Raven was shockingly extravagant with her pin money—were all safe in her reticule at home. There was nothing, now, to placate the growing mob of dirty-faced brats other than courage and cool resourcefulness. She doubled her hands into fists, turned, a little, so they stopped dead in their tracks, waved her fists threateningly in the air, and hoped for a miracle. None occurred, of course, so she took advantage of their first surprise by darting off the paving and into the road.

She stumbled, a little, for she could not help looking back as she made her move, and was sent sprawling headlong into the street. The crowd would have followed her but for the crunching of wheels against cobbles and the urgent whinnying of horses but a fraction above her head. Then there was the thud of metal and a splintering of glass before Primrose could look up and take full measure of what she had done. A gentleman dismounted—she could tell that from the sleek lines of his coat and the gleam of hessians on cobbles—before she was hauled up from the ground in an unceremonious tug that left her gasping. She gasped all the more when she realized that her tormentor was Lord Rochester, and that he had her in a steely grip by the scruff of her neck.

"What is the meaning of this, whelp! I could have run you over under my wheels! You are not hurt, I take it?"

Primrose shook her head, but her throat was too dry to talk. The crowd was larger, now, but she no longer worried about the street urchins. There was a man behind Rochester who looked angrier even than my lord. "Beggin' yer pardon, yer honor! The varmint shall be made to pay. My cart collided with your chaise when it halted and just look at the damage! A right whipping he shall have, pleasin' yer honor and that I vouch for!" He glared at Primrose, who stiffened under his gaze. "You shall not stand for a week when I have done, you careless whelp! Why, the veriest simpleton knows to stand clear of traffic. I shall have your hide, me lad, you see if I don't!"

Lord Rochester glanced impatiently at the crowd and at the boy before him. He was shivering in his scanty clothes and though my lord's fury was unabated, he had it in his heart to be merciful. There was something in the boy's bearing that spoke of pride. Mindful of the time, he froze the gentleman's bluster with a simple stare.

"Your gig collided into mine. I believe it is *I* who must demand compensation in this matter."

The man glowered. "Pleasin' yer honor, if yer had not stopped for this varmint I would not have collided into your rig! See, my windows are smashed and the axle . . ."

"Confound your axle. Will a sovereign fix your axle?"

The man's eyes grew cunning. "Then there are the windows . . ."

"Two sovereigns, then, and I will hear nothing more about the matter." The marquis withdrew the promised coins and handed them over without a thought.

"My lord, the boy needs to be punished. I will see to his whipping . . ."

"Lord, man, have I not said there is an end to it?" My lord's customarily mild tones took on an edge.

When the man still seemed undecided, not used to being bested, but unaccustomed to traffic with the gentry, my lord waved his hand irritably.

"If it soothes your nerves *I* will see to the boy's punishment. I believe he will not again err in this matter." Rochester's tone was suddenly grim enough for Primrose to take fright. She moved a little under his firm grip, but was crushed to find that his fingers tightened, silently, at the gesture.

The man hovered on the brink of indecision. He handled his coins and eyed the marquis assessingly. Despite a careless demeanor, my lord had the boy in a vicelike grip and his sinewy muscles were not disguised by the absurdly tight fit of his cloth. It was just possible, he supposed, that the gentleman could give a beating that matched the one Josiah Hadley had meant to mete out. Indeed, it might go worse for the boy, for my lord had chipped his paintwork besides losing two sovereign into the bargain.

There was no doubt, Josiah thought, about the strength of his jaw or the meaning behind the tight ridges across the expanse of his chest. They spoke of a masculine power that boded ill for a boy about to take a thrashing. The man nodded briskly, cast a last, disdainful glance at the varmint, and turned an inquiring eye again, on Rochester.

"Go! You have my word on it."

Josiah Hadley pocketed his coins and waved away the throng of onlookers. His pride was satisfied, for there was something in my lord's bearing that made him take him at his word. He unhitched his team and set about moving the cart off the road. Primrose was inclined to take her chances and run, for she did not quite like the firm set of my lord's chin or the unrelenting grip he had of her collar. His fingers brushed against her neck and felt warm, and unbearably masculine. She wondered if he would carry out his threat and thought, with horror, that he just might. She flexed her body, slightly, but it was as if my lord had a second sense. His grip tightened though his tone remained neutral as he ordered her into the chaise.

Miss Chartley was about to argue but she caught sight of her tormentors in the distance and thought the better of it. Without a word she climbed up the boards into the familiar barouche—painted, as she saw by day, a bright royal blue.

The doors closed almost before she was achingly aware of his form against the squabs. He hardly glanced at her as he called an order out to his coachman and consulted his fob.

"Hurry, man! We cannot afford any further delays."

The coachman nodded and soon the well-sprung chaise was away from the hustle of Burlington Street. Primrose closed her eyes and thought furiously. Rochester obviously had given her no second thought. If he'd recognized her, he would surely have held her more tenderly, would not have suffered her to fear for her very life, though in truth he had probably saved just that. If she revealed herself to him now, in all her town grime, he might take her in disgust, for she was very far from the belle of Almack's. She was caught now, in even more of a compromising position than she had then. *Then* climbing into the marquis's chaise had been an unwitting mistake. *This* exploit was willful folly.

She bit her lip and held her peace, praying the good marquis was too caught up in his errand to take much note of a street urchin.

He was, for even now they were turning into my Lord Barrymore's street at a spanking pace. Rochester addressed her sternly, and the set of his chin sent a brief shiver down Primrose's spine that was not altogether fear.

"Stay here, whelp! I shall deal with you shortly. And be very sure that if you escape it will be at your peril."

Primrose nodded, eyelashes downcast, for she did not think she could look Rochester boldly in the face when she was so enmeshed in deceit. Besides, though it had been dark when they had last encountered each other, there was still a chance he might recognize her.

He nodded, a brief glimmer of light behind his alert, dark eyes, then he descended the chaise with an instruction to his coachman. Primrose thought it was an age that she waited. She told herself sternly that nothing else mattered but that Lily was safe. She was on the shelf anyway; it was Lily's reputation that must be preserved at all costs.

Part of her—a little part—smiled at how impetuously Rochester had responded to her summons. She could not have asked more of him were it her own self that had needed saving.

His face, when he returned, was bleak, and his tone curt as he ordered the horses to commence to a posting station not twelve miles from the city. Primrose gasped, for she had not anticipated this, and she must surely be ruined if ever she survived the ordeal. She bit her lip and endeavored not to capture his attention. My lord spoke quickly to his coachman and she strained to hear the conversation.

"The servants within swear my lord Barrymore was not provisioned for a trip to Gretna."

"The cur, for it was then not marriage on his mind, but a villainy far greater. Did they say where he might be headed?"

"Dorchester? Then onward, for there is no time to spare."

Primrose could not hear further, for the wind caught her at a disadvantage. My lord must have had a better idea of what he was at, though, for he nodded briskly and ordered that all speed be made to a certain posting station some twelve miles northeast of the city. Primrose clenched her fingers tightly as orders swirled above her head.

"Be swift, mind, and have a care to the horses. It shall not do us any good if they are winded and it is a few hours still till nightfall."

A few hours. Surely Barrymore would not be so dishonorable as to ruin Lily in broad daylight? But if he were pressed for funds, he might be driven by desperation. Primrose shivered. How *could* she have so blithely judged him to be of good character? Rochester was right. She was not suited to be a chaperone. It was her laxity that had permitted Barrymore to take Lily up in his chaise. If she had denied him, Lily would even now be nibbling on marzipan at Raven Place and contemplating *Daisy's* romance with youthful sighs. She looked out the window and was hardly aware of a tear that rolled out of her slate gray eyes, dampening the muddy shirt points that Rochester had so recently laid hands upon.

My lord, lost in his own thoughts, did not notice either. When she sniffed, however, he found himself regarding the ill-favored varmint with mild interest.

"Do not weep. Though you shall undoubtedly be punished, as I have promised, it shall not go as ill with you as had master *Hadley* had the mastery of you."

Primrose startled. She had not thought to address him this trip. Indeed, she dared not, for if she spoke he would know at once that her speech was not lowly enough to be that of a street child. So she folded her arms and glared at him defiantly, an act that had my lord Rochester's lips twitching, for in truth he could sympathize with the errant lad. Time enough *he* had been up to mischief and awaiting discipline from my lord Hereford, the marquis before him.

Then his attention was arrested by the glint of copper. There was something of the shade that pleased him, for it reminded him of that *other* copper-curled person, for whom nothing but the sanctity of wedlock would wholly satisfy his desires. Even the slender wrists and the high bones of the cheek were like, but of course, other subtle differences were too innumerable to mention.

My lord sighed at his fanciful nature and stared out the window. He thought he heard a similar sigh from the other seat and smiled. Mayhap the lad was glad he had other matters to occupy his attention. He would teach him that he was a hard master, not easily disobeyed, then turn him over to the stable hands. Doubtless he could earn his keep in some way. There were always hay bales to be fetched and carried and stables that needed sweeping. Better that, surely, than a life of crime that would doubtless be his lot if he was set down on the streets again.

Primrose eyed him cautiously, then dropped her hands demurely in her lap. Not the stance of a youth but then she was not practiced at subterfuge. My lord eyed her, puzzled. The lad had slender wrists, lily white as though they had not seen the seedier side of the docks or the coal mines or the slums. He seized one, caught by a sudden strange fancy. The shock in the lad's eyes were mirrored only by his own, for in that touch there was something indefinable, something between them that was more than man or master.

The youth flushed a little and jerked his hand away. My lord ignored the gesture, for he was most perturbed, caught up in some fanciful delusion that he would doubtless chuckle about on the morrow. "By the saints," he thought, "I am likelier drunker than I thought." The marquis, having partaken only of a few light brews, was harsh on himself.

The child drew his beaver down over the curls, but shivered, all the same. Rochester threw him a blanket, which was received with a grateful smile, but again no words. The smile was enough, however, to send the gentleman's pulses racing quite extraordinarily. It was direct and echoed in the eyes, albeit fleetingly. My lord could not mistake the whisper of a smile through dark, copper-toned lashes. They curled long and luxuriously across the lids and even under the beaver's brim they were too exquisite to carelessly ignore. He drew in his breath.

By God, if he knew no better he would think . . . but no! The lad had none of the delectable curves that had been such a sore temptation to him in the lamplit chaise at Almack's. Even now, he could recall Primrose's dark velvet gown, cut low enough to tantalize, yet more modest, he had to regret, than some of the *other* confections that were being worn that year. No, he'd had just chance enough to glimpse soft rounded curves cupped by velvet and laced in by slivers of organdy. Smooth, and soft to the touch he would guess, though even *he* had not dared presume that far. The child was hugging the blanket to him so he could not compare, but really, such comparisons were absurd; he would have noticed from the outset. Or *would* he have?

Doubt suddenly overcame Gareth. The urchin was wearing a jerkin, after all. Perhaps, even now, beneath the thick green wool those heavenly curves were struggling against the cramped shirt he had so ruthlessly tugged at. My lord felt a tightening about his elegant satin breeches that was really quite perverse, but the thought intruded upon his consciousness too forcibly to be ignored.

He regarded Primrose intently from beneath hooded lashes. What could she be playing at, he wondered. If it *was* Primrose facing him with impunity from under the brim of that far-fetched beaver, she would have much to reckon with, for the fright she had given him. God, the thought that she even now could be wed or bedded with Barrymore made his fists clench quite wretchedly.

If she had put him through that shocking misery, then still had the unmitigated gall to masquerade as a street urchin and place her life—not to mention reputation—in the veriest danger, she would have a lot to answer for. They were ten miles, still, he judged, from the inn.

Time enough to have the horses turned round if this was all a prank. Time enough, if it was not, to discover the truth at all events. God knew, he needed his mind to be occupied whilst there was this moment of forced in-action. Though the carriage was moving onward quite steadily, Gareth felt hamstrung by the enforced wait. He might as well occupy himself to some purpose.

He leaned forward, suddenly, ostensibly to check the catches on the carriage doors. As he did so, he was assailed by a scent memorably sweet and shockingly provocative to his senses. Musk and jasmine . . . he had his answer.

Eighteen

"You shall not get away with this!" Lily sobbed in impotent anger.

Sir Rory smiled gently, but his blue eyes were slits and granite hard. "Oh, but I shall, my little passion flower."

Lily did not answer, so he continued. "It is true that the *last* time I attempted this, I was ill-prepared. Fortunately, I am not so puffed up in my own conceit that I do not learn from my mistakes. See, I have not brought, this time, some lame, low-stepping nag. I have a chaise and pair, now, a very different thing, I am certain you will agree."

He eyed her scowl complacently and patted her leg. Lily felt her skin crawl beneath the gay, brightly rosetted morning gown, but she chose not to squirm. She may have been young and foolish, but she had learned a little, at least, of dignity and bearing. It would be unbecoming to squirm, besides being pleasing, no doubt, to her captor.

It was at the tip of her tongue to tell him triumphantly that all was in vain, for she was wed already. The thought made her mouth curve, a little, in secret triumph. She fingered the gold band but newly placed upon her finger and frowned. If her tormentor were to notice, it might not go well with her, for she would lose the advantage of surprise. Also, if he knew she were wed and the ransom lost to him one way, he might choose the other, more despicable way. He may ransom her body to Raven and despoil it himself. The thought made her shudder. Surely he could not be so vile! But yes, she thought he could.

All his innuendoes about her being good and becoming his wife started to make horrible sense. With great courage and infinite regret, she pried the ring from her finger whilst he stared at the dust clouds and let it drop, silently, behind the squabs. She could have wept, then, for it was like tearing herself asunder from Barrymore. Without the warm weight of comfort on her finger, she was subtly more vulnerable. She turned her head and looked silently out of the other window. She could not see a thing, for the horses were cantering so swiftly upon the country road that the dust was prodigious. She only hoped they were ditched.

In a different chaise altogether, two horses had slowed, at Lord Rochester's command, to a mere trot. Primrose looked up in surprise. "Why are we slowing, sir? Your mission is urgent." In truth, if he was uncertain before, he was certain now! The baggage had forgotten to be silent and so her feminine, delightful, and quite impeccable tones were revealed to him in all their glory. My lord had never been so thankful or so genuinely angry at one and the same time.

"Come here." His tones were soft, but his eyes were uncompromising and Primrose felt a sudden clutch of fear in her heart. Had he recognized her? Had he taken her in sudden disgust? She peeped at him, desperate to divine his intentions. My lord gave nothing away but merely beckoned to her. She went rigid and as silent as the grave. If he had *not* recognized her, she must take very good care not to let such a stupid slip occur again. In deep Cockney tones that made my lord smile despite his very real anger, she begged him to continue on his way.

My lord regarded her, for a moment, then called to the horses to stop. They allowed a country gig to pass, then instantly slowed at a clearing.

"What am I to do with you, lad?"

His voice was quiet, but Primrose felt a wealth of hidden meaning behind the tones that she could not begin to untangle. She caught at his last word, then, and breathed a sigh of relief. Lad! So he had *not* pierced her flimsy disguise, then. She shrugged her shoulders inquiringly and bit her lip. It would not do to imperiously command my lord to return to his mission. Nothing could possibly be more hazardous to her masquerade. She must wait, servilely, for him to say his piece and hope that he made up speed thereafter.

"I am in great haste, lad, there is a gentleman, you see, that I must kill."

Primrose looked at him in shock. Kill Barrymore? Had she directed him to be so precipitant? She thought not. She swallowed a protest in her throat and regarded the luxurious finish of the beechwood floor.

"He has abducted the woman I love and I intend to have vengeance."

Primrose looked up, then, for her heart smote her badly. Love Lily? She did not know my lord *knew* Lily, let alone loved her! She flushed, for in her fluster she could not remember all that had passed between them in the chaise and she wondered if she had revealed herself—or her love—to him. If she had, she must take care to hide it from him in the future.

My lord, regarding her in silence, for a moment, despaired of any response but the rising color to her temples. Now was the time, if ever, for her to admit her trick, yet like some wanton, she did not! And still he loved her, those copper lights peeking out from that appalling head-gear. . . .

"I love my lady dearly, and I shall avenge her myself, but if ever I catch her entangled in a web of deceit, I shall punish her as I shall punish you now."

Still, there was no response, but for a strangled choke my lord found hard to interpret.

"Come here, lad, for it is time that you felt the sad effect of your carelessness this day." Primrose was not so naïve as to misunderstand his meaning. She almost choked, even as she felt her heart beat miserably faster.

"Not now, sir! After!"

"What, afraid to take your punishment like a man? Be thankful I have not called the coachman to drag you out-side and whip you with the cold lash of his carriage crop. *That*, and likely worse, would have been your fate had I not rescued you this morning."

Primrose nodded, for she was not too green to know that in this, at least, Lord Rochester spoke the truth. She felt a strange trembling, though, as he continued on ruth-lessly.

"I promised Josiah Hadley that you would be punished, and punished you shall be, though your rear end smarts two days from the enterprise."

Primrose colored. Though Grandfather had certainly schooled Lily and Daisy upon occasion, that fate had never, thankfully, come upon herself. It had always been a blessing, moreover, that no matter how wrathful Grand-father's birch had been, the sisters had always been sin-gularly well cushioned by a plethora of hoops and useful linen petticoats. Though Raven had grumbled about this feminine advantage, he had never been so fierce as to order them removed. Primrose's garments suddenly seemed absurdly scant, the boy's breeches hugging her curves in a manner she had hardly paid attention to when hastily dressing. Now, she was aware of my lord's eyes upon the thin, lightweight cloth. His hands, encased in excellent doeskin gloves, seemed large and uncomfortably forbidding.

The man's eyes were upon her, his chin firm and uncompromising. She bit her lip. If Gareth truly loved Lily, then revealing herself to him in these rags would be mortifying. He would take her instantly in disgust, be forced to have her for sister-in-law. Primrose tried not to think of all that had passed between them. To do so would be to weep. Her face must have revealed something of her turmoil, for Rochester's eyes softened.

"Hush, child." The tone was gentler, but when Primrose hesitated, the frown reappeared. He had stopped his carriage that she might confess. And still, despite all threats, she did not. The silence seemed endless. His lordship, at a loss, summoned up his anger like a mantle of protection against this woman who had wreaked havoc in his life without so much as a by-your-leave. Now, of course, she was willfully deceiving him. He stubbornly ignored his impulse to kiss her into oblivion.

"Come here." Again, the steel in his normally pleasant accents. His intention seemed appallingly clear.

Primrose quaked. "Can you not school me after?"

"After *what*, if I might be permitted to inquire?" The tone was suitably scathing.

"After you have killed that gentleman?"

"After I have killed the gentleman I shall doubtless be caught up in embracing the lady." No, he would not spare her blushes. If she would have him believe her a boy, then he would talk to her as one.

The honorable Miss Chartley barely refrained from squirming, whether from the vision he conjured up, or from the threat to her person, it is not possible to accurately conclude. Suffice it to say that her color was high when he finally touched her. It was a clasp quite different from that which she had previously encountered. Her eyes were impossibly bright as she struggled for the words that would secure her instant release.

My lord continued. "And you, you varmint, will have made your escape. No, I do not drive one mile more until I have fulfilled my promise to Josiah Hadley. You will find, to your discomfort, that I am a man who keeps my promises."

He tapped on the chaise and gestured to the coachman. "Have a break, Simon. There is a stream but a few steps from here. Take up your lunch and wait for my call."

The coachman tapped his cap at Rochester, grinned curiously at the urchin within, and needed no second bidding. They waited in silence until the man was gone. Now Primrose could *certainly* not tell him the truth, for they were miles from anywhere and entirely unchaperoned. Rochester waited, hoping that Primrose would quail under his glare and yield first. He had no taste for this type of bullying, but his anger was still high, and she persisted in this charade, allowing him to think hellish thoughts of what might be becoming of her at the hands of the good Viscount Barrymore.

"Tell me your thoughts."

Primrose's eyes widened and her throat ached. How could she tell him? Tell him that she loved him, that she was miserable, mortified, maddened with hopelessness? Impossible. So, she said nothing. He called her to him quietly. Misunderstanding his intention, she rebelled.

"No!"

"No?" The marquis stared at her hard, so Primrose remembered his earlier threat about the coachman and his lash. Heart beating faster than ever she could dream, she questioned him unsteadily. "After . . ."

"Yes?"

"After you have done this thing, you will continue your chase?"

"Of a certainty."

"Then I shall do as you say."

Rochester sighed. And still, she did not trust him. Then there was the veriest touch of warm pink skin brushing against his shirt as she moved toward him. It was outrageous, this teasing of his. He would have to yield defeat and release her, for she was now, in truth, trembling. He was being grossly unfair—a cad, he supposed, but oh, how he *wished* she would trust him! Still, confidences could not be forced; they were precious gifts to be given freely or not at all. Sighing, he shook his head, dark curls lingering over his temples. Then he pressed her back into the velvet cushions. He was disappointed, but disappointment could not overshadow his admiration. She was both brave and true, not to mention very, very, very lovely. He had been unwise to send Simon away. She offered a terrible temptation.

Primrose regarded him steadily, her huge eyes asking more than she knew. They were wet with unshed tears, yet she held herself calmly. She was admirable. Oh, admirable! He would be blind not to see it. The marquis relented. It was time enough for the charade to end. No matter how she teased and troubled him, yet she was indomitable in spirit. Suddenly, all of the anger was gone. His lips twitched.

"You may stop trembling, my dear, for, though I am loath to admit it, I swear that I shall never lay hands on you so long as I live."

Primrose stared at him. His words were simple, yet so sincere that she forgot his previous rather dire threats to the contrary and regarded him closely. Her heart soared at his altered tone, though she was still abundantly confused.

"I do not understand, my lord."

"Oh, but I think you *do*, my little urchin. Come here, while I remove that despicable headgear of yours. A pearl-

trimmed bonnet from a decent French milliner will become you more. I shall see to it just as soon as the banns
have been posted."

Primrose, for once, was speechless. Could he be mistaking her for Lily? But surely not, when Lily was so strik-
ingly featured and unmentionably beautiful. Was he run
mad, then? She had little time to ponder this possibility,
for she found herself on his side of the chaise, again.
This time, in a singularly fast but entirely maidenly fashion she had no objections to at all.

"My lord!"

"I thought we had agreed on Gareth."

His voice was soft and mischievous as he removed the
offending hat and cast it on a vacant seat.

Primrose gasped, for he was certainly not mistaking her
for Lily, now. She had just time enough for air before he
was kissing her ruthlessly and his hand, once more, was
on her spine.

"Stop!"

"Good God, Primrose, you are a strange creature!
When I threatened to spank your pretty little derriere,
you say nary a word, but when I kiss you, you yell stop!"

"In truth, my lord, if my wits are wandering you have
only yourself to blame! And when I think what you have
put me through, this day . . ."

"Yes?"

Her eyes sparkled. "I believe I shall marry you after
all. It will be fit punishment for you to be leg-shackled
to an ill-tempered termagant."

He released her, then, and laughed. "But why the charade, Primrose? I received the most urgent note from one
of your sisters, saying Barrymore had ridden off with you.
I was beside myself with rage and worry. Then I find you
masquerading as a street varmint and nearly causing yourself grief of the first order . . ."

"I had no notion you would respond so quickly. And the letter, my lord, was from me."

Light dawned. "From you? But why so cold, my little love? You signed it a curt 'Miss Chartley,' for all the world as though we were strangers."

Primrose blushed.

"We were."

"After what passed between us at Almack's we were *strangers?*" His voice was incredulous and so harsh Primrose began to think, again, about the nagging ache to her rear.

"You might have wished it so, my lord."

"Foolish girl! I went directly over to Raven Place and formally acquired permission to court you."

Nineteen

There was a moment where the wind blew into the carriage and the horses whinnied, but Primrose heard none of these things. She stared, instead, at Gareth, Lord Rochester, and asked herself quietly whether she was dreaming. She thought not, for the man was regarding her with such a smug smile upon his distinguished countenance that she felt ready to throttle him. One did not wish to throttle in dreams.

"Permission to court? From Grandfather Raven?"

"The very same."

She digested this news in silence. "How did you tell him we'd met?"

Gareth's eyes gleamed a little. "I did not. It infuriated him mightily."

Now Miss Chartley was pleased to chuckle, for it seemed to her that Lord Rochester was more formidable by day then he was by night. She had a taste, she found, for formidable men, especially ones that were wickedly handsome and glanced at her as though at any moment she might expect to find herself bedded. She flushed furiously at the thought.

How the mighty had fallen that she, Miss Primrose Adelaide Chartley, fabled for her common sense and prosaic character, should have come to this. She disentangled herself from his grasp and sat up.

"Did he curse you?"

"I believe so."

"Did he throw a pitcher of barley water at you?"

"No, but I believe, at one time, he threatened to."

Primrose sighed in satisfaction. "Then it is well. He must like you exceedingly."

My lord smiled and would have proceeded with the delightful task he had set himself—poor Simon by the river would have had a long wait—but for a sudden urgency in Primrose's eyes.

"We must set off at once!"

"Whatever for?"

"Barrymore still has Lily in his clutches. Nothing has changed."

"Oh, but it has. It was *you*, you see, that I thought he had set his sights on."

"What matter it? One of us is still at risk."

"Only of being wedded out of hand. Barrymore warned me he might do such a thing. I thought he was speaking of you and nearly split him with my own dueling sword." Rochester's tone grew suddenly grim and Primrose could not help smiling.

"Yes. Laugh, but I tell you it was a close-run thing for him. But for the fact that he is a rather beguiling character that I actually quite admire, I would probably even now be up before the assizes."

"For his murder? Come, come, you exaggerate. But pray, don't let me stop you. Continue with this fascinating tale at once!" Primrose's heart was now brimful of joy, for she knew that Rochester would not dally thus if there was true cause for alarm.

"Being a civilized soul, I merely agreed to invest a fortune in his coal mines and assist in whatever way I could with the design and implementation of a steam-based rail engine. Primrose, we shall be pioneers of a new era, for I believe that very soon there will be a railroad across the length and breadth of the country. Imagine that—what will it mean for our postal systems, for our ability to travel without changing horses, without . . ."

"Intriguing, my lord, and one of my pet interests, as I think I may have informed you the other night. However, if you can just veer, possibly, more to the point . . ."

"Shrew!"

Primrose allowed herself a small smile. "So instead of running him through with a sword . . . ?"

". . . I gritted my very fine teeth and rather icily informed him to withdraw his claim. I also mentioned that you were all removing, shortly, to my town residence, there to be sponsored by my mother."

"Thus increasing his haste! My lord, are you sure it is wedding he intends?"

"Undoubtedly."

"For his stab at the Raven's Ransom?"

"Very possibly."

"Then let us make haste at once!"

Rochester cleared his throat. "I can tell you, however, that whether or not he is influenced by the ransom, I believe him to be wholly in love. Therein lies his salvation, for I had it in me to pity him. I know what it is like to love a Chartley sister."

"But not the same one."

"Not the same one."

Primrose sighed. "A lifetime ago it was Lily I thought you loved."

"A lifetime ago? Only a carriage ride ago, you silly girl."

"It felt like a lifetime."

"Is that why you did not reveal the truth to me?"

Primrose nodded.

"My poor girl! You nearly got spanked for that."

"Right properly, too, I warrant."

"No, I have not the temerity."

"Fustian! I was quaking in my boots. It is very thankful

I am that you made me that promise. I shall hold you to your word."

"I nearly always keep my promises. I believe I told you that several times this ride."

"And very ominous it sounded to me, too! Now let us get going, sir, before I change my mind and select myself a meeker husband."

So saying, my Lord Rochester moved forward and very gently, teasingly, did something to mistress Primrose that caused a blush to rise to her forehead and a soft "Oh!" to escape her lips.

"You prove your point, my lord. I hope you are not always so inventive in your arguments."

"Oh, but I am."

"Then we shall be arguing a lot when we are wed."

Gareth stopped his rather seductive actions and grinned.

"Indeed, I *count* on it!"

"Very good. But for the moment, you shall meekly oblige me and get going!"

"Why?"

"Because I have a mind to see Lily wedded."

"She is likely that already."

"Then I have a mind to wish her happy."

Gareth regarded her, for a moment, warmly. "We shall make haste, then, for I doubt Barrymore will be pleased to see us if we arrive toward nightfall."

"It is not *comme il faut*, you mean, to break in on an abduction?"

"No, I believe that is perfectly acceptable so long as you do it politely. Etiquette, however, does *not* permit breaking in on . . . pardon your blushes . . . postabduction seduction."

"I see. How remiss of me not to have perceived that finer point for myself."

"Yes, very remiss. Simon!" The marquis raised his voice.

"My lord?"

The voice came from a suitable distance.

"Make haste, if you please! We continue!"

Whilst the coachman leapt up to obey Lord Rochester's command, Primrose tidied what she could of the jerkin and knee breeches and looked ruefully at her erstwhile captor.

"I never thought I would be so vain as to wish fervently for a gown. A gown, a gown, my kingdom for a gown!"

"Yes, well I don't deny you look comelier in one!"

"Brute!"

". . . But you *feel* infinitely better in knee breeches. I shall insist upon them in the bedroom."

"You don't try to spare my blushes, do you?"

"No, why should I? They are delightful."

Primrose ignored him, though she felt a delicious happiness creep into her heart.

"Remember, to the coachman I am still a street urchin."

"Very well, you whippersnapper! And what shall I tell Lily?"

"Oh, Lily will know at once! She will be in peals of laughter at this escapade, for she has always said that since I have ever been good and proper and commonsensical, I shall one day fall into the very *devil* of a scrape!"

"She was right, then."

"Yes, she was right." Smiling amicably, Primrose scanned the road for any sight of the inn.

"Damnation!" Sir Rory cursed as the team was brought to a sudden halt. It jarred Lily terribly, for the chaise was not well-enough sprung and she had pins and needles from sitting with her back rigid and her fingers clenched for a good half hour at the minimum.

Sir Rory paid her no notice, but descended from the chaise in acute annoyance.

"What is it?"

"Reckon as I don't know, sir. The 'orses are sweatin', like."

"They'll keep. They were fresh when I left London."

"Mayhap they need water, like. We can turn back to the inn . . ."

"Out of the question! Is that why you stopped, you blunder head?" Sir Rory Aldershot glared at his man, who stepped backward a pace.

"Not *me*, pleasin' yer honor! The left beast is a might skittish, like. Took a stumble, I reckon."

"Careless handling, then! Now get going!"

Sir Rory swung himself up again and eyed Lily with sharp dislike. He was just thankful he'd had the foresight to ply Barrymore with burgundy, for they were not making good time and he had no wish for any mishaps.

Lily could have kicked herself for not thinking of the weapon he'd carelessly left lying behind the cushions. Oh, if only she had retrieved it! She might never have the opportunity again. She could have almost moaned with dismay, but remembered, of course, to maintain her dignity. That was the only small satisfaction she *had* against this vile man!

The journey began again in silence, Aldershot more concerned about the time than about baiting her. The slower the progress, the more likelihood there was of being pursued. He called to the driver.

"This is not a country picnic, man, move it, I tell you!"

"I tell you, I *can't*, pleasin' yer 'onor! The team be not stable."

"Nonsense! They are as well matched as can be. You are merely being specious."

The driver, having no idea of the insult being thrust at him, defiantly continued, though his face was black with a scowl and his hand heavy. Of a sudden, the carriage swayed precariously. Lily was thrust to the side, her shoulder jammed against the door as the wheels ground to a screeching halt.

Aldershot cursed. His door was jammed so he leaned over Lily to try hers. She recoiled at the touch, but the man was too incensed to notice. The driver jumped down from his perch and went round to the front of the team. Aldershot followed, without a backward glance at his victim.

"God's truth, you are a veritable cow hand! Have you no notion how to handle a team?" He glared at the driver, fuming.

"Don't glare at *me*, sir! Reckon they've been pushed too hard, that's wot."

"Nonsense!"

"Then *you* drive 'em, me lor'! The left 'orse feels lame."

"Impossible! You are just an addlepated gudgeon, for I inspected them myself this morning."

"It is *lame*, I tell yer!" The coachman folded his arms and glared at his master. "Lame, lame, lame!"

"You are hysterical." Aldershot cuffed him soundly and examined each bit.

Lily, finally, had her chance. Quick as lightning she changed seats and felt for the weapon. She prayed it was not a sword, for she had not the foggiest notion how to wield such a thing. Her hands touched cold steel. She breathed a sigh of sudden elation. A pistol!

Very carefully, she primed the thing, for had not Lord Raven insisted she know about such matters despite her earnest and youthful protests? Well, she never really had the hang of it, but by God, she would make shift now! Carefully, cursing her modish, delectably expensive morning gown and all its tiresome petticoats, she shifted her position and waited. When Aldershot returned, she would shoot him. She waited calmly as she heard raised voices at the front of the chaise. Good! They were out of sorts with one another, for it was a sad and undeniable fact that she was facing two men with only one pistol shot.

Fetlocks were being inspected. She peered out of the window and fiddled with the handle of the door. They were not so isolated as it would seem, for there was a crofter's cottage nearby and evidence of a recent fire. She wondered whether she should scream and thought the better of it. Surprise—and a pistol—were her only true advantages. Screaming would make her forfeit one at least.

Now it was the hooves being examined. Eight in all . . . her eyes wandered to the bundle of wood lying in neat bundles by the embers. Chopped so precisely with that ax . . . she could see the wood splinters of each log, a dull yellow against the darker brown bark. Then suddenly her wits were about her.

She descended the chaise quickly, so the wheels creaked and the springs jerked. The horses stepped backward, too, so the surprise she so valued was no longer one of her advantages.

"Get back in." Aldershot left off his arguing and advanced angrily toward Lily. In a split, hysterical second, Lily had an irreverent thought. "At least he did not call me passion flower." And then she was all business.

Hands steady, she demanded that Aldershot stand back. And his man, too. Sir Rory saw his danger immediately.

"Don't be so foolish. You do not know how to use that thing. Put it down."

"Tell your coachman to stand next to you."

"I shall do no such thing."

"Then I shall shoot you."

"You wouldn't dare!" For an instant, Lily was sorely,

sorely tempted. She would aim for his nose, not his heart, for surely that was the ugliest of his features.

Then she remembered herself and called his bluff. "The pistol is primed, you may note. I would have the greatest satisfaction shooting you, sir, but first, I require your coachman."

The coachman needed no second telling. He left off fussing about the colts and stepped forward with speed. When he saw Lily, a splendid vision in the most delectable gown he had ever seen, he knew at once that Sir Rory had taste if not sense. When he said as much, with a little grin in Lily's direction, she dimpled, though her hand remained firm.

"Was it lame?"

"The *'orse,* ma'am?" The coachman was very respectful to young ladies with pistols. Lily nodded.

"Oh, aye. It was the shoe. Musta slipped off on the road, like. Colt's got a bloody big stone in 'is 'oof, saving the language, miss."

"Shall I shoot it, to put it out of its pain?"

Aldershot winced. He believed in Lily's beauty, not in her sense and certainly not in her ability to handle a weapon. Still, he would rather she shot a horse than him. And *then* he would teach her . . . God's truth, how *could* he have left the thing lying about for her? But then, as he told himself, any decently bred maiden would not think to touch such a thing.

"No, ma'am, the 'orse can be spared. Save yer bullet for them wot needs it."

A decided dimple now appeared in Lily's creamy, heavenlike cheeks.

"Be silent, you fool!" Sir Rory could have stamped with rage. In the event, he remained still, for the dastardly pistol was now directed most pointedly at his nose, if not his heart.

"Stupid widgeon!" He choked on the words and shifted his weight to his other foot.

Lily just smiled.

It did not take Barrymore a fraction of a moment to realize something was amiss. Though the burgundy lived up to its promise, it paled on the palette when Lily did not reappear smartly.

"You there!" Barrymore snapped his fingers peremptorily, for he did not like the smirk on my lady innkeeper's face or the shifty manner in which she hurried past him.

"Aye?"

He noticed the defiant lack of "my lord" as she addressed him, and grew alarmed. "Where is my wife?"

"Your *wife*, me lor'?"

Too late she applied the necessary title. Barrymore was too incensed to notice.

"I believe that is what I said."

The woman tittered unnecessarily. "She is off, me lord! Saved from a night of carnal sin, she is."

For the first time in his debonair, happy-go-lucky, devil-may-care life, Denver, Lord Barrymore, wished to commit cold-blooded murder. This he very nearly did with his own two hands were it not for the fact that he was interrupted from his goal by the innkeeper himself.

"My lord, I believe I can explain . . ."

"Get this woman out of my sight and explain as I saddle a horse."

The innkeeper bowed and gestured to his wife, whose bluster suddenly dissipated in the face of her spouse's very tangible wrath.

"He would have despoiled an innocent virgin . . ."

"Stop blabbering, woman! They were married this day.

And much good that is going to do us with your interfering, meddlesome ways . . ."

My lord did not favor them with the courtesy of listening. He strode out and was just selecting, from the medley
of horses available, a suitable mare, when a grubby hand
pulled at his impeccable ruby red morning coat. This was
a feat in itself, for the superfine clung to Lord Barrymore's form as closely as a second skin. It did not yield
easily, but the grubby hand was tenacious and it was little
less than a second before the viscount turned to see the
cause.

"Yes?" His tone was uncompromising and the boy
thought to cut his losses and run. Still, he was an enterprising lad and not inclined to scrub basement floors at
the expense of a gentleman's penny.

"Lose 'is shoe, 'e will."

"Beg pardon?"

"Bloody great 'orse will lose 'is shoe. I knowed it at
once."

Barrymore looked at him closely. He wiped his nose
on his sleeve and sniffed.

"*Who* will lose his shoe?"

"Didn't I tell yer? That gentry mort's 'orse it will. Made
off wiv the lady, mind, but they won't go no how wiv a
shoe like that."

Denver's heart leapt for a moment. The boy began to
make a certain sense.

"How do you know?"

"I walked them, like. The left 'orse seemed a little lame
and I looked."

"Why did you not tell the gentleman?"

"No time for no changes. Said so 'imself."

"Did you tell him about the shoe?" The boy grew sul-
len with all the questioning. He sniffed again.

"He didn't ask, like."

"Good, *good* lad!" Denver felt the strangest impulse to

kiss the varmint. He was not so far deranged as that, however, but he *did* draw from his pocket a coin far too unsuitable for a youth of his size and criminal predilection. It was the last coin left to him as he had trudged somberly to settle his debt with Raven. The child gasped at the sight of it, but Barrymore's mind had already turned to weightier matters. He selected the mare, apprised his men about the circumstance—Standish blanched to the roots of his hair—and set off at a canter after Sir Rory Aldershot and the only thing that meant more to him than Lord Raven's Ransom, the raven herself. Lily, Viscountess Barrymore, his raven-haired wife.

Twenty

Sir Rory Aldershot had been careless. Now he was stuck, in a unique position, between a little waif of a thing and the barrel of his own, most excellent, gun. In the circumstances, he chose to remain stoically still, but hard lights glinted in his granite eyes. Though they were as blue as the sky, yet they were as cold as my Lord Raven's icehouse. He ground his teeth together as Miss Chartley—how was *he* to know that she was already the Viscountess Barrymore?—took aim for the tip of his rather splendid nose.

"Do me a favor," Lily addressed the coachman without looking at him.

"What, me, ma'am?"

"Yes, you. You look to me a nice strong creature. Tie him up, will you?"

The coachman thought a moment, for his processes were sluggish, then grinned. "Aye, that I will gladly, but I have no rope."

"Use strips off a traveling rug."

"There *is* none."

Sir Rory's eyes bulged at this conversation.

"You double-crossing dog! I shall have your hide for this!"

Lily ignored him. So, too, she was pleased to note, did the coachman.

"Any suggestions?"

"Your . . . petticoats, ma'am?"

"My . . ." Lily blushed.

"No, I think not. Much as I would not hesitate to use my undergarments for such a worthy cause as this, I believe it would be foolish. I would need both hands."

"I will tear them off meself, ma'am."

"Ha, I *warrant* you would!" Sir Rory smoldered at the man's insolence, but was still wary of the gun. Lily was a confoundedly unpredictable sort of female. She would need schooling, when this nonsense was concluded with. It was only a matter of time before she made a mistake. Unfortunately, time was something he could ill afford. He bit his lip angrily.

"Now, now, Sir Rory, don't be impertinent!" The light of laughter touched naughty Lily's eyes now. She addressed the coachman, but her gloved hands remained as steady as rock.

"I believe I shall pass on your offer, sir. Even *I* balk at the impropriety of having you reach for my undergarments."

Sir Rory gasped at this unmaidenly comment. Lily continued, with an impish smile hovering about her full, delectably inviting lips. "Besides," she said, "I am conscious of the fact that my pistol might wobble. Steady, steady, you know." Sad to say, the sweet viscountess was beginning to enjoy the high drama. It was amazing how collected one could be on the correct side of a primed pistol.

The coachman grinned his alternate appreciation and rampant regret. Still gazing at Aldershot, she addressed the menial once more.

"Make yourself useful, if you will, with that ax."

He looked a query, which she noticed from the corner of vivid, emerald green eyes. She did not turn her head in reply, for her gaze was still fixed firmly upon the tip of Sir Rory's aquiline nose. The nostrils twitched.

"Go on, then, fetch it. It is a passing fine ax."

The man obliged, but looked puzzled. So, too, did
Aldershot, who had thought he had Lily's measure. Now
he was at a loss. He shifted to his right foot, then shuffled
again to his left. He wanted to consult his fob, but the
stupid widgeon might set the pistol off by mistake. So,
he waited.

"Got it?" Lily's voice was almost merry. Sir Rory eyed
her suspiciously as the man nodded.

"Good. Then start chopping."

"Chopping?" The coachman looked at the fire logs in
bewilderment.

"Not those, sir! *Those!*" Lily indicated the carriage
wheels with a quick flick of her hand. Aldershot moved
forward, but the gun was trained on him again in an
instant.

"Not so fast, Sir Rory! I might shoot your foot by mistake!"

Aldershot decided not to take the risk. His eyes nearly
popped out of his forehead, however, when the coachman
understood what she was about and began to chop the
great round wheels with masculine zeal.

"What in the blazes are you doing?"

"I should have thought it obvious, sir. I am rendering
any further journeying useless."

The coachman snickered a little, so Sir Rory kicked
him roundly with the point of his civilized top boots.

"You are fired, man!"

The coachman stared a moment, then wreaked silent
revenge by his continued devastation of the carriage
wheels. It was a singularly enjoyable task, for Sir Rory was
a petty man and he was being regarded with satisfaction
by the prettiest little nymph he had seen in years.

"Did you hear me? You shall be turned off without a
character. I shall be *damned* if anyone will employ a hap-
less nobody with no references!"

"Oh, you are so wrong, Sir Rory!"

Lily smiled sweetly.

"Be quiet, you vixen! You know nothing of such matters!"

"Oh, but I do."

The carriage gave a great groan and sank to the ground, back wheels helplessly aloft. Lily addressed the coachman calmly.

"That will be fine, sir. You may start on the back two. I want this wood to be good for nothing but sticks. Won't the crofter be surprised to see how industrious we have been? He shall have enough firewood to last all the winter. A fitting repayment, I believe, for the use of his ax."

Sir Rory took a cautious pace forward. Lily seemed too amused to notice, so he took another.

"Uh, uh, uh! Naughty, naughty."

The pistol was leveled, again, at his nose. What an appalling child!

"Did you say you have turned off your coachman?"

"You heard me."

"Very good, he may consider himself hired once more."

"Over my dead body!"

Lily looked at him consideringly. Then, in a rather haughty tone that quite suited her magnificent features, she addressed him.

"If you like, though that will not be necessary. Lord Barrymore requires only that he can handle a team and obey my commands."

"Lord Barrymore? You flatter yourself."

"I think not." Lily's voice was deceptively gentle.

Sir Rory raised his brows fleetingly. He would not argue with the silly wench. Now she was opening her berry red lips.

"We were married, you see, only this morning."

There was a moment's stillness. Then the unwelcome information finally filtered through to her abductor.

When he hissed vituperously and clenched his fingers into a taut, uncomfortable fist, Lily thought he understood.

"So you see," she continued lightly, "the viscount will be seeking me shortly. I shouldn't much like to be in your shoes when he finds me, should you?" Her voice danced as lightly as clouds.

"Climb under the wreckage."

"Beg pardon?"

"Climb under the wreckage. Since I cannot bind either of you, I must hope that the weight of half a barouche will keep you occupied awhile. Yes, you, too, Master Coachman, one can never be too careless of one's trust these days. But this I promise you: if you engage not to permit this worthless piece of flesh to escape, you shall very soon be wearing Barrymore livery. My word on it."

At which the burly man grinned a toothless smile—or in truth, there was evidence of some back molars, but these were of little account—and pushed Barrymore under with him.

Lily waited until she was perfectly certain both would have a fair time struggling to lift the remains of the interior. Just to be certain, she packed some of the chopped wheels about in places, so that splinters alone would offer sufficient enough hazard. Then, with a careful click to decommission the pistol, she lifted her skirts and ran as if her life depended on it.

Lord Valmont cantered across the plains with a merry twinkle in his dark, rather rakish eyes. Without his cloak and bandanna he looked rather regal upon his steed, but he trusted this would not weigh too greatly in his disfavor. After all, a gentleman born could not *help* having prize Arabian mares or his coats tailored with impeccable precision by Scott.

He was wearing a riding coat of dashing blue velvet, trimmed in the military style with gold buttons and epaulettes of fine West Sussex braid. His finger flashed, briefly, with the light of a cabochon sapphire, and his neckerchief was tied, rather carelessly, in a cheval knot. Daisy could not have dreamed up a more dashing hero for herself, though his pockets were not filled with daggers or poisons, but rather with sugarplums hastily plundered from his mother's living room dish.

The sun was dropping steadily from the sky, though it was still cheerfully light and the clouds were drifting away in lazy streams. Still, there was a way to traverse before the welcome lamps of London were lit and he was able to keep his assignation at Lord Raven's residence. When he crossed the familiar Westenbury plains, he reined in a little, for the inn was busy with ostlers at this hour and he had no wish to be embroiled in carriage accidents, or to have to negotiate his way past any lumbering stage-coaches.

His eyes narrowed slightly as he caught sight of a wreck on the northbound road. Dash it, he would have to stop to help. It would be unthinkable to pass such a thing and not offer assistance of some sort. He glanced down at his elegantly wrought fob and suppressed a small sigh. At this rate, Daisy dream Daisy would have to watch the sun ushering in one more velvety night without him. He cursed.

"Ahoy, there! May I help?"

"God, you stupid dolt, of course you can! Get this thing off me!"

My lord rode a little closer and gasped a little. The wheels of the ill-sprung chaise were chopped to ribbons. No accident, this.

" 'Ere! We don't want no rescuin', sir! You ride right on, hark yer!"

"Silence, you clod-hopping son of a street whore!"

"Oy! Forgivin' yer 'oner, but I shall knock the teeth out of yer for that!"

My lord watched with interest as the carriage seemed to shake and quiver on its hinges. He could not see much beside a tangle of legs, but what he *did* see was sufficient to cause a wide grin to cross his remarkable features.

"How remarkably edifying! That you, in there, Sir Rory?"

He heard nought for answer but an outraged splutter, so he deemed it a suitable moment to carry on his way. After all, he was not partial to being called a "stupid dolt" when offering assistance. Further, he had never liked Sir Rory Aldershot, Esquire and possibly never would.

He assumed a jaunty whistle as he kicked in his heels and urged his wonderful Arabian steed on to something between a canter and a cautious trot. Only a horseman as skilled as Lord Valmont could achieve such a paradox, but indeed, Armand thought nothing of the feat, just as he thought nothing of the outraged bellows issuing from the shell of the chaise. A night outdoors would doubtless do Sir Rory the world of good. He was the most unconscionable fribble Lord Valmont had ever been duty-bound to greet. Too bad Quimby was but a stone's throw from the Westenbury estates. Valmont grimaced, then found his eyes widening in surprise. The trot turned into a full-out canter as he skirted the road—to avoid any traffic from the inn—and cut across the verdant meadows that bordered the pathway.

A lady was running—faster than he'd ever had the felicity of seeing a female do, her skirts held fast in her hand, and her raven locks streaming down her back—flying, he thought, briefly—before being tangled in a branch of a chestnut tree. He had only time to hear a varied and rather colorful oath before coming up to her from behind.

"May I be of assistance?"

Her eyes widened in panic, then relaxed almost instantly. Lord Valmont noted they were a splendid green and were accompanied by a delightful dimple when she smiled.

"You!"

"I might say the same! We appear to meet in rather odd circumstances." Lord Valmont did an exaggerated bow from the saddle of his horse. Lily's gaze wandered past him.

"Did you see . . ." Her eyes clouded.

Valmont scowled. "Sir Rory Aldershot and company?"

"Yes."

"Don't look so stricken. They were in the most delightful pickle. Sir Rory looks likely to lose his teeth, for he was *not*, sadly, endearing himself to the other rapscallion in the chaise."

Lily grinned, jerked her head upward, then winced.

"Ouch!"

"Hold on." Lord Valmont's foot hardly touched the stirrups as he leapt to the ground and began untangling the silky, dark strands from the prickly twigs. His horse remained perfectly still, save for a few nibbles of the long grass.

"Be quick!"

"I shall be as quick as I can, but your hair is so soft, it tangles."

"Cut it, then."

"What?" Armand gazed at her in astonishment.

"They shall catch up."

"Then they shall have me to reckon with." Valmont's jaw hardened.

"You really mean that!"

"But of course I do!"

"The beastly wretch will turn you over to the authorities."

"What?" Valmont looked puzzled until he remembered his fearsome role of cutpurse.

"Oh!" He smiled. "The boot shall be on the other foot, Miss Chartley. I am sorry to disappoint you, but I fear I may have misled you a little. I am the Honorable Henry, Mortimer, James Armand Garcia, eighth Viscount Valmont. At your service. Naturally."

Lily gasped. "The Earl of Westenbury's son?"

"You read your *Debrett's*, I see. The very same."

"Then Daisy . . ."

"Yes, it is very sad, but she will learn to live with it, I hope. Being a viscountess is no bad thing. One becomes accustomed."

Lily giggled. "It is not Daisy I worry about but Grandfather. He will be furious!"

"Ah, the family feud. Still, indigestion was always a good thing for Raven. Too much harmony and he may wallow in a decline. You are running away, I take it?"

Lily nodded. "In a manner of speaking . . ."

"Very good, then, for we shall *share* his wrath! Hop on behind and I shall have you home in no time."

"With my reputation in tatters! No, I thank you!"

"This from a lady perfectly willing to chop off her hair. Base ingratitude!" Armand smiled, but acknowledged she had a point. Inwardly, he cursed. A fine fix he was in when carrying Lily home would mean her ruination. Compromising his future sister-in-law seemed singularly maladroit under the circumstances. He searched about wildly for an answer then shaded his eyes narrowly as a dust cloud appeared on the horizon.

The thundering of hooves confirmed to his quick senses that this was no idle ostler from the inn, or stray postboy out for a quiet canter on the downs. He pushed Lily from the tree and grabbed the reins of his Arabian. He had no wish to frighten the powerful beast.

"You devil! I shall split you alive if you have touched so much as a hair on her head!"

Barrymore's golden head bobbed from his borrowed mare. In less than a second he was on solid English soil, fists clenched.

"Lily! You are . . ."

But his words were drowned by a flood of tears and laughter that relieved him so greatly that he had little time to spare for the bemused Valmont. Instead, he whisked his beloved off her feet—thus exposing a very pretty pair of ankles—and kissed her soundly. Then he pressed her to him again before eyeing the Honorable Henry, Mortimer, James Armand Garcia, eighth Viscount Valmont in some inquiring surprise.

"You are not Sir Rory Aldershot."

"I am relieved you can distinguish the difference, sir. I do not approve either of Sir Rory's tailor or of his unfortunate habit of wearing puce in company. In short, I fear, Sir Rory is a fribble."

"And you are not." Barrymore's eyes crinkled in sudden amusement. It was easy to be amused, he found, when he was cradling his wife.

"Certainly not! I, I fear, am a veritable pink of the Ton! You have only to note my impeccable tailoring . . ."

"Scott, if I mistake it not."

"Indeed." Armand bowed.

"I prefer Weston. And why, sir, were you making free with my wife?"

"Your wife?" Armand startled.

Lily giggled. "I hope you are right, my lord, when you say one becomes accustomed. I have been a viscountess these several hours and am not accustomed yet!"

Armand's brow cleared. Saints alive, the lovely Lily was wedded! He was not going to be compromising her this day, after all!

"My felicitations. Barrymore—yes, I met you once at

Burtons—I must most earnestly desire you to take over from here. I am due to enact my own elopement at sunset and fear I shall be unforgivably late!"

"Then by all means go!"

"You will let me pass unspit? I touched *several* strands of your lovely wife's head, this day."

Barrymore caught the mirthful glance his impish scamp of a wife shot Valmont and scowled. "Then let the reckoning be later! Right now, I have business with my wife."

"Very good, my lord. Sensible, too. And now, adieu."

He had no sooner mounted than Lily extricated herself from Denver, Lord Barrymore's fond embrace, and emitted a sudden, rather unregal whoop of surprise. "Primmy! That was Primmy's hair if ever I saw it!"

Barrymore looked resigned. "Miss Chartley?"

"Yes, in that chaise. It is tumbling out of our horrid charades hat. I saw it distinctly."

"Many people have hair of that color. Can you not have mistaken it?"

Lily looked scornful. "Gentlemen know *nothing* of fashion. I tell you, Primmy's copper color is unique!"

"But that is not Lord Raven's chaise. It has a golden crest upon it."

Lily shaded her eyes and squinted toward the inn, outside which the chaise had drawn to a very neat stop.

"I can't precisely see, but certainly it is not Grandfather's. His livery is different. *Look!* There is a man in there!"

Barrymore shot Valmont a resigned glance. It was filled with such unspoken apology that even Armand, anxious as he was to set his *own* affairs in order, was forced to grin.

Lily looked alarmed. "Gracious heavens, do you think she is *also* being abducted?"

The gentlemen peered into the distance. Both seemed

inclined to think not, for now another gentleman was emerging in a very orderly manner. He was deplorably attired, of course . . .

Lily gave a shriek. "It is Primmy! Oh, I do declare it is Primmy in our play clothes! Oh, come at once! This is beyond belief amazing!" With never a thought for the two handsome—if somewhat bewildered young men paying her court—she once more took up her skirts and headed directly for the inviting portals of the White Dragon Inn.

It did not take long for the story to unfold, but by this time, Lord Valmont had missed his sunset deadline and was staring with dismay out the twilight window. Lord Rochester had procured, upon the instant, the best private parlor the inn had to offer, but the question of Primrose's reputation was now being hotly disputed. There was no telling *who* may have seen Miss Chartley in the marquis's closed chaise. If she had been remarked at all, returning past nightfall in an unwedded state would be fatal.

Lily seemed to think Primrose's copper-colored hair was fatal and my Lord Rochester, upon deep and earnest consideration—which caused Primrose's color to heighten to a remarkable degree—was forced to concur.

Presently there came upon the door a rather timid knock and as Rochester sought to cover Primrose as best he could, the handle turned.

"What in tarnation? This is a private parlor!" As Rochester protested, Barrymore stepped forward in surprise.

"Your reverence! I thought you had departed long since! Come in, come in!" This the archbishop did, with a very sorry tale. He had wandered through the gardens, lost track, a little of the time, and discovered, to his horror, that "some elegant sprig in a confoundedly close-fitting morning coat"—had stolen his prize mare. Since it comprised half of his carriage's team, he could not move an inch until the rapscallion returned.

At which, the Honorable Viscount Barrymore looked distinctly uncomfortable, Lily stared at her husband hard and the Viscount Valmont, no slow top, burst into an outright chuckle.

"Sprigged the nag, did you?"

"Well, what would *you* do?" Barrymore sounded indignant. "The rest of the mares were sorry little beasts without an ounce of speed between them."

When apprised of the tale, the archbishop's brow cleared and he murmured that abduction was a shocking thing and doubtless the Lord worked in strange ways. If it was *his* beast that had been the saving of her ladyship, then he must needs be satisfied.

Whereupon Lord Barrymore apologized most contritely—though his merry blue eyes lost none of their twinkle—and promised that even now the mare was being watered and fed. The archbishop harrumphed a little at this, but seemed mollified enough to take the seat that was offered him and he even nodded a little at the prospect of a fine cup of Bohea tea. Then Armand, eyes wickedly gleaming, suggested that the clergyman might once again—and maybe yet again, before the evening was done—prove his worth. The party stared at him, puzzled. That was for a fraction of a moment only, however, for Rochester's eyes widened in quick comprehension.

"The very thing! Primrose, my dear, if you could dispense with pomp and circumstance, we might save your reputation yet!"

"What of the marchioness?"

"Fiddlesticks! She will be so relieved to see me legshackled to the *right* Miss Chartley she will not grumble at the shimble-shamble manner of the service."

"But have you a special license?"

"No . . . but. . . ." Gareth, Lord Rochester, looked

pleadingly in the archbishop's direction. As he had hoped, the matter of the special license was waved away by his reverence, who, despite shuddering a little at Primrose's unorthodox attire, nevertheless deemed the couple worthy of his matrimonial blessings. Consequently, he signed all necessary parchments with a flourish of ink and the only obstacle to wedded bliss was thus summarily overcome. And so, clad only in knee breeches and a sadly flopping hat, the very sensible Miss Chartley became, like her sister before her, a peeress of the realm.

Twenty-one

Daisy had long since finished her tammying. Growing alarmed at Primrose's absence, she broached the subject with Grandfather Raven, who merely pinched her cheek affectionately and bade her "mind her own business." This said with a wink and a guffaw she found mystifying, but which her good nature did not allow to question.

Instead, she tiptoed up to reach Lord Raven's wizened cheek and there placed a timid kiss upon the leathery skin. Lord Raven was so taken aback he could only say "Ha!" and "Humph!" but Daisy smiled to herself, knowing he was pleased. She guiltily hoped he would feel the same way on the morrow, when she told him she was wed. Doubtless he would work himself into a fit of rage, but since that had never harmed him before, Daisy took leave to hope her disobedience would soon be forgiven. After all, if she were not now being wooed so steadily by a myriad of fortune hunters all after the Raven's Ransom, there would have been no need to rush into the thing.

But now. . . . any moment Grandfather might betrothe her to some unsuitable upstart who cared more about the treasure trove than her. Armand, she trusted, with a small, secret sigh of contentment, was different. He may need the ransom, but he also needed her. His eyes would not glow like hot coals when they gazed upon her if this were not so. She quietly closed the oak door behind her and crossed the gallery. Sadly, she was accosted by an under butler, who took leave to tell her that a handful of callers had just arrived. Further, Mrs. Bartlett was out of cream puffs and sweetmeats.

Daisy had just time to straighten her gown, whisper that slivers of bread with soured cream and some of the game salmon would just have to suffice, when she was accosted by one particularly bold suitor. He had strolled out of the receiving room and into the long gallery with the hope, he declared, of "catching a glimpse of a starry-eyed maid with pools of blue." Daisy nearly snapped back that he was mixing his metaphors besides wasting his time, but faultless good manners intervened. She therefore nodded at the under butler and gently led the rake—she suspected he was such, for he cast her an appraising glance filled with a deplorably languishing look—back to the receiving room.

The afternoon seemed singularly tedious without the support of her sisters, whose absence was remarked upon repeatedly until her head ached. She was just coming to the end of a long string of polite excuses when the time chimed on the great-grandfather clock in the hall. Heavens! It must be close to sunset!

Abruptly, she put aside one of the posies that had been pressed into her elegantly gloved hand and moved toward the balcony. It was true that the sky was pinkening, and the sun dipping down beyond the far fir trees.

"Oh, *do* excuse me!" She turned around and nearly fell into the arms of Sir Richard Bridgewater, who had recently been betrothed to a speckle-haired heiress. Sadly, she had eloped with a footman, leaving poor Sir Richard in dun territory and urgently in need of a wife. Well, an heiress to be more precise about the matter.

"My dear Miss Chartley! Allow me to steady you!" Sir Richard placed his ringed fingers upon her scalloped sleeves. They were warm and slightly given to fat, though the moment was so fleeting Daisy may have been doing him an injustice.

"Sir! I am fine, I thank you."

"Nonsense, Miss Chartley. You look faint. Come, we shall take a stroll on this balcony whilst the others fight over your fair charms. The air shall do you good." Sir Richard seemed to feel it was *more* than the air that would do her good, for he took the liberty of slipping his arm about her waist. Daisy was indignant.

"Sir!"

Sir Richard removed his arm huffily. "How quaint, Miss Chartley! You should go out a little more. I believe *most* young society misses are not so coy."

"Then court them, instead, Sir Richard. I believe I make poor company. My head aches." Daisy amazed herself at her waspishness. Fortunately—or unfortunately, as the case happened to be—the good Sir Richard did not, apparently, feel its sting.

"All the more reason to stay out on this balcony. It is very close within."

"And close without." Daisy grew bold. Surely he could *not* ignore this pointed rudeness?

But he did. The sky was darkening to purple before Mrs. Bartlett marched in and ordered—yes, ordered—the visitors out. One look at Daisy's pained expression was enough to set the housekeeper on her mettle. With a few sharp words that were interspersed with "chaperone" and "unsuitable" and "not wishing to offend" and the like, the rabble—including, even, the reluctant Sir Richard Bridgewater—had called up their horses and chaises and hackney coaches. Some half hour later, they were all gone.

"You are a godsend, Mrs. Bartlett!"

"Now don't go talking fustian, Miss Daisy! It is off to bed with you, with a hot posset. You look peaky."

Daisy eyed herself in the cheval glass. It was true that

she was pale, and her glorious guinea gold locks seemed to make her features appear whiter, even, than they truly were. She sighed. If Armand came . . .

If? What was this if? She did not doubt that he would come, and that right quickly, if the first star was anything to go by. Suddenly, her blue eyes regained their sparkle and a little color crept into her cheeks, though Mrs. Bartlett still eyed her frowningly.

"You are a dear, Barty! I won't be needing a hot posset, for I feel better already! Now please, *please* help me to select something wonderful to wear!"

"Your shift and a nightgown, young lady!"

Daisy giggled.

"And what is so funny, might I ask?"

But Daisy could not very well tell Mrs. Bartlett—who had known her since leading strings—that Armand had rather lasciviously suggested the very same. Doubtless, though, he had not had Mrs. Bartlett's severe starched linens in mind.

So she shook her head meekly and promised "to be a good girl and run along." Which she did, astonishing her maid by pulling out half her wardrobe and rifling through a dozen kid gloves, muffs, bonnets, and shawls until the poor girl thought her demented.

When Daisy finally mumbled that she was "to meet a gentleman—but hush," little Annie's curiosity was more than satisfied. Indeed, she set herself to expertly selecting out a satin court gown—never worn—with a band of azure silk across the bust line. The color exactly matched Daisy's favorite draped undertunic, which was held in place, as usual, by crisscrossed ribbon bands. The open overdress that flowed into a deep sapphire silk was pinned closed across the hip by Grandfather Raven's fifteenth birthday gift to her—a jewelled brooch encrusted, modestly, with pearls. Hem and cuffs were of embroidered azure satin and sparkled as she moved. Daisy—dream

Daisy—had never looked better. Annie wished to set her hair high up in a chignon, but Daisy, on a sudden, intuitive whim, shook her head. Thus it was that her glorious bright hair was allowed to tumble, unpinned, across her shoulders and down a dainty, perfectly straight back. It did not escape entirely, however, for it was subjected to a hundred strokes at least of a very demanding brush, so that when Daisy was done, it gleamed like sunshine, or like the purest of spun gold. The room had long since been lighted by wax tapers, and only the moon now shone through the drawn curtains.

Daisy startled. It was late, then! Past sunset, certainly. She could not remember when she had last heard the hall clock chime. She dismissed Annie with a pleasant "thank you," then waited for the door to click before diving behind the damask drapes and opening her long French window. It creaked as she peered out into the darkness. There was no sign of a rider or even a horse. She sighed, wondering if she was truly even more foolish than Lily. Fancy being so puffed up in her own consequence that she could think that a man like Armand . . .

But wait! There was a commotion below stairs, she could swear it. She strained her ears to listen but could hear no more than a whisper of deep voices. Sir Richard Bridgewater again? Perhaps he had left his silver-headed walking stick, or else his ridiculous beaver topper and fur-lined gloves. She would not risk going down and encountering him again. If she strained her ears, she could hear footsteps up to the gallery level. And more, beyond. *Surely* he would not be so presumptuous as to enter into the residential wing? But then, the Raven's Ransom addled *everyone's* wits.

Sir Rory Aldershot was a prime example. Daisy wondered whether she should lock her chamber. Perhaps she was being missish but with her sisters away . . . She heard a door slam. Grandfather *Raven's* door, unless it was one

of the sundry linen cupboards that lined that wing. Dared
she peek? She wondered. For a moment, she was entirely
at a loss, for she longed to know what was happening,
yet was terrified to leave the window, lest she miss Armand's clandestine arrival. In the event, her curiosity got
the better of her, for far from locking her door, she
opened it a crack. A flicker of light warned her that
Grandfather Raven's door was in truth ajar. She waited,
a little, at sixes and sevens, not knowing whether to follow
her instincts and investigate, or wait, as she had planned,
for her handsome, oh-so *breathtakingly* wonderful cutpurse. No, she could never think of Armand as that . . .

She smiled and moved closer to the window, her decision unconsciously made. In the candlelight her ears
flashed with the diamond drops she had fastened on, and
her hair was a wave of pure, luxurious gold. She was aware
of none of these things as she gazed with longing at the
blackness outside. *More* than Venus and the first evening
stars were out, now. There was an abundance of flickering
points of light and the sky had changed, again, from purple to a velvety black. The moon was a gibbous—half crescent, half full. She shivered, wondering how far below
there—if at all—stood a rider and his mare. She did not
know how long she stood at the window, for her heart
was filled with a deep yearning. Strange, tumbling emo-
tions seized at her and held her entirely in their thrall.
Some were deliciously pleasant, others more deeply poi-
gnant whilst others yet, seized at her very being and whispered of matters she had yet to learn the sense of. Her
mouth parted, slightly, and she felt the azure ribbons
tighten against her soft, untried breasts. Strange how her
heart was beating! As if she could feel his presence in
this very room . . . she whirled around and startled at
the shadow cast upon her door frame. It was more ajar,
now, than it had been. That was her last thought before

being embraced, quite scandalously, in her own bedchamber.

It was Armand who cast her from him, gently, with a teasing smile on his wide, sensuous lips and an unconscionable grin that caused her to pout prodigiously and announce that he would be well served if she called out an alarm.

At which he only laughed, his teeth gleaming white in the half light.

"Did you doubt I would come?"

"No!"

"Not even a little?"

Daisy dropped her eyes.

"Oh! A little, then, you fickle maid!"

"It is past sunset!" There was a tiny reproach in her tone.

"If you have been decked out in all this finery since *then,* my little dove, I can understand your annoyance. By the by, you look . . ." He gazed at her assessingly.

"Bridal?"

He grinned. "There is that, but no. You look . . . you are going to think me *appallingly* unimaginative but the only adjective that rises to my tongue-tied palate is . . . beautiful."

Daisy laughed. "I can live with that."

"Can you? How about breathtaking?"

"That, too."

"Good, for I would hate to be tedious. And now, my love, I am going to disappoint you vastly, I fear."

Since his words rang with a lazy confidence that set Daisy to shivering quite deliciously, she did not pay too much attention to the content of his words.

"Vastly?"

"Vastly." He nodded with decision then whisked her off her feet, so she must needs throw her arms about his neck to steady herself. She giggled, then put a guilty hand to her mouth. She must be quiet, lest Grandfather Raven or any of the house staff hear her.

"I cannot elope with you this night."

Daisy's eyes fluttered open. They had closed the minute his lips had brushed across her brow.

"No?"

"No."

She swallowed. "Then put me down, sir, for you have taken a great liberty with my person."

Lord Valmont felt her back straighten against his palm. He laughed. "Oh, ye, of little faith! You doubt me still! We cannot elope, my dear, for Lord Raven greatly desires to be of the wedding party. Insists, in fact."

Daisy looked wondering.

"You are pleased to tease!"

"Indeed, I always am! But this time, my dearest Daisy, dream Daisy, I speak only the truth. If you step down the corridor, you will find his chamber bursting with people."

"You speak in riddles."

Lord Valmont laughed. "Then let me be plain, Daisy dearest. In order of precedence, the Marquis and Marchioness of Rochester, the Earl of Raven, the Viscount and Viscountess of Barrymore, and the most reverend Archbishop of Westenbury, all await your pleasure."

Daisy frowned. "Now you are *certainly* making no sense!"

"Then come with me and allow light to dawn!"

And Daisy, being a sweet and timid young thing, took Lord Valmont's gloved hand in her own, satin-clad one, and finally—finally—obeyed.

"Ha!" Lord Raven was in his element. "What took you so long?"

He glared at Daisy, but the gleam of amusement was unmistakable.

"Fie, sir, that you should ask such a question!" Three lords protested in unison whilst two sisters—even proper Primrose—chuckled merrily.

Daisy blushed a deep crimson and looked likely to answer, but Lord Valmont stopped her with an imperious sweep of his lordly hand.

"Hush, child! If my lord is such a ninny-hammered clodpole as to not suspect what kept you, let him forever remain in ignorance."

"Impertinent jackanapes! If you have compromised the girl, you shall . . ."

". . . wed her." Lord Valmont's tone was firm. "Sadly, I have not compromised her . . . yet, but since I have every intention of doing so, let us proceed at once."

Whereupon the archbishop, who by now, after a long, trying, but singularly edifying day, had at last learned his cue, rose gracefully and announced that if the special license was to hand, they might proceed.

Rochester eyed Valmont doubtfully, but it seemed the young sprig was up to the rig, for he produced it from his waistcoat with a flourish and turned warm eyes upon Daisy.

"Daisy, dream Daisy, would you consent to being my wife?"

Daisy nodded.

"Though I am not a villain, not a cutpurse, not even on weekends, a highwayman?"

Daisy blinked. "Not even on weekends?" Her mouth was soft and kissable, her round, cornflower eyes rounder even than Armand remembered. He sighed, regretfully. "Not even on weekends."

Daisy thought hard. "Then Lord Raven's Ransom is essential to you!"

"A scurvy *pox* on Lord Raven's Ransom! The only thing essential to me is *you!*"

Lord Raven, *most* put out, stepped upon his gouty foot. "What do you *mean*, a pox on my ransom?"

Lord Valmont ignored him.

"I shall marry you, Armand, even if we are poor as church mice."

Lord Valmont smiled. "Not likely, my dear, but I honor you for the sentiment." He pulled off the cabachon cut sapphire that graced his finger and removed a soft, satin glove. Then, slipping the heavy jewel—too large, but Daisy did not mind—effortlessly onto her person, he continued in a conversational tone.

"Would you mind, very much, being Lady Valmont? One day it shall be the Countess of Westenbury, but since it is my mother who now holds that honor, and my father who is the current earl, I hope that shall be in the very distant future."

Lord Valmont never *did* get to hear Daisy's answer, for Lord Raven was roaring that his leg hurt and if they intended to have a wedding they had better get on with it right speedily.

And so they did.

Postscript

The jewelled tricorne hat still molders in the closet along with Lord Raven's other elegant trifles. The earl called for it at *once*, after the marriage of Daisy, the last of his famous granddaughters, all wed upon the selfsame day.

Sadly, his undutiful kin would have none of it. Neither would his scoundrel grandsons-in-law, who all, in unison, demanded that he "burn the stupid thing."

Thus Raven is still stuck with his riches and is plotting, to this day, which unsuspecting grandchild to bestow them upon.

He still glowers at Lord Valmont and roars at Denver, Lord Barrymore, who won his wager fair and square by selecting Lily over the king's ransom. Even the mild-mannered Marquis of Rochester has had pitchers of lime cordial flung upon him upon occasion. All admit, however, that the earl has mellowed with time.

The Countess of Westenbury thinks Daisy much, much preferable to a " 'igh kicker" or even a "moonkey." They are the best of friends and outdo each other only in the matter of romances, where Daisy prefers Gothic and my lady wavers delightfully between Byron, Scott, and some of the more excessive French writers.

Gwenyth, Dowager Marchioness of Rochester, deprived of the privilege of sponsoring the Chartley sisters, is instead turning her illustrious attention to Raven himself.

She bickers and scolds quite horribly, but rumors have been rife for some time about nuptials. . . .

Finally: The viscount's coal mines are thriving and "Raven's Rail"—powered by one of the first multitubular boiler engines of its kind—has surpassed all expectation. Denver, Lord Barrymore, is no longer emptying his pockets of bills. As his very fine valet Hoskin puts it, "He has the luck of the devil himself."

Discover the Romances of
Hannah Howell

Experience the Romances of
Rosanne Bittner

__Shameless $6.99US/$7.99CAN
  0-8217-4056-3

__Unforgettable $5.99US/$7.50CAN
  0-8217-5830-6

__Texas Passions $5.99US/$7.50CAN
  0-8217-6166-8

__Until Tomorrow $5.99US/$6.99CAN
  0-8217-5064-X

__Love Me Tomorrow $5.99US/$7.50CAN
  0-8217-5818-7

Put a Little Romance in Your Life With
Betina Krahn